BURN IT ALL DOWN

NICOLAS DiDOMIZIO

LITTLE, BROWN AND COMPANY
NEW YORK BOSTON LONDON

Copyright © 2021 by Nicolas DiDomizio

Hachette Book Group supports the right to free expression and the value of copyright. The purpose of copyright is to encourage writers and artists to produce the creative works that enrich our culture.

The scanning, uploading, and distribution of this book without permission is a theft of the author's intellectual property. If you would like permission to use material from the book (other than for review purposes), please contact permissions@hbgusa.com.
Thank you for your support of the author's rights.

Little, Brown and Company
Hachette Book Group
1290 Avenue of the Americas, New York, NY 10104
littlebrown.com

First Edition: May 2021

Little, Brown and Company is a division of Hachette Book Group, Inc. The Little, Brown name and logo are trademarks of Hachette Book Group, Inc.

The publisher is not responsible for websites (or their content) that are not owned by the publisher.

The Hachette Speakers Bureau provides a wide range of authors for speaking events. To find out more, go to hachettespeakersbureau.com or call (866) 376-6591.

Cataloging-in-publication data is available at the Library of Congress.

ISBN 978-0-316-49695-7 (hc)

Printing 1, 2021

LSC-C

Printed in the United States of America

For Mom

one

LUKE: Joey
LUKE: come on babe
LUKE: I'm sorry
LUKE: ok?
LUKE: you win
LUKE: helloooo
LUKE: stop icing me out
LUKE: you're being crazy!!
LUKE: this is a complex situation

I should have known it would end like this. Luke was nothing if not a carbon copy of every other hypermasculine asshole I've swiped right on over the past four years. The only difference is that he's the first one who didn't run screaming the second I slipped the word *boyfriend* into a post-hookup conversation.

"I never liked that prick," Mom says. I'm pretty sure it's a lie, but I appreciate the gesture. "He was always so cocky."

"It's my fault." I toss my phone across our ratty pleather couch so she can analyze the texts for me. She's wearing a black spaghetti-strap tank top, and her shiny gold GIA necklace bounces against her Jergens Natural Glowy skin as she reaches over to pick it up. "I ignored all the red flags."

The earliest one appeared in flirty conversation more than ten months ago, when he told me his childhood hero was Tiger Woods. A stone-faced athlete with a known fidelity problem! What the hell did I expect? Meanwhile, my childhood hero was Monica Lewinsky.

"Hmmm." Mom stares into the dim light of my phone. Watching her absorb Luke's empty words makes me picture them all over again in my head. Which makes me want to scream and/or sob and/or get violently drunk. I'm sure all three will happen in time. Probably within the next hour or so.

I pour myself a glass of the cheap red wine we popped open a few minutes ago. "What do you think?"

"I think he's out of his goddamn mind." Her voice drips with trademark New Jersey sass. "'A complex situation.' Really? Like keeping it in his pants is the Riddle of the fuckin' Sphinx."

I knew she'd be furious for me. Emotions aren't something Mom and I are capable of experiencing separately. They're always shared.

"And then he has the nerve to call you crazy." She pours a glass for herself and shoots me a look of caution. "Promise me you won't justify that with a response."

Of course I won't. If there's anything I've learned from being on the *other* side of this couch all my life, it's that "crazy" is a word shitty men use to deflect attention from their own shitty behavior. It calls the validity of your pain into question and pivots the fight into a new direction by forcing you to defend your sanity. Before you know it, an entire hour of screaming and crying and dish-throwing has somehow just passed. *Wait,* you finally stop to ask yourself. *Why is my sanity even a topic of discussion right now? He's the sociopath who's been lying to me every day for the past year.* But now you've already screamed and cried and thrown dishes, so your entire argument falls apart faster than the porcelain shards of a freshly hurled salad plate. It's textbook gaslighting. And I'm not gonna fall for it.

"Don't worry." I tug at my navy-blue Rutgers sweatpants. "I would never."

Luke gave me these pants after I got my acceptance letter last month. I didn't want to apply anywhere—being a stand-up comic doesn't exactly require a formal education—but my Nonna is desperate for me to be the first in the family with a college degree. So I figured I might as well just pick the school my boyfriend goes to. You know! Like a real dumbass.

"*'You win.'*" Mom's still going at it with the text analysis. "What kind of bullshit is that? Acting like his half-assed apology is some kind of prize." Her shiny espresso hair flutters as she shakes her head in disgust. "This bitch."

Her insult of choice triggers a bittersweet Luke-memory from just a few weeks ago.

"You guys would love Joey's mom," he told a few of his buddies over chicken wings. It was a Saturday and I was spending the weekend with him on campus. "She's dope. Her name is Gia and she's, like, young and hot. And she calls everyone 'bitch.'"

I laughed so hard I almost spit out my Diet Coke. He was so right. To Mom, everyone falls into one of two distinct categories: *this bitch* or *that bitch*. The former is a razor-sharp insult; the latter is a God-level compliment.

"She's never called *you* a bitch," I replied.

"Not to my face," Luke answered with a grin.

The sweetness of this memory burns to a crisp as I realize how prescient it was. I have to rub my eyes to ward off a threatening wave of tears.

"Do you think it was me?" I ask. Mom is obviously going to answer with an emphatic *no*, but I can't help posing the question. I've never felt good enough for Luke. Which is probably why I loved him so much. "Am I too young? Too low-key fat? Is my voice too gay? Maybe it's because I don't know anything about golf."

"Joey!" She hits my arm with her perfectly manicured hand. "You're eighteen. You're literally a twig—not that it should matter if you weren't." Her throat catches for a second, but she quickly composes herself. "And who cares if you don't like golf? There's nothing wrong with you. Or your voice. Okay? He's the one with the problem here."

"Yeah, yeah." It's just that Luke and Joshua (that's his "straight" roommate) both have these manly voices. The kinds of voices that are never *not* sure of themselves. You know what I mean? Whereas mine is basically an audible question mark. I could literally be robbing a bank and it would still sound like I was asking for permission. *Put the money in the bag, motherfucker! I mean...if you want to. No? Okay. Yeah, no. That's fine. This was a stupid idea. Sorry. Please don't hate me.*

"So walk me through it," Mom says. "How did you find out?"

"Joshua's girlfriend messaged me on Instagram." I guzzle the remaining contents of my wineglass. This wouldn't be my first choice of alcoholic beverage for an occasion of this magnitude—I'd rather have a shot of tequila or maybe an IV of vodka—but Mom always keeps Luna di Luna in stock at home. It's basically like water for us. What? We're Italian. "She walked in on them while they were going down on each other."

"No! Seriously?" she asks. "*While* they were—"

4

"Yup."

"At the same ti—"

"It was an active sixty-nine situation, yes."

"How do you know?"

"Obviously I grilled her. She gave me all the details."

"Oh, babe." Mom curls up under our Christmas-themed throw blanket (please note that it's currently April) and sighs. "I'm so sorry."

"I just can't believe this is even happening to me," I say. "I thought I knew Luke. You know? This is something one of *your* boyfriends would pull, not—" Oh. Damn. That came out way judgier than I meant it to. "Sorry. I'm not saying Richard would ever...you know." Awkward silence. "How are things going with you guys, anyway?"

"We're fine." She graciously doesn't acknowledge the fact that I just clocked her as a hopeless asshole-addict. "He's out of town for work again 'til next Tuesday."

See what I mean, though? Richard is exactly the type of guy you'd expect to be a cheating scumbag! Always traveling for "work." And don't even get me started on his marital situation. He's separated but not divorced from his wife, because somehow he can't find the time or money to close the deal. Meanwhile, he owns several businesses and drives a brand-new Tesla. But every time Mom brings it up, he gets mad at her for picking a fight. So she never brings it up. I've tried telling her how fishy this is — especially since it's been almost two years at this point — but she insists I just don't get it. Her connection with Richard is special, marriage is complicated, and other assorted bullshit justifications.

"Where is he now?" I ask.

"San Francisco." Mom bites her glossy lip and wipes a strand of hair behind her ear. "I mean, yeah, it's still frustrating. Sometimes

I feel like I've been waiting forever." She pauses for a second before continuing. "But we're in the home stretch. He knows I'm dying to move into that house."

That's the other thing. Richard owns this HGTV-ass McMansion out in Short Hills, but he wants to wait until his career calms down and I go to college before he and Mom start living together. Short Hills! That's basically the capital of rich-people New Jersey. Meanwhile, Mom and I live in Bayonne—the exact opposite of rich-people New Jersey—and we still struggle to get by on her hairdresser tips and the money I get from my part-time job stuffing cannolis at Mozzicato's Bakery. Richard knows the move would be a huge life upgrade for her. Why won't he just let it happen already?

Sometimes I worry it's because he doesn't want it to happen *ever*. Like he's just keeping Mom on the back burner until he finds someone more wifeable. You know: hot, basic, chill, dumb. Not that Mom isn't gorgeous—I've always said she looks like a brunette Lady Gaga—but "basic" and "chill" are entirely foreign concepts to her. And she's definitely not dumb. Nonna's always telling me about what an amazing student she was in high school. At least until junior year, when I decided to set up shop in her uterus.

"You really don't think he's lying to you about anything?" I ask.

I know I shouldn't be pissing in her Richard Cheerios just because *my* boyfriend ended up being a dishonest douche canoe. But I can't help it. I don't want to see her get hurt again. Especially now that I know firsthand how horrible it feels.

"Don't start with that shit." Mom rolls her perfectly done smoky eyes. "I've told you a million times. Richard is different."

Luke was supposed to be different, I think but don't say out loud. *So what do either of us really know?*

"Sorry." I take another swig of wine. "I'm just all messed up from the Luke thing."

Speaking of Luke, my phone is buzzing.

"I don't even wanna look," I tell Mom. She grabs it from my hand as it buzzes again. And again and again. "*You* read them."

"You sure you don't wanna?" she asks. *Bzzz.* I nod and drink. *Bzzz.* She soaks up the new messages and her face instantly goes all grim. Damn. This must be worse than the first batch. "Honestly, Joey? Fuck him. You're done with him, right?" *Bzzz.* "I'm deleting the conversation."

"Wait!" I kind-of-maybe shriek. "Don't delete anything."

She jumps off the couch and holds the phone out of my reach. "Joey, listen! You're better off keeping his ass on mute."

"I will!" It's obviously now imperative that I read these texts. "I just wanna see what he wrote first."

"Joey." She skips across the living room and almost knocks over our chintzy Walmart floor lamp in the process. "Trust me."

"Mom, seriously."

"I am serious," she snaps back.

"Come on," I whine.

I know! I'm pathetic. But the past ten months are now flashing before my eyes. A hundred identical visions of Luke in the driver's seat of his tricked-out Subaru: his perfect jawline accommodating a smirk, messy black hair peeking out from under his New Jersey Devils hat, strong hands gripping the steering wheel like he's in full control of not just his car but every other car on the road as well. There was something so safe about being his passenger. Can I really afford to lose that?

And who knows? Maybe these new texts have some kind of surprise explanation that will magically fix everything once I see it. *Bzzz.* Or maybe they're just as bad as Mom is making them out to be—in which case I should also definitely see them. Right? For closure.

Bzzz.

"Just give me the phone!" I wail. "Please?"

"Joey—"

"Mom."

It's like a game of one-on-one basketball as I chase her around the living room and she expertly blocks me from getting even the slightest grip.

"Joey..."

"MOM!"

We finally just collapse on the floor at the foot of the couch, exhausted and drunk. But I have to admit the whole scuffle was weirdly therapeutic. We're even giggling a little bit.

"Fine," she says. "Here."

"Thank you."

"Just remember what I said." She rubs my arm like I'm going in for surgery or something. "Fuck. Him."

I look down and immediately notice that almost every text starts with the word "you." Probably not a great sign.

LUKE: you wanna be like this, fine

LUKE: you're always the victim

LUKE: Poor Joey

LUKE: it's pathetic

LUKE: you always say I don't care about your feelings lol
    but that's because you ONLY care about your own
    feelings

LUKE: you've been accusing me of cheating since day
    one anyway, so screw it, you got what you wanted

LUKE: you have no idea how unattractive your constant
      insecurity is
LUKE: you and your mom deserve each other

"Joey…" Mom starts.

"It's fine," I say, but of course it's not. I feel hollow and heavy at the same time—like I've just suffered multiple gunshot wounds and my body doesn't know which one should start bleeding first. I ignored Luke for a total of—what? Six hours? And that's all it took for him to completely give up on me. Not just give up, but *unleash*. "Whatever."

"He always lashes out like this when you fight," she says. "Don't even worry about it. In an hour he'll be texting you, 'I'm so sorry, my temper got the best of me—'"

"*I'm* the one who should have a temper right now." My voice cracks. How many dishes can we afford to lose? I would love to smash a few right now. "This isn't just another fight, Mom. He cheated. And he's never said *this* kind of shit to me."

"I hope you know how wrong he is." She pours herself another glass and squeezes my wrist. "There's nothing wrong with you. Or us. He's just a prick."

He's just a prick. Funny. That's exactly what she used to say about Brooks White when he and his friends would terrorize me every day back in middle school. Actually? Luke always kinda reminded me of Brooks. How fucked up is that? It's probably why getting him to be my boyfriend always felt like such an achievement. It was like a delayed seal of approval from every popular jock who's ever called me a *fag* before.

And now it's been ripped away.

"Oh, my God, Joey. Don't cry." Mom places her glass down

and wipes a streak of eyeliner from her cheek. "Now you're making me cry."

Shit. I didn't even realize I'd let myself go. I look down at Luke's texts again in an attempt to transmute my sadness back into anger. It's not that hard to do, actually — I just stare at the word *pathetic* until a current of rage begins to crackle in my bones.

"Remember the Leo incident?" I ask her.

"Joey…" she ominously warns. "Don't even think about —"

"Why not? I have to do something to get back at Luke! This is just" — I catch my breath before it gets away from me and I melt back into a puddle — "it hurts so much."

"I know it does." Mom's hand oozes pity as it rubs my back. "But we don't do stuff like that anymore. Remember? It was stupid. I could have gotten us into so much trouble. We're lucky Leo let it go the way he did."

Leo is one of Mom's exes from…like seven years ago, I guess. He cheated on her and we got him back by trashing the hell out of his luxury condo one night when he was out of town. It was epic. We took two baseball bats and four cans of spray paint and exorcised our anger from wall to wall to wall. Mom even burned a few of his precious Giants jerseys in his bathtub. I honestly thought the building might burn down, but she turned the shower on and somehow prevented the fire alarm from making even a single *bleep*. A professional!

I didn't understand the gravity of Mom's pain at the time, but the experience moved me nonetheless. All these years later, I can still see the flames — flickering, waving, dancing through a pile of charred menswear in the middle of the marble bathtub — so vividly in my mind. I would kill to create some new ones right now.

"I'm supposed to just let Luke get away with this?"

"Trust me," Mom says. "Trashing his place won't make you feel any better. It won't fix anything."

"I really think it will."

"Let's be realistic." Mom sits up and tosses the blanket aside. "The kid lives on a college campus, for Christ's sake."

She has a point there. We'd never make it past the RA in the lobby.

Damnit.

"Then maybe we can egg his car," I say. "Or slash his tires." I drop my shoulders in desperation. "We have to do *something*."

"Jesus." Mom lets out a sad little laugh. "I've created a monster."

two

It's Monday — the first official weekday of spring break. I was supposed to spend this week with Luke on campus for a laid-back
staycation kind of thing. Instead I'm sitting on Nonna's outdated
kitchen counter, nibbling on a Stella D'oro biscotti and trying to
cure my hangover with a giant mug of dark roast coffee. "Volare"
by Dean Martin wafts out from her ancient kitchen radio. I usually love when she plays this song, but right now it's a little too
cheery for me.

"You look like you've aged ten years since last week," Nonna
says to me as she hovers over a pot of lukewarm water on the
stove. She's dressed like the anti-Mom, which is to say in loose-
fitting pastels. "Please don't tell me you stayed up all night crying
over that *stunad*."

"Of course I didn't," I lie. "I just had a bad night's sleep."

I wish I could blame my haggard appearance on an all-nighter
spent bashing Luke's headlights in, but Mom stood firm in her
conviction that it was a bad idea. So instead I retreated to my
room and made a half-hearted attempt at writing some new material for my hypothetical stand-up act. My plan was to add a page
or two to the running list of jokes I've got going in my Notes app,

but I couldn't come up with a single word. One of the reasons I love comedy so much is because it's a way to avoid pain and choose laughter instead—but *this* pain refuses to be avoided.

At least I restrained myself from answering his texts. What was left to say after his vile tirade against me, anyway? It was almost like he'd been saving that outburst in Drafts for months, waiting for the right time to hit Send. Maybe he and Joshua got caught on purpose. Maybe they're in love. Maybe he's been wanting to break up with me all this time and just didn't know how to go about it. I guess we had been fighting a lot. Maybe I missed something? Maybe—

"It's all your mother's fault," Nonna says, as if she knows I'm searching for answers in my head. Not that this one is at all helpful. According to her, every problem I've ever had is Mom's fault. "You look scrawny." She flicks a pinch of salt into the pot. "When's the last time she fed you?"

"I don't know." Which is probably why it's past noon and I'm still hungover. In the midst of all the drama last night, Mom and I never had the chance to incorporate any solid foods into our wine-a-thon. "How is *this* Mom's fault, though? Luke is the one who cheated on me. She had nothing to do with it."

"She's the reason you're like this!" Nonna says. "For the past year all I've heard is *Luke, Luke, Luke.*" She lightly slaps my arm. "What about *Joey?*"

"What about me?"

"You give these boys too much power—and you learned it from her." She delicately stuffs the pot with a bundle of uncooked linguine. "You don't need a man. Look at me. I've been alone for eighteen years. You don't see me crying."

"That's different," I say. "You just refuse to get over Nonno."

Nonno had a sudden heart attack and died when I was a baby.

"Because he was a good man." She side-eyes me while adding more linguine to the boiling pot. "Not like these *chadrools* you and your mother go for. I swear, you think any dummy walking down the street with a *pisello* dangling between his legs is God himself. And you." She points at me with a piece of raw pasta. "You have a *pisello* of your own! What do you need another one for?"

"Nonna, *ew*." I almost choke on my coffee. "I really don't need to hear you talking about my . . . *pisello*."

"Oh, please. Who do you think was changing your diapers while Gianna was off at beauty school? Anyway. All I'm saying is you should learn from your mother's mistakes. Otherwise you won't know how to keep a good man once you find him." She stirs the pot. "Let's not forget about poor Marco. I could've strangled your mother for what she did to him."

As if I could ever forget about Marco. He's the closest thing Mom's ever had to a healthy relationship. And the closest thing I've ever had to a father. Up until I was in fourth grade, the three of us lived together in a cute little townhouse on Franklin Avenue. It had an upstairs and everything! We played Scrabble as a family on Friday nights and even went grocery shopping on a semi-weekly basis. Can you imagine? It was all so wholesome I could puke. Mom tried really hard to be happy with him, but she eventually broke it off because he was "too boring." I was furious with her at the time — especially because the guy she dated after him was Leo, of all people — but I like to think I'm mostly over it. Nonna, not so much.

"She didn't *do* anything to him." I shift my weight on the counter. "There just wasn't a spark."

"You two and your 'spark.' You know what a spark gets you? Burned." She makes one of her over-the-top hand gestures. "Marco would have been a good husband."

That's probably true. But here's the thing I've come to realize about Marco. He was a total Nice Guy. He didn't have any of that Asshole Mystique™ Mom and I find so irresistible. Getting a Nice Guy to fall for you is kinda like getting into community college. Probably a safe choice, but not exactly a self-esteem boost.

Luke? He was like getting into Harvard for me. Which I guess means that last night was the admissions office officially rescinding their offer. And then pissing all over my application just to rub it in. You know what? This metaphor sucks. I don't even care about college! All I'm saying is that ever since I started dating, I have been able to better understand why it didn't work out between Mom and Marco. Anyway, moving on...

"It's not like Marco ever proposed," I respond. "And even if he had, would you really want your daughter to be trapped in a love-less marriage for the rest of her life?"

"Of course I would!" Nonna says. "Then at least you would still have a father."

"You're so dramatic," I say. "Marco's not my father."

One of the only things I do know about my father is that he was nothing like Marco. And everything like Leo. *Same shit, differ-ent dick* is how Mom would put it. The only difference is that Leo didn't refuse to wear a condom and then try to assault her into a miscarriage after her egg said "sure, whatever" to *his* unrelenting sperm. (Is that not how conception works? Listen, I'm gay.) I think she had to get an actual restraining order at one point—it was such a toxic situation. We don't really talk about it.

Nonna turns her kitchen faucet on. "You know what I mean. Marco is a good Italian man. Not like that disrespectful *medigan* she's been wasting her time on."

"She says she's happy with Richard."

"I'm her mother and I've never even met him." Nonna rinses

her hands in the sink. "You trust him? I don't trust him. I've seen pictures. He looks like he's full of *merda*."

Richard is handsome in a middle-aged suburban kind of way—like a guy in a Supercuts ad or something—but his face definitely has a shady vibe. You know those moments when you're crying and/or vomiting on the bathroom floor (as one does) and you randomly look over at the toilet from a certain angle and the seat looks like it's giving you a smug grin? That's Richard's mouth, basically.

"Aren't you at least excited for when she moves to Short Hills?" I ask. "It's gonna be like a whole new life! Who knows, maybe I'll live there, too... now that I'm not going to Rutgers."

Nonna straightens her posture and gives me the facial expression equivalent of a bitch-slap. I guess this answers the question of how she'll react to the news that I'm thinking about forgoing my college education to ensure I never have to be within a hundred yards of Luke ever again.

"I hope you're kidding," she says. "I've already cosigned on the loans—"

"Sorry." I shouldn't have brought it up. I really don't wanna have this conversation right now. "It was a dumb joke."

"Oh, Joey." She narrows her deep-brown eyes at me. They look just like Mom's—if Mom were thirty years older and spent a little less money at Sephora. "You've got to be stronger than this."

"That was why I had Luke." I can't believe I'm even saying this out loud. I really am hopeless. "He was strong so I didn't have to be."

"You think he was strong?" She scoffs. "You think *men* are strong? Men are weak." She scoffs again. "They're just better at not admitting it."

"Uh-huh."

Nonna puts the finishing touches on her linguine with clam sauce and forces me to eat three heaping bowls of it before she leaves for her part-time florist job. I'm just heartbroken enough to not care about carbs, so I oblige without resistance.

Know what I think is the worst part about getting cheated on? The humiliation. It's like the whole world gets to see how bad you are at being loved. I wonder how many of Luke's friends knew before I did. Probably all of them. As much as Luke tried to incorporate me into his life, I never really felt like I fit into it. They probably all laughed at what a gullible dumbass I was behind my back. How did they manage to look me in the face every weekend for almost a year? They can all go choke on dicks. Especially Joshua.

I remember this one time the three of us went out to Topgolf — a restaurant-slash-driving-range where you can reserve a small section with friends and take turns hitting golf balls.

"You gotta keep your left arm straight on the backswing," Luke gently instructed me after my first attempt resulted in a complete whiff. "And focus your eyes on the ball."

"Thanks, babe!" I fakely chirped back through my teeth, wondering why I agreed to participate in the first place. I'm generally less coordinated than an inflatable tube man outside a car dealership. "Got it."

But I didn't get it. I just whiffed again and then gave up.

"This is brutal," Joshua quipped as he took my place at the tee. It took him about five seconds to execute a perfect shot. "Boom! Thank you. Next."

And then it was Luke's turn.

"Just watch me," he proclaimed as he stepped onto the artificial green turf. He looked so hot in his Rutgers hoodie and athletic shorts. If he were a guy at my school, he'd have definitely been straight and popular. I always had to pinch myself to remember that he was both gay and *mine*. "This is how it's done."

A crisp pop reverberated in the air as his club hit the ball. His shot was even more perfect than Joshua's—the ball lifted and soared all the way to the back of the stadium-lit driving range like it had just shot out of a tiny little cannon.

"You make it look so eas—" I started.

"My man!" Joshua interrupted before I could finish my sentence.

He jumped over to Luke and gave him an obnoxious high five. Then they bumped chests like only two bros can, their respective pairs of arms protruding behind them as their fit bodies enjoyed a microsecond of direct contact. Once their feet landed back on the ground, Joshua grabbed Luke's left shoulder in that way straight guys grab each other's shoulders. You know? That quick grab—almost like a mini-massage—that says, *Way to go, man*. Or something. I don't know. That's a language I've never been able to speak. So I just rolled my eyes and scrolled through my Notes app from the sidelines.

Looking back, it was all so poetic I could fucking scream.

three

I was fifteen when I lost my virginity to a sketchy-hot Wall Street guy in downtown Jersey City — an experience fueled not by teenage love but instead by shame, fear, and a perilous thirst for male attention. You know! The usual.

It was so fucked up. He was probably in his late thirties, (older than Mom, which, in retrospect: *ew*) and even though I lied about it on Grindr, I'm sure he knew I was underage (which, also, in retrospect: *ew*). Second thoughts swirled through my mind for the duration of my Light Rail ride to his neighborhood, but I swallowed them all down like some kind of nasty medicine. In the end my nerves were outweighed by desperation and horniness. I mean, he answered the door wearing nothing but a pair of Under Armour gym shorts.

His sleek condo smelled of teakwood designer candles and weed. I hoped the latter meant he would be mellow and easy to talk to, but alas, not so much. He started aggressively kissing me — my first kiss! — before I even had a chance to ask him for his real name. Then he got his teeth involved, which caused my bottom lip to bleed. I tried to be chill, wiped the blood on my sleeve like I was Brad Pitt in *Fight Club* or something.

Honestly? I didn't hate it. I was kissing a real, live man. It was a dream! Like I was starring in my own movie. Granted, *Fight Club* is a violent meditation on American angst and I would have ideally preferred more of a Hallmark-y situation. But what are you gonna do? He kept kissing me. I closed my eyes and pretended we knew (and maybe even cared about) each other.

Things escalated quickly from there. His energy was wolflike — strong and hungry and full of this weird sexual anger. I held my breath and stared at the burning candle on his cherrywood nightstand as his hands gripped me. The words *wait* and *stop* banged around the walls of my mouth but never made their way out. I figured he had already made his mind up, you know? And I wasn't stupid. I knew what I was getting into by going there. I just hoped it might've played out more romantically. Like maybe he'd open the door and it would be an instant-soulmate situation. We'd cuddle and talk and he'd tell me he loved me and *then* we'd move on to the sex. Wow — okay — you know what? I take back what I said just now about not being stupid. I was a total dumbass.

So basically I just kept staring at his nightstand until it was over, at which point he wiped a bead of sweat off his forehead and rushed me out immediately. Something about work the next morning. (It was a Saturday.)

My lower lip was still numb as I made my way home that night, which was fitting because so was everything else about me. I checked Grindr to see if Old Man Wall Street had sent me any messages in the half hour since I left his place — maybe something that could make me feel better about what had just happened — but his profile had completely disappeared. I'd been blocked.

Mom was off from work the next day, so naturally I broke down and told her everything. Or — not exactly everything. I lied and said he was a kid from Saint Peter's Prep, because I knew if I told her I had hooked up with an actual adult she'd either murder him or try to get him arrested.

But I told her the important stuff. Like how I felt this strange mix of disgust and worthlessness from his rejection, tinged with a kind of pathetic comfort from the fact that he had at least found me fuckable in the first place. She admonished me for not seeking her advice *before* I threw myself into such an emotionally combustible situation, but then she hugged me and told me it would be okay. We drove down to the Shore later that day (even though it was late winter) and ate fast food on the cold, empty beach.

"I was so relieved when I found out I was having a boy," she told me, stretching out her yoga-pant-covered legs on the tattered blanket beneath us. "I figured it would mean you could never make the same mistakes I did. Not that *you* were a mistake—but, you know." She paused for a moment and steadied her voice. "I guess I should have realized that just because you can't get pregnant, doesn't mean you can't get hurt. I hate that I couldn't protect you from getting hurt yesterday."

"Yeah." It occurred to me that I was only a few months away from the age she was when she had given birth to me. This seemed impossible. "Me, too."

"You aren't cut out for these hookup apps," she said. "And that's a good thing. You deserve a guy who will love you, Joey. This world is full of pricks who will use and abuse you if you let them. But you don't have to let them, okay? Don't let them."

So naturally I proceeded to spend the next two years *letting them.*

I know! But I truly believed that each new guy who crossed my smartphone screen was just *one* hookup away from falling in love with me. You have to blow a lot of frogs before you find a prince, right? So that's what I did—except replace *frogs* with *noncommittal douchebags* and *closeted straight guys*. But then I met Luke last summer. Finally! Someone who didn't kick me out of bed at the end of our first time together. Instead, he kept his arm around me and let me play with his chest hair until we both fell asleep. I immediately claimed that space—his Rutgers dorm room, his squeaky old mattress, his Old Spice–y armpit—as my own. He said *I love you* three weeks later. The Hallmark prince I deserved.

And now look at me. I'm right back where I started—literally. Mom wanted to cheer me up after she got off work earlier, so we've returned to that same beach. It's a little warmer than it was that day three years ago, but it's still the offseason. The sand, ocean, and sky all have a sad emptiness about them.

"Did you hear from Luke today?" Mom asks between bites of dollar menu fries. "Did you text him?"

"Nope and nope." I feel just as numb—in a different and worse way—as I did the last time we did this. "I was at Nonna's earlier, so she distracted me for a while."

"What'd she have to say about it?"

"Just the usual." I force a half-chuckle. "It's all *your* fault—"

"You know what?" Mom puts a hand up to cut me off. "I don't know why I asked."

"I have a random question." I pop a fry in my mouth and wash it down with some watery Diet Coke. Mom hates the topic I'm about to bring up, which is why I normally wouldn't. But a tiny plus side of being heartbroken is that I know she feels too bad for me to get truly annoyed by anything I could say right now. "What was Nonno like? I was thinking today about how I've only ever heard *Nonna* talk about him."

"Oh." Mom sighs and looks the other way as a light gust of

wind blows her hair halfway across her face. "I don't want to ruin whatever perception of your grandfather she's given you. Especially since I know it's a positive one."

"So you're saying he was an asshole?"

"To me? Kinda."

"What did he do?"

"He just wasn't always the nicest person." Her tone has a very *I'm-not-talking-about-this* quality to it. "That's all."

"Nonna loved him," I offer. "So there's that."

"If you wanna know the truth, I don't think she was happy with him. Her entire life revolved around taking care of his entitled ass. Cooking for him, cleaning up after him, shopping for him. It was sad to watch. He did whatever he wanted and she didn't say *boo*. If he had been caught cheating on her? Forget about it. She wouldn't have even confronted him. It was like she didn't have a voice."

"Okay—wow." The thought of Nonna not having a voice doesn't compute for me. I've always viewed her as one of the most outspoken people in New Jersey. Which says a lot! Jersey is kinda known for its ridiculously outspoken people. "Are you saying that Nonno cheated?"

"I'm just saying he didn't respect her. It wasn't until after he died that she canonized his memory like he was some kind of saint." She scoffs. "Anyway. I always swore I wouldn't settle for that kind of relationship. I promised myself I'd have a voice. If a guy pissed me off, I'd let him know about it."

"I'd say you've kept good on that promise."

We share a laugh over this, probably both thinking about all the melodramatic fight scenes she's engaged in over the years. But then I think about Richard and how Mom has been quietly waiting around for him to get a divorce before their real life together can start. Maybe she's a little more like Nonna than she realizes.

I breathe in the crisp ocean air and dig my greasy fry fingers into the sand behind me. The sun is starting to set over the water in the distance — all pink and orange and blurry. It would be a perfect Instagram post, but I can't go on there because then I'd have to scrub Luke from my grid to make the breakup official. Not that I have any followers outside of Mom and a few coworkers from Mozzicato's. Oh God. *Work.* I took the week off for spring break, but I'm gonna have to go back eventually. All I ever did behind that stupid pastry counter was gush about Luke.

"I think the hardest part of this whole thing is knowing that it's *over*-over," I tell Mom. "With past fights, there's always been that underlying knowledge that we'll make up and it'll be fine."

"You don't want it to be fine with a guy like him," Mom answers. "You're still young. You don't need to make *all* of my mistakes, okay?"

"Would it be a mistake to —"

She throws a fry at me. "Don't text him."

"Who said anything about texting him?" I ask.

"That's where you were headed," she says. "I know you."

I huff because she's right. "I just don't get how easy it was for him to snap at me like that. And then to not text me all day today. It's like the entire past ten months were wiped out instantly, you know? Am I seriously *that* easy to stop loving?"

"Don't talk like that!" She squeezes my shoulder. "This isn't about you. It's about him being too stupid to realize what he has." She corrects herself. *"Had."*

I'm back in that aching space between pissed off and sad. Fifty-fifty on whether I wanna sob or scream. I consider punching the sand, but then I think of that dumb expression *Go pound sand* — which is something Luke used to always say — and *great!* An involuntary tear has now fallen. I jerk my hand up to wipe it off, and — oh, awesome! Now I have sand in my eye.

"You all right?" Mom pouts her lips at me in pity. "Let it out."

"No, it's just…sand…" I dig my wrists into my eyeballs until I've released enough tears to wash it out. "I'm fine."

"I promise this will get easier in time," she continues. "You'll come out of it smarter and stronger. And the next time you're talking to a guy and you see those red flags, you won't ignore them. You'll get out quick and trust that you can do better." She pauses. "The worst thing you can do is *know* a guy is bad for you but still jump in and try to make it work anyway."

That last part hangs in the salty air for a few seconds too many.

I wish I was better at taking her advice.

I wish *she* was better at taking her advice.

four

Notes App / Stand-Up Ideas:

Growing up, adults always loved to ask me why I didn't have any friends. As if it were a deliberate choice—I just woke up one day and decided to be a loser. It was demoralizing to always have to be like, "Nope. This is me trying!"

***

I just couldn't relate to other boys my age. They used to ask me stuff like, "What's your favorite toy to play with?" and I'd be all, "Ummm.. my mom's hair?"

Here's a question. Will I ever be able to put together an act that *doesn't* make me cringe so hard my dick shrivels up into a sad little piece of tortellini? All my jokes suck! Nobody wants to hear an awkwardly tall gay guy whine about what it s like to grow up without any friends.

I throw my phone across the bed in a fit of frustration. I have such a love–hate relationship with my Notes app. Sometimes the jokes flow so easily my fingers can barely keep up. Other times the screen taunts me, a backlit reminder that I'll never be good enough. I'll never get to live out my fantasy of writing an act so good that I get up on stage one day and just kill it. You know? An act so funny and perfectly delivered that everyone in the audience has no choice but to love and respect me.

I know, I know. It's an idiotic thing to fantasize about. I've seen enough comic interviews on YouTube to know that everyone bombs in the beginning. But maybe I'll be the exception! (Did you think my delusional expectations were limited to romance? Listen, I contain multitudes.)

Anyway. It's almost ten and Mom's still not home. Should I be worried? I'm kinda worried. We got back from the Shore more than two hours ago, and then she ran back out for a quick CVS run. That should have been a thirty-minute situation at most. Especially on our budget.

Just as I'm about to reach across the bed to retrieve my phone, I hear the front door open and slam shut. The sound is followed by the smell of . . . cigarette smoke?

Shit. Something bad must have happened. Mom hasn't smoked in years. I creep out of my room and see her attempting to open a new bottle of Luna di Luna at the edge of our peeling Formica countertop. Her hands shake, her cigarette dangles. She can't get a good grip. Jesus. This is an entirely different woman than the one I had a heart-to-heart with on the beach a few hours ago.

"Mom! What's going on?" I leap toward her and grab the bottle before it falls and creates a bloodbath on the linoleum. Those magnum bottles are like sixteen dollars, you know. "What happened?"

My gut tells me it's Richard and his bullshit. I really hope I'm wrong.

"It's Richard and his bullshit." Mom takes a final drag of her cig and places it in a half-full mug of dirty water in the sink. "I don't even know where to begin. I just feel so" — and now they're coming — "extremely" — yep, she's crying — "ugh" — aaaand I'm crying — "stupid."

Having such easily triggered tear ducts is exhausting. Like, really? We're about to have another night of bawling? This is getting to be ridiculous.

Maybe I should add it to my act. *My mom and I cry so much, it's amazing either of us ever has to pee.*

I finish opening the wine, pour us a couple of glasses, and guide her to the couch so we can sit down and discuss. It's a déjà vu moment for sure. "Here."

"This is bad." Her voice is steady and grim. "Like, really bad."

"I never liked that prick." I take a sip of wine and center my breath. "So what happened?"

"*You were right* is what happened," she says. "He's been living a double life. He was never gonna finalize the divorce. He was never gonna settle down here. He—"

"How do you know this?" I ask. "What the hell happened at CVS?"

"The house." She takes a frantic sip. "I got a Zillow notification for a new listing in Short Hills. It was his house. *Our* house. He put it on the market."

"Mom," I say. "I thought we agreed to stop looking at real estate porn online. It only makes us feel bad about ourselves." I pause for a second as I realize the true weight of what she just told me. "But oh my God. Seriously? You just found out from the Zillow app? He didn't say anything?"

"Nothing." Her voice goes up an octave as she punches one of our stringy Big Lots throw pillows with her free hand. "Nothing! So I called him from the parking lot."

"And what did he say?"

She places her wineglass down and reaches into her purse for a fresh cig from her shiny box of Newports. She knows I don't approve, but I slap her hand to solidify my position.

"What?" she says. "This is an extenuating circumstance."

"So is lung cancer." But I sip my wine and let it go. "What happened when you called him?"

"He got pissed at *me*." She takes a drag, and it does seem to help her relax. "Said I shouldn't have been snooping on him. As if real estate listings are top secret or something. Can you believe that?"

"Yup." I shake my head, thinking about Luke's outburst from yesterday. "I can."

"And then—" she's interrupted by her own impulse to gasp for air while holding back a sob. "And then—"

"Oh, my God, what?"

"He dumped me." She almost breaks down again but finds her strength in the filter of her cigarette. "I should have been the one dumping him, and he dumped me. You should have heard his ass. Going off on this rant about how I'm 'the most high-maintenance side bitch he's ever had.'" She flicks an ash into one of the empty wineglasses we left out last night. "I was like, *'side bitch?'*"

"Shut up." I wish I could save her right now. I wish I could get Richard in a room and just torture him. Like some *Saw* movie shit. "Who was the . . . main . . . bitch?"

"His wife!" she shrieks. "He *hasn't* been traveling all over the country for work. He's just been splitting his time between here and their house on the West Coast."

On some level I've always known this would be the inevitable culmination of their relationship. It was almost too easy to see coming. The idea of her (or us) ever actually living in Short Hills always seemed like more of a pipe dream than an actual future.

But despite all my skepticism, I still wasn't prepared for the pipe to burst. I wanted Richard to prove me wrong. For Mom's sake.

He picked the wrong day to prove me right. Between him and Luke, the current of rage that's been crackling in my bones since last night has now escalated into full-on explosion territory. My body won't be able to contain it much longer.

"I'm so sick of being treated like shit by these guys," I tell Mom. "We need to do something. Don't you wanna *do* something? To get back at them?"

"Joey." She narrows her watery eyes at me. "We already talked about this."

"Listen." I sit up and my back stiffens with determination. "I know you're nervous about getting in trouble. But we have both made so many stupid decisions based on these assholes. And they could care less. Someone has to hold them accountable!"

"Joey—"

"You know that documentary we love about Monica and Bill?" I ask. It's time to evoke our lifelong folk heroine. "Remember how everyone bashed Monica like she was some kind of homewrecking slut? Even though *he* was the one who kept buying her gifts and stringing her along with empty promises and lame excuses?"

Not to mention the fact that he was fifty and *literally the most powerful man in the world*. Monica was basically a kid—only a few years older than I am now.

"And then there was Hillary," Mom bleakly adds. "Standing by him the whole time." She lights another cig and refills our glasses. "*Fuck Monica,* right? As long as the perfect blond wife for-gives him."

Good. She's getting worked up. I can totally sway her.

"That's what I'm saying. It's not fair." I gulp my wine until the glass is empty and take a big breath. "We have to do something to make it fair."

Mom purses her lips as I continue my descent into drunken-ness, guzzling the rest of the wine directly from the bottle. Hope-fully all those beach fries will provide a starchy enough base to keep me from throwing it up later.

"So what do you say?" I ask. "Don't you wanna have a *voice*?"

We stare at each other for a moment, then down at our empty wineglasses on the coffee table. The fake wood is stained with watercolor-y red splashes from our sloppy pours.

"Fuck it," she finally answers. "You're right."

"Yes!" I wrap her up in a big messy hug. The current of rage in my bones instantly feels less suffocating—like it'll soon have a chance to escape my body. "I'm so ready to fuck shit up."

"I think the baseball bats are all the way in the back of the bathroom closet." She peels herself up off the couch and flips her hair back so it falls perfectly over her shoulders. "We're gonna need to get some new spray paint, though. I'm sure the cans we have under the sink are expired by now."

five

"Are you sure you're okay to drive?" I ask Mom from the passenger seat of her dinky old Nissan. As if we're not already barreling down the turnpike. "We had a lot of wine."

"*You* had a lot of wine." Her eyes are fixated on the road and we're not swerving, so that's promising. "I'm fine! Here." She tosses her phone at me. "Put some music on."

"What should I—"

"*The Playlist,*" she interjects. "Duh."

"Oh, my God, right."

The Playlist is our genre-spanning collection of highly pissed-off breakup anthems. Mom put it together years ago in the wake of the Leo debacle. The songs have always been like musical comfort food for us—audible evidence we can't be *that* damaged if so many other people have been through the same experiences we have. I dig through her Spotify and refamiliarize myself with the selection:

"You Oughta Know" by Alanis Morissette. "Before He Cheats" by Carrie Underwood. "Ring the Alarm" by Beyoncé. "Bust Your Windows" by Jazmine Sullivan. "Never Again" by Kelly Clarkson.

"Crazy Ex-Girlfriend" by Miranda Lambert. "Picture to Burn" by Taylor Swift. "Breakin' Dishes" by Rihanna.

Our plan tonight is to pull a "Before He Cheats" on Luke's car and then go to the Short Hills house for an explosive "Breakin' Dishes" moment.

If you've never heard "Breakin' Dishes" before, just know that it is perfection. You can *feel* Rihanna's rage as she informs her ex that she's gonna fight him, break his dishes (of course), burn (and bleach) his clothes, and then blow the entire house down. At one point she sings, "I ain't demented," then chuckles and says: "Well, just a little bit." Queen! I press Play.

"I forgot how much I love this song." Mom slaps the steering wheel and gives her own demented laugh. "Rihanna is *that* bitch."

I roll my window down and stick my face into the cool nighttime air. Something about the wind blowing against my all-cried-out eyes makes me feel more alive than I have in days. I'm ready to smash some headlights.

"We gotta get in and out of that parking lot as fast as possible," says Mom. "Anyone sees us, we're fucked."

"Totally." I settle back into my seat. "We'll do the quiet stuff first. Key the doors and slash the tires. Then you can get back in the car and get ready while I smash the headlights and windshiel—"

"Don't mess with the windshield," she interrupts. "We're not *criminals*."

"But Mom!" I protest. "The windshield is the most therapeutic part of the whole thing. Remember when Beyoncé did it in that big yellow dress in *Lemonade*?"

"Beyoncé has money," she dryly replies. "She can do whatever she wants."

"You don't understand," I tell her. "It would barely even

count as a crime. Luke *already* has a big-ass crack in his windshield. He's getting it replaced soon —"

"I said no." Her eyes remain focused on the road as her voice shoots me down. The whole vibe almost reminds me of a normal mother–son exchange, like from a family sitcom or something. "Plus it would probably set off his car alarm. Let's just stick with gentle vandalism on this one."

"Oh, good point." I guess I can let it go "I didn't think about the alarm."

A few more angry breakup songs later and we're pulling into the Rutgers campus in Piscataway where Luke lives. This place has always reminded me more of a giant shopping-plaza-slash-office-park than a traditional university campus. Lots of big, modern buildings. Not many of those charming brick castle-y structures or perfect green lawns you always see in college movies.

"Left," I say, as we approach a sign with a list of facilities and arrows. "He's in the Livingston Apartments."

Being in this environment with her is surreal. I always felt like such a different person during my Rutgers weekends — like someone with friends and a life. Even if the friends were Luke's and the life was a lie. Now I'm just here as . . . *me.*

"So this is where you're gonna be living in five months." Mom is going about two miles per hour. "It's bigger than I expected."

I think about the exchange I had with Nonna earlier and feel a heaviness rise in my throat. I don't want to disappoint her — especially after she's already committed to help out on the loans — but my vision of life on this campus was completely predicated on being *with* Luke. It occurs to me that he didn't just ruin our relationship. He ruined Nonna's family dream.

I can tell that Mom is reading my mind as I silently stew.

"We'll figure it out," she says quietly.

37

"Here!" I motion for her to turn right. "This is his parking lot."

She pulls in and stops perpendicular behind Luke's beloved Impreza. The spot he chose is only five cars away from the heavily lit back entrance of his building, which isn't ideal. It would have been better if he parked in a faraway dark corner of the lot so we could really have some privacy. But I guess vandalizers can't be choosers.

"Of course he'd park so close to the entrance," I say. "The asshole."

"At least he's not in a handicapped spot." Mom opens her door and looks around. "We're far enough away from the cameras. Let's go."

I pick up our two pocketknives from the floor below me and toss one to her. Seconds later I'm hovering over Luke's passenger-side door, peering into the same beige leather seat that used to make me feel so safe and wanted.

I pull on the handle. It's locked.

This is when it hits me that there's no turning back. Even if I did want to stoop to an entirely new level of desperation and forgive Luke for everything he's done, there's no way he'll forgive me for everything I'm about to do. I pull up my phone and look at his text rant from yesterday for last-minute confirmation that I'm making the right decision.

you have no idea how unattractive your constant insecurity is

you and your mom deserve each other

Yup.

He can definitely go fuck himself.

I shift my gaze to his back window and see his golf clubs splayed out across the seat, which takes me back to that night at Topgolf.

Pshhhhh.

I'm jolted back into reality by the sound of Luke's driver's-side tire deflating. I walk around to the side and see Mom's tiny frame crouched down in her black hoodie, digging her pocketknife out from the tire in question.

"Come on!" she whisper-screams. "We don't have all night."

Right.

I run back around to the passenger side and let every emotion I'm feeling travel from my hand to his tire. It's weird that the expression is "slashing" tires when you really have to make more of a stabbing motion to get the desired result. That rubber is thicker than a bitch!

Pshhhhh.

And now: *Eeeeeet.* I drag the knife against his doors as I crawl my way from the front to the back, still crouched down like an undercover agent or something. Save for the light scraping and deflating noises, Mom and I are being remarkably quiet. Good for us.

Crack.

Drip.

I feel something gross and sticky slowly ooze onto the top of my head.

"Oh, my God, ew!" It's egg. Mom cracked an egg on the roof of his car and it is now in my actual hair. "Mom! Hello? I'm right here! Now I have egg on my head."

"Whoops." She laughs. "Here." She tosses me a few eggs. "Take it out on Luke."

Right as I begin to press one onto his trunk, I'm blinded by a set of swirling orange lights about fifty feet away at the entrance of the lot. I squint to get a better look.

"Shit!" I say. "It's campus security."

"Be cool." Mom wipes a strand of hair out of her face and tucks it into her hood. "He hasn't even turned into the parking lot yet."

And then he turns into the parking lot.

"Excuse me!" Mom yells out loud, jogging toward the security officer. She sheds her hoodie in the process and ties it around her waist, revealing a tight white tank underneath.

"What are you doing?" I whisper. To myself. She's already gone.

The officer stops his cart at the entrance as Mom approaches him. My elbows vibrate in fear as I lean them against Luke's keyed, egged, and tire-deflated car, doing my best *nothing to see here* impression. Mom presses her weight against his cart and starts giving him a speech. I wish I could hear what she's saying. I keep leaning, extra casual, praying that he can't see anything. Calm. Cool. Collected. He looks over at me.

Shit.

Then Mom looks over at me.

She's . . . smiling? I hear them both laugh.

"Thanks so much!" She slaps the top of his silly little clown car. "Have a great night."

Mom prances back as if everything about this situation is chill and normal.

"Oh, my God." I breathe the heaviest sigh of relief. "How'd you get him to leave? Did you flash him or something?"

"I just told him you were my son."

"And?"

"That you had a flat tire, but we called AAA and they're en route." She smirks. "But yeah. Having a pair of boobs probably helped." She wiggles back into her hoodie. "That guy seemed like a fuckin' perv. Okay. Let's get out of here before he comes back."

"Can you pop your trunk?"

"Why?"

"Spray paint," I explain.

"Fine." She rolls her eyes and jumps into the driver's seat. "But hurry up." The sound of her car's engine starts buzzing into the air. "We gotta go."

I know I told Mom I wouldn't smash anything, but that was before I reread Luke's texts. How can I let him off with just a couple flat tires and key scrapes? I need his car to be mangled, like my heart.

So I ignore the spray paint cans and go straight for one of the two Easton aluminum baseball bats we laid out in the trunk earlier. The feeling of its rubber grip in my fingers takes me right back to that night in Leo's condo. I think for a moment about how other boys' baseball bat memories are probably all rooted in normal activities like Little League games and piñata birthday parties. There's gotta be a joke in there somewhere. I make a mental note to jot something down on the way to Richard's.

"What are you doing?" Mom barks. "Gentle vandalism only! The alarm. Remember?"

"I'll be quick." I give her my best shruggy apologetic face. "I promise."

"Stop—"

I turn back toward the front of Luke's car and channel every ounce of strength I have into my wind-up—mentally zooming through our entire relationship, from the first kiss to the final text—and smash the hell out of his driver's-side headlight.

The air remains quiet.

"No alarm!" I brag to Mom. "See?"

"You got lucky—now let's go!" she snaps as quietly as possible. "People definitely could have heard that."

I look back at her and sincerely mouth the word *sorry*.

I climb on top of Luke's eggy front hood and survey the uneven crack that's already in the center of his windshield. Somehow it's doubled in size since we first noticed it a couple weeks ago. With luck, maybe I can triple it.

I execute another impeccable wind-up—closing my eyes this time, thinking about all my future plans that have morphed into giant question marks over the past two days—thinking not about just Luke but every man who's ever made me feel bad about myself—from my middle school bullies to my nameless father to the Grindr creep who made my lip bleed—and hurl my entire body weight into a swing of the bat directly against the glass. I'm hypnotized as the existing crack swiftly expands out in every direction. The entire windshield is now covered in a spiderwebby mosaic of jagged white lines.

"Joey!" Mom yells. "What did you just do?"

Still no alarm. So I wind up again and give the windshield one final whack. The last one felt too good to not do it again.

This time the glass crumbles like a fresh biscotti. That passenger seat I used to feel so safe in is suddenly covered in a zillion tiny glass fragments.

I drop the bat to the ground in a daze. Mom pleads for me to get back in the car. I can barely hear her over the sound of Luke's alarm, which I've finally triggered with that last whack. The mixture of siren and horn creates a blaring dissonance—echoing throughout the entire parking lot in a tortuous loop—reminding me of the mistake I've just made.

six

"Have you lost your goddamn mind?" Mom screams as she zooms through the campus in search of the nearest exit. It's 12:01 a.m. and I'm officially a criminal. "I told you it would set off the alarm! That security guard was barely around the corner."

"I'm sorry." The last thing I wanted to do was add yet another layer of stress to our night. "But it didn't go off after I smashed the headlight! I figured it must've been broken or something." I watch out my window as we almost miss a key intersection for our escape. "Left! The on-ramp is like a mile down the road after you turn."

She doesn't exhale until we're back on the turnpike.

"Luke's gonna know it was us," she finally says. "Let's hope he doesn't press charges."

"He won't." As if I know how Luke would respond to a situation like this. "His parents will fix it for him. He knows we're broke."

"Right." Mom shoots a cautious glance at the rearview mirror.

"There's no one behind us." I press Play on her phone. "We're fine."

The first song to come on is "Bust Your Windows" by Jazmine Sullivan.

"Oh, my God," I say. "It's—"

"Your theme song," Mom blurts.

We burst into laughter like a pair of cackling witches. I turn the volume up and absorb Jazmine's lyrics. She's unapologetic—singing about how what her ex did to her was much worse than a car repair bill, but she had to do *something* to make him hurt. Preach!

"Holy shit." I wipe a validated tear from my cheek. "This song is almost too perfect."

"She's *that* bitch."

As the song fades out, it occurs to me that we haven't yet sketched out a plan for Richard's house.

"How are we gonna get inside?" I ask. "You're positive there won't be anyone home?"

"He's in California." Mom lights a cigarette with the hand she's not using to steer the car. She's basically back to being a full-blown nicotine addict at this point. "Who else would be there?"

I don't say anything. The answer is obvious.

"There's no way he had *two* New Jersey side bitches," she says. "I think I'd have at least picked up on that." Her voice shakes with insecurity. "Trust me. The house will be empty. I know the code to his garage. We're fine."

"He has one of those garage door opener keypads?" I ask. "God. That's so upper middle class I could puke."

Mom smirks. "Wait 'til you see the granite kitchen island."

"Shut up." Seriously, though. What's up with rich people and their big-ass kitchen islands? *You already have a countertop and a kitchen table! Why do you have to breed them?* "I'm gonna have so much fun spray painting it."

Richard's exit appears practically out of nowhere. After a few left turns, we approach a random stoplight in the middle of his otherwise residential (and poorly lit) neighborhood. It's yellow, but Mom isn't reducing her speed.

I glance out the side of my window and see a jogger — sporting a pair of black stretchy pants, a purple Reebok hoodie, and oversized headphones — round the corner from the street perpendicular to us. She's clearly oblivious, jamming out to her running playlist and headed directly toward the crosswalk we're about to plow through.

"Mom, slow down!" I squeal. "There's someone about to cross. Look!"

"Fuck me." She slams on the brakes. We jerk into a stop directly under the traffic light. The jogger snaps out of her haze, drops her phone on the pavement, and comes to her own screeching halt right in front of our headlights. She's blond and middle-aged. "*This* bitch," Mom hisses. "Who goes for a run at this hour?"

The bitch in question picks up her phone from the ground, gives a half-wave, and continues on her journey. You'd never guess we almost just mauled her.

"She should at least be wearing some reflective gear." I turn the music off. "Damn."

"Right?"

Mom tosses her burnt cigarette out the window as I maneuver my head under the windshield and look up. My cheek is basically glued to the dashboard, but it's the only way I can get a glimpse of the traffic light dangling above us.

"Okay." It turns green. "Go."

Mom switches the headlights off once we're on Richard's block. An eerie darkness consumes the interior of the car now that the radio display and speedometer are no longer backlit. It's accompanied by an equally eerie silence. I feel like we're tiptoeing down the street.

"Here it is," she whispers.

I notice a FOR SALE sign on the (sizable) lawn as we pull into the driveway. I peer out the window and take it all in: two-car garage, tidy white railing framing the front porch, dark window shutters against light vinyl siding. It's all so HGTV — the kind of house some rich bitch with a million dollar budget on *House Hunters* would complain is "too cookie cutter" while Mom and I scream at the TV in a shared fit of life envy.

We sit in silence for another few moments.

"I feel so stupid." She looks straight ahead at her hands, still on the steering wheel even though the car is in park. "This house —"

She stops herself from finishing the sentence. Probably because she knows she doesn't have to. I'm feeling it all, too. This house was supposed to be the finish line. Moving into it would be proof that Mom's relationship with Richard was truly different. Proof that she could see all the long distance periods through to their eventual happy ending. Proof that she was indeed wifeable — totally capable of being one of those million-dollar-budget HGTV rich bitches. Even if the budget wasn't technically *hers*. It would be close enough.

There's a fog of sadness in the air. Damn. I really shouldn't have turned off the music. It totally stalled our momentum.

"You put up with way too much from him." I rub her shoulder. "Remember that night last year when he didn't show up?"

I could be talking about any number of nights — Richard was always blowing her off — but I have a feeling she knows which one I mean. It was a hot Friday in August. We shared the bathroom mirror as we both got ready for our respective weekends away from the apartment—her in Short Hills, me in Piscataway. Luke was picking me up at nine. Richard hadn't texted Mom since they made their plans on Wednesday. She'd spent all day becoming flawless for him anyway—hair, manicure, wax, everything. Even with her makeup only half done, she already looked like she belonged on the cover of *Vogue Italia*.

"Is this normal for you guys?" I looked at her through the mirror while aggressively massaging store-brand apricot scrub into my T-zone. "Not texting for two days?"

"He's in his forties." Mom didn't break focus from her eyeliner application process. "He's not attached to his phone like we are."

Fast-forward to nine o'clock when Luke texted me to let me know he was parked on the street outside.

"Are you okay?" I asked her, gathering the rest of my things for the weekend. "I don't know how you haven't been blowing up his phone."

"If I do that, I'll look like a crazy person." She blinked twice and stuck the cap back on her Maybelline liquid liner. "What I need to do is act like it doesn't matter to me."

"I think you're taking this whole 'chill girl' thing a little too far." I couldn't help but think about how a pre-Richard Mom would have been screaming obscenities into a dude's voicemail for pulling something like this on her. "You shouldn't have to play these games! It's been more than a year with him. Haven't you at least earned the right to be annoyed by the fact that he's MIA after you've spent all day getting ready?"

She lowered her perfectly shadowed eyelids in shame. "Yes."

"Text me when you hear something." I was halfway out the door. "And if he doesn't show up, please give him shit." I gave her a hug. "Actually, give him shit either way."

She took my advice and they ended up fighting for the entire weekend. He turned it around and made *her* feel like she was wrong for not trusting that he had a valid excuse for his silence. "Flights get delayed and phones die." She accepted this line as law from that point on, reminding herself of it whenever he showed up late or blew her off, desperately looking forward to the day when they'd live together and this kind of thing would become a nonissue.

And now here we are in front of their would-be domicile, realizing that day will never come.

"All those times I should have said something." Mom bows her head. " 'Flights get delayed and phones die.' I'm so —"

"Stop saying that." I comb my fingers through her hair. It's soft, shiny, straight. Maybe those bargain keratin treatments *are* just as good as the real thing. Sometimes I miss her curls, though. When I was little I would wrap them around my tiny fingers and let go — entranced by how they'd always bounce back into shape like little springs. She hasn't worn it like that in years. Guys like Richard always prefer it straight for some reason. "You're not stupid. You were just gaslit."

"Wait here." She unbuckles her seat belt. "I'll wave at you once I'm sure we can get in."

"Shit. I just realized I dropped my bat in the parking lot after smashing Luke's windshield."

"Whatever." Mom shrugs. "I'll whack. You spray."

She slinks out of the car and up to the front of the garage — stealthily, like Lara Croft in *Tomb Raider*. A pair of motion-activated floodlights turns on and illuminates the entire front of the driveway. Oh, no. I almost snap my neck turning to scope out every other driveway on the street, terrified they'll suddenly be filled with nosy neighbors in silk pajamas. (That's what rich people wear to bed, right?)

But thankfully, the glow is perfectly contained to the ten-foot radius directly in front of the garage doors. We're fine. The houses in this neighborhood are about a hundred times more spread apart than they are in Bayonne, where you can literally stick your arm out your window and into your neighbor's kitchen.

Mom got the door open! I gather my bundle of supplies and do a *Tomb Raider* creep of my own. The first thing I notice upon entering the empty gray box of Richard's garage is a set of golf clubs resting in the corner. *Perfect*. I swipe one to use as a replacement for the baseball bat I no longer have. The floodlights — which were also illuminating the inside of the garage for us — tick and turn off. Everything goes back to black.

"Please be open, please be open, please be open," Mom quietly chants as she twists the door handle leading into the house. "*Yes*."

"I have to pee." I enter the first bathroom I see and place my Walmart bag and golf club on the marble counter. My reflection in the wall-spanning mirror is a damn travesty. I'll admit that I normally have some degree of dark-circle action happening under my eyes, but it's on a whole other level right now. You can tell I've been intermittently sobbing for the past thirty-six hours. It's not cute! And, oh, my God — my hair. Random clumps of it are glued together from the sticky residue of the egg. Gross. I turn the faucet on and try to rinse it out over the sink.

All of a sudden I hear a cacophony from the other room. I turn the water off. Mom must have started without me again. *Clank. Clank.* I'm guided down the hall by the faint glow of dim track lighting. I find her standing in the open-concept kitchen, chucking dishes across the living room like Frisbees. The shiny hardwood floor at the bottom of Richard's stone fireplace is peppered with chunky ceramic confetti. Rihanna would be proud.

"Gimme!" I giddily command.

"You know what really kills me about this?" Mom hands me a bowl. "It's that I *knew* better than to trust his ass. But I did anyway."

"Fuck him." I hurl the bowl at the fireplace and watch the pieces burst and scatter. It's entrancing to hear the room go from total silence to *clank* and back again. I grab myself another bowl. "Fuck all of them."

"I just thought, 'You know what? I've never been with a big-shot successful guy like this." Mom picks up a plate. "Maybe Richard's right. Men like him are *busy*." She thrusts her entire body weight forward on her throw. "Yeah." The plate explodes against the stone and shavings rain down onto the floor with the rest of the wreckage. "Real fuckin' busy."

Mom steps away from her pitcher's mound and grabs a can of spray paint from the Walmart bag. I stand back in awe as she unleashes it all over the kitchen—on the counters, stainless-steel appliances, cabinet doors. Her approach is abstract: random lines, squiggles, zigzags with no rhyme or reason. She's a pissed-off Picasso in skinny jeans and mascara.

"I'm going upstairs." She tosses the can at me.

I barely catch it. "I'll meet you up there."

Just like the rubber grip of the baseball bat earlier, the chemical smell of paint fumes in the air transports me back to that day at Leo's. Somehow the stakes feel higher at this house. I guess it's just that much bigger. In large letters all over the kitchen island, I spray:

The jet black graffiti against the tan-white granite gives me chills.

Bzzz.

My phone.

Shit. It's Luke.

LUKE: WHAT IS WRONG WITH YOU

Bzzz. Bzzz. Bzzz. Fuck. He's calling. I hit ignore and quickly respond to his text.

ME: what are you talking about? I'm sleeping

My pulse quickens as I watch the three dots next to his name bubble ominously.

LUKE: campus security just woke me up and showed me
    my car

It's been at least an hour since we set his alarm off. What the hell has that security guard been doing this whole time?

ME: Someone keyed it or something?

This is something someone with absolutely no idea of what happened would say in response to the context clues Luke's given so far, right? Right? Right?

LUKE: it's DESTROYED
LUKE: you need serious help
LUKE: you're fucking crazy

There it is again — the C-word. Because *God forbid* I have any feelings whatsoever about the fact that he ran my heart through a meat grinder.

ME: go to hell Luke — I WISH it was me
ME: I've been in Short Hills all night
ME: maybe it was Joshua
ME: or some other guy you've been fucking

The back of my throat burns with rage. A part of me feels genuinely offended that he's so quick to assume I would do something so unhinged as to destroy his car in the middle of the night. (The fact that his assumption is correct is neither here nor there.) But a bigger part of me is more concerned with building a case for my innocence.

I send him a GPS location tag as ironclad proof that it couldn't have been me. I'm more than thirty miles away from the scene of the crime.

LUKE: so u ignore my last texts for two days and
        suddenly respond now
LUKE: interesting

Fuck. He has a point. If Mom were here when he texted, I'm sure this is the first thing she would have warned me about. Damn her for going upstairs without me! What is she even doing right now?

LUKE: they're pulling the security footage
ME: good for them

I put my phone in my pocket and pick up the golf club, channeling my ire into my grip. I almost wish I could just send Luke a link to the music video for "Bust Your Windows." What he did to me was *so much worse* than what I did to his car. How could he not understand that?

I look around for something good to demolish, but the space is surprisingly sparse and open. There are only essential furniture pieces — no lamps, no vases (a vase would be so good right now), no cutesy home accents. This really would have been the perfect blank canvas for Mom to decorate if she had ended up moving in as planned.

I turn the corner toward the front entrance of the house and finally spot the perfect target: a crystal chandelier dangling over a random table in the foyer. It's off, but the crystal is shining in the darkness — reflecting all the fragmented brightness it can muster from the kitchen lights down the hall. I admire the beauty of it all for two seconds before stepping back, putting my hood over my head for protection, and going berserk on the thing.

It's raining shards of crystal. I'm reminded of the inside of Luke's car after I obliterated his windshield earlier. It's like I'm standing in the middle of a (highly disturbed) snow globe.

By the time I'm through with it, the chandelier resembles a bush that got run over by a lawn mower. I drop the club on the ground and shake the debris off my hoodie.

It occurs to me that the upstairs is too quiet. Shouldn't I have been hearing an equal amount of destruction from above? I drop the golf club to the floor and barrel up the beige-carpeted stairs, casually spraying the walls with black paint as I go. It's dark in the hallway, but there's some light peeking out from beneath a door down the hall.

"Mom?"

I push the door open and see her zooming back and forth

between two doors on opposite sides of the room. She's possessed — maniacally transferring loads and loads of clothing from the walk-in closet to the master bathroom.

"This fucking bastard," she says. "Look at this!" She drops her current load of clothes to the floor and bends over and rummages through the mess, apparently in search of a specific garment that isn't there. "Ugh!"

She collapses on the floor, buries her face in her hands, and whimpers.

"You okay?" I ask. What a stupid question.

"Yeah." She exhales and snaps out of it. "Or at least I'm about to be." She leads me into the bathroom. The extra-deep soaking tub in the corner looks like the menswear bargain bin at JCPenney, if JCPenney bargain bins were filled with designer labels. She digs around until she finds what she's looking for: a black bra. "Double D! This isn't mine *or* his wife's. I looked her up online and she's flatter than a goddamn Olsen Twin."

"I'm glad I just destroyed his chandelier."

"I thought I heard something down there." She tosses the bra back in the bathtub. "Nice."

Something has snapped in her. The version of Mom that gave sage beach advice and warned against smashing Luke's windshield has been dying a slow death all night long — but this bra was the final nail in the coffin. She has absolutely no more fucks left to give.

"So are we —"

"Yup." She goes back to the bedroom to grab the clothes she dropped on the floor a few moments ago. She comes back and slaps them into the tub with the rest. "What else should we burn? Anything?"

"Uhh . . ." I scan the beautiful en suite. Once again not much more than the basics. There's an almost-full bottle of Listerine by one of the sinks (of course this bathroom has two sinks). I pick it up. "What if we pour this over all the clothes?" I ask. "This is, like, super-flammable, right?"

"Only one way to find out."

I douse the clothes in the minty green liquid.

Mom grabs a book of matches from under the sink. "I used to love taking baths with him in here."

"Oh, my God, TMI." Even we have our limits with the personal details. "I do not need to picture you in here with Richard's old ass."

"His *crusty* old ass," she adds.

"I will vomit. Let's just light this shit on fire already."

"There's a smoke detector right outside the bathroom door," Mom says. "We can't let it get too crazy."

"Should I take the battery out?" I ask.

"Oh, right." Her face relaxes. "Yeah, do that."

Normally I'd be gentle when performing this kind of task, but in this case I just rip the alarm right off the ceiling without caring if I break something in the process. I pluck the 8-volt battery from its compartment and toss it on the floor.

Mom is tearing a match out of the matchbook when I get back.

"Wait!" I dig into my pocket and grab my wallet. It's dark-brown leather, from Banana Republic. Luke gave it to me as a birthday present just last month. I empty its contents into my pocket — twelve dollars, school ID, license, debit card — and throw the wallet on top of the heap. "This ugly-ass waste of leather can go to hell."

Mom looks at me with sad eyes like she totally gets it. I do the same for her.

"Here we go."

She strikes the match and throws it into the tub. The tiny flame lands on the sleeve of a sweater and immediately fades out.

"Well," I say. "That was anticlimactic."

She tries again, personally holding the flame directly to a piece of Listerine-y dress shirt until the fabric finally catches fire.

This time it works.

The white-yellow-orange starts slowly—creeping its way through sleeves and pockets and collars. We stand still, entranced by the wandering flames. I can't pinpoint the exact stitch that causes the fire to accelerate, but soon enough our faces are totally illuminated by this blazing bundle of Calvin Klein before us.

I grab Mom's hand.

This feels like the perfect form of closure for our respective situations. All the lies, pain, drama. Our invalidated pasts. Our canceled futures. *Burn it all down.*

"Shit." Mom lets go of my hand. "Do you smell that? It's like...burning pl—"

"Plastic." I'm jolted back into the moment with the realization that something is very different about this fire than the one we made at Leo's. It's bigger, brighter, bolder. "You don't think the actual tub is melting. Do you?"

Mom frantically zips to the faucet to turn the shower on.

Except—oh, my God—how did we not notice that this bathtub is *a standalone bathtub*? There is no showerhead hanging above to save us.

The shower is totally separate and on the opposite end of the bathroom!

"Shit!" Mom screams as she turns the regular bath faucet on. Cold water drips out, barely impacting a single flame. I cup some of the water with my hands and splash it toward the fire, but somehow it only seems to make things worse.

"Fuck, Mom!" A five-ton slab of dread plummets from my head to my chest to my knees. This can't possibly end well. "How many times have you been here? You've seriously never noticed that there's no shower over the tub? Seriously?"

"Jesus, Joey, I don't know! Of course I noticed. I've used that shower a million times. I didn't put two and two together." Her arms flail in panic. "Romantic baths and revenge fires are kinda on opposite sides of my brain."

For all the high-end finishes in this godforsaken place, the developers failed at installing a melt-proof tub. This thing is very much turning into sludge before our watery, smoke-filled eyes. That five-ton slab of dread in my body is increasing in weight by the second, by the flame.

"Does he have a fire extinguisher?" I ask. Mom just looks at me in a way that indicates she has absolutely no clue. "Shit! Oh, my God. Oh, my God."

"Maybe downstairs?" she adds. "Fuck. I don't know, Joey!"

It feels like we're on a speeding train that has gone off its tracks. There are no brakes. There is no safe way to exit. All that's left to do is violently crash into something.

"We gotta get the hell out of here," I say. "This fire is gonna hit the bones of the house and the whole place is gonna burn down."

"It's just a bathtub fire!" Mom cries. "There's gotta be a way we can contain this."

Right as she says that, an attack of angry flames flares out at us. Sparks fly everywhere. There's a mess of melted plastic and pipes where the bathtub used to be. A single wood plank is exposed, burning like a campfire log.

Suddenly the smashing of Luke's windshield seems tame.

Even a little cute.

seven

"Shit! Shit shit shit shit!" Mom's face is a wet, eyeliner-streaked crime scene as she paces back and forth in a panic. We're downstairs in Richard's kitchen and have now confirmed that not only does he lack living room furniture (and basic human decency) — he also doesn't own a fire extinguisher. "What are we gonna do?"

"He can't *not* have a fire extinguisher!" My eyes dart back and forth between Mom, the big open pantry that we just raided, and the ASSHOLE I scribbled on the kitchen island earlier. I hear a loud *thud* from somewhere upstairs. "What was that?"

"I don't know!"

Meanwhile, the thick smog of smoke we hoped was confined to the master bathroom has made its way down the stairs and is now wafting into the kitchen. A nearby fire alarm starts blaring. I curse myself for not thinking to disable all fire alarms in the house before we decided to commit arson. But of course we didn't *decide* to commit arson, which — oh, my God, wait, shit, fuck — *we just committed arson.* How is this happening? All we wanted to do was ceremoniously burn a bra and a wallet! Not an entire McMansion.

Mom looks at me with frightened, desperate eyes. I'm sure it's because she, too, is coming to the realization that our only option at this point is to get the hell out of here before the fire spreads even more and Richard's neighbors are awoken by the alarms or the flames or both.

"We gotta go," I declare through a smoke-induced cough. It's getting difficult to breathe through the haze. This is, like, the opposite of air. "Even if we do find an extinguisher, we can't go back upstairs. This place is actively falling apart."

"I'm so sorry," Mom cries. "I'm so sorry, Joey."

"What are you talking about? Now is not the time—"

I'm interrupted by another *thud*. Who knew fires could be so loud? It's like the house is begging, screaming for help.

"Oh, my God." Mom wipes her eyes and grabs her keys from her hoodie pocket. "Come on."

Thud. This is the loudest one yet, and it jolts us into movement. We sprint through the garage and jump into the car—a hotbox of adrenaline and fear. I can't steady my hand enough to click my seat belt in, so I give up. I look over at Mom and see that she didn't even bother trying in the first place. She starts the engine. The dashboard dings with an alert telling us to buckle up.

Mom throws the car in reverse. I wanna yell at her to go faster but I'm distracted looking up at the house. The roof appears to be intact, but there's a cloud of smoke escaping out from under it. It's only a matter of time before this fire rages out of control like one of those disasters you see on the news.

The car crawls down the street with its lights off. Mom clicks her seat belt in and I follow suit, if only to make that seat belt alert shut up already. The instantaneous switch from relentless dinging to total silence is sobering. Neither of us can muster a single word, so we remain mute.

I have no idea where we're going. Is Mom even capable of

driving safely in her current state? I'm definitely not. My brain involuntarily starts to workshop a stand-up joke about our predicament — something about how all we wanted was to have a "Before He Cheats" moment, but somehow ended up with "Jesus Take the Wheel." I could almost laugh if my face weren't frozen with shock.

Mom's hand shakes as she attempts to control the steering wheel and light a cancer stick at the same time. I would normally refuse to assist (and therefore enable) her, but this feels like a true extenuating circumstance. I grab the lighter and hold it up to her cigarette until it flames — this tiny little version of the very thing that is currently threatening to eviscerate both of our lives.

"Listen, Joey." She clicks her headlights on once we're a good mile away from the house. She suddenly sounds sure of herself. "I'm gonna call the cops and tell them there's a fire. Then I'm gonna turn myself in for —"

"No fucking way!" I have absolutely no idea what our next move should be, but hearing her say that out loud makes me abundantly certain of what it should *not* be. "Are you insane? We'll go to jail. This is a major crime."

"You think I don't know that? Christ." She can barely grasp her cigarette firmly enough to flick an ash out the window. "Listen to me. We aren't going to jail. Maybe I will, but — I swear to God — you're going to be fine. You'll live with Nonna if you have to. You'll go to college. You're gonna have a *normal* life. Okay? I'll say it was an accident and that I did it alone. The car, the house, everything. This is all my fault anyway. You have your future to —"

"No!" is all I can manage to squeak out before the air escapes my lungs. The thought of a future without Mom feels like a black hole. Losing her would be like losing a limb. Or a sense. I'd be armless and blind. "You can't do that. There's no way they won't know I was with you."

"Why? Just say you were at Nonna's all night. If you're ever even questioned." She finally manages to flick an ash, but her hand is still shaking. Hopefully that means she has some doubts about this incredibly stupid idea. "If I confess," she continues, "it will be an open-and-shut case for them. If I don't confess, there's gonna be a whole investigation. And then we'll both be screwed."

"No one will ever believe you did this alone!" Okay. So not only do I not want to lose her, but I'm also pissed at her for even thinking that I'd *want* her to take the fall for this. As if I'm such a baby that she has to make some kind of grand sacrifice to protect me from the repercussions of the house we just accidentally set on fire. I'm not a child! I knew what we were doing. I basically convinced her to do it in the first place. "Think about it. How did you unscrew that fire alarm? How did you smash that chandelier? There's no way a five-foot-tall woman could have done all that damage herself!"

"I'm five-three, bitch."

Mom's deadpan delivery makes me laugh. "Maybe in your knockoff Jimmy Choos."

"Ugh," she moans. "I don't know what to do, Joey. This is bad. This is real bad."

"I know."

The car goes quiet once again as we zip up the interstate, an alternating blur of lights and trees and smokestacks gliding outside my passenger-side window.

I remind myself that despite the brief laugh we just exchanged, we're still felons without a plan. My mind races from possible alibis to defenses to straight-up fantasy scenarios that would somehow absolve us of any responsibility for our actions whatsoever. I

Google "jail time for arson" and then immediately clear my browsing history because *Oh, my God, what if my Google searches are pulled up as evidence in a hypothetical future investigation?* I consider Googling "can the police find your browsing history even after you've deleted it," but decide not to, because if the answer to that question is *yes* then I might as well just dial 911 on myself right fucking now.

"It was an honest accident," Mom offers. "We had no idea the tub would melt like that. That has to count for something."

"I really don't think it does." I vividly recall all the havoc we wreaked on that house before the fire got out of control—the dishes, the island, the chandelier, the premeditated removal of the fire alarm—and am convinced there's no way anyone would believe we didn't know exactly what we were doing. "We left our mark all over that stupid house."

"Oh!" she says. "What about that security guard at Luke's parking lot? If we do become suspects, maybe he can be our alibi and vouch that we were nowhere near Short Hills tonight. I had that whole conversation with him, remember?"

Shit. Luke.

My entire face numbs as I remember that I sent him my GPS coordinates. *Who the fuck does that?* A thoughtless moron who wants to be arrested in the very first episode of the Netflix docuseries about their crime. That's who. In my attempt to prove my innocence of one crime, I implicated myself in another—far worse—one.

I wish I could go back to that moment in Richard's dark hallway when Luke texted me. I would gladly admit to everything. *Yes, it was us. We've been in Piscatway all night.* Oh, my God. Being guilty of *only trashing a car* sounds like such a blissful dream. I'd kill for that set of circumstances right now. Wait—hold on—that was just a figure of speech. I wouldn't *actually* kill someone. (Now that I'm a criminal I feel the need to clarify.)

"Joey?" Mom asks. "You all right?"

And now I'm the one who's shaking. I press my fingers into my eyes and drag them down my cheeks in an attempt to inject some hope into my face.

"We're getting ahead of ourselves talking about alibis and investigations," I say. "Think about it. How is this gonna play out? Let's say the entire house burns down — that would mean all the evidence is burned down with it. They'd never even know the place was trashed first! But even if the house doesn't burn down, how would they connect the dots to you and me? It's not like they have our fingerprints in the system."

I realize my argument would be a lot stronger if it weren't for the concrete proof that I delivered straight to Luke's inbox earlier. But even then...how would *he* end up being looped into a random fire investigation in Short Hills? Unless he talks to the cops about his car, and then *they* connect the dots. But those are totally different cops, different towns, different districts. They don't talk to each other. Right? Or — fuck — do they? I wish I could Google it, but I'm afraid to Google literally anything right now. Other than maybe something like "best pie recipe for a mother and son who have been sitting at home in Bayonne all night doing absolutely nothing illegal."

"It won't take much," Mom replies. "Richard is gonna ask himself, 'Gee. Who in New Jersey would want to *burn my house down*?' and then — ding, ding, ding! 'Gia Rossi. The high-maintenance side bitch I've been stringing along for the past two years, who I finally dumped today.'"

"It could have been another side bitch! What about the Double D bra? Maybe she snapped."

"Right," Mom cracks. "So it's either me or Big Tits McGhee. A grand total of two suspects. Very reassuring."

"Or! Maybe *he'll* suspect it's you or Big Tits McGhee, but he won't actually say anything to the cops. Because then his wife would find out that he's been cheating on her. Maybe he'll just let it go."

"People don't just let stuff like this go."

Our debate is at a standstill, but the car's still moving. My shoulders instantly relax as I peek out the window and realize we're approaching our exit. Being this close to home somehow makes me feel like I can trick my mind into believing tonight didn't actually happen. *We never left Bayonne. We sat on the couch Googling pie recipes all night long.*

I look at my phone. It's three in the morning. No new texts since I heard from Luke pre-chandelier smashing. The emptiness of my screen reinforces this comforting feeling that nobody knows and nobody ever will. Maybe we *can* just go on living our lives and everything will be fine. We'll proceed with our daily routines tomorrow morning as if it's just another Tuesday. Luke's car and Richard's house will be cold cases—unsolved mysteries. Those happen all the time. Right? Maybe? Please? God? Jesus? Take the wheel.

"Has Richard called or texted you?" I ask. "Has anyone?"

"Shit, I don't know." Mom uses her non-steering-wheel hand to pat down her hoodie and jean pockets. "My phone's not on me."

"No! Please don't tell me you left it at the hou—"

"I don't know, Joey." she yelps. "I don't think I used it at the house. Did I? Fuck. Is my purse in the car? I don't remember. It would be in the backseat. On the floor."

Panic floods my system all over again as I reach into the backseat and poke around until my hand feels the sensation of faux leather.

"It's back here." I dig in and feel through all kinds of random objects—makeup compacts, Advil bottles, approximately two zillion lip balms—everything but an iPhone. I turn on the flashlight app of my phone and twist my body backward so I can get a better view of the backseat floor. "No phone."

"Tell me you're kidding."

"I'm not."

We might as well just drive to the nearest cliff and gas it at this point.

"Joey!"

"Me? What the hell were you thinking bringing your—" I spot her sparkly pink phone case peeking out from behind the driver's seat. "Oh. Thank God. I found it."

"You almost gave me a heart attack! So what's it say?"

"Hold on." I swipe in her password and run through her notifications, instantly relieved by the absence of a missed call from 911. As if it would actually show up as 911 on Caller ID when the police call to tell you that you're wanted for arson. "This is good. No missed calls. Some junk email. A Bath & Body Works coupon. Adriana liked your Instagram post from yesterday. You just have one text. From...Marco?"

Mom exhales in relief, which tells me her thinking is just as twisted and delusional as mine was a few minutes ago: *Notification-free phone! We're in the clear!*

"Marco says, *Hey G, I miss you*, and—wait. Why is he texting you?" I think back to my conversation with Nonna earlier. Maybe she was right. Mom should have never left Marco. Nice Guys might be boring, but they also don't inspire felonies. This suddenly strikes me as a reasonable trade-off. "What's going on? Are you guys talking again?" I scroll up in the conversation, and there's one message prior to his. From Mom, five hours ago. It just says hi. "Oh, my God. You initiated this! You *hi*-ed him!"

"Calm down." Mom flips her blinker and gets off our exit. "I was buzzed from the wine and feeling like shit about myself because of Richard. And you remember Marco — he was always good for a self-esteem boost. That's it. You know he lives all the way in upstate New York on Lake Whatever-the-Fuck. Just delete the conversation."

"Fine." I sneakily respond with miss you too. It's a shady move, but whatever. Our lives are at stake and something tells me that keeping an open line of communication with him right now might actually be beneficial.

Mom turns onto our block. I stare out the window at the flickery street lights and McDonald's fry sleeves lining the sidewalk. Short Hills' worst nightmare. I swear to God. Why couldn't we have just torched one of our neighbors' houses instead? They probably would have thanked us.

"No cop cars," Mom says. "That's gotta be a good sign."

I'm kind of annoyed that she's jolting us back to reality by being on the lookout for cops, but also relieved, because, well, there are no cops. I even feel allowed to be exhausted — which I totally am. Being this close to my bed induces a vigorous yawn.

"Let's just go upstairs and get some sleep," I suggest. "Maybe one of us will have a brilliant idea in the morning. Or maybe we'll wake up and all of this will just go away."

Mom parks the car in our narrow shared driveway and gives me a sad chuckle. "Yeah." Her side profile is stunning as always under the faint glow of a nearby streetlight, but there's a tightness to her temples that suggests she's still holding back tears (basically her resting state at this point). "I'm so sorry."

"Enough with the apologies—"

"This is my fault. I'm a bad influence—"

"Mom. Stop." I refuse to let her continue down this road. Especially because it still makes no sense to me why she keeps acting like this whole night was her idea. I would never even think to blame her for anything that comes out of this. Even if we both go to jail. "Can't we just try to get some sleep?"

She quietly accepts my plea. We get out of the car and crawl up to our apartment—in the front door, through the kitchen, past the empty wine bottles on the living room coffee table—and retreat into our respective bedrooms. I can hear Mom crying on the other side of the wall, which would destroy me if I weren't so depleted of the emotion, adrenaline, and general will to live that's been keeping me going all night long.

I collapse onto my bed and close my eyes. It's amazing how the most trivial anxieties can sometimes keep me up for hours at night, and yet right now, in the aftermath of incinerating a million-dollar house, my mind is just like *fuck it*. I slip out of consciousness immediately. Barely aware that it's happening.

eight

A relentless beam of sunlight slices across my shoddy old Ikea dresser. I grab my phone from the kitchen-chair-functioning-as-a-nightstand beside my bed and squint at the display. Eight in the morning. My chest thumps as if I just had the worst nightmare of my entire life. Then I remember everything.

"Mom!" I yell as I run out of my bedroom. "Are you awake? Are you okay?"

"Just got up." She's in velour yoga pants and a white tank top, waiting for her coffee to brew at the kitchen counter. "Not okay."

"Any calls or texts?" I ask.

"None. You?"

"None." We stand there in weighted silence for a few beats until I finally muster up the courage to suggest the inevitable. "Should we turn on the news?"

We flip through all the local channels. Everything is politics, sports, crime of the non-arson variety, and weather, weather, weather. It's gonna be unseasonably hot and sunny all week. Awesome! So great to know that Luke and I would have had sterling conditions for our spring break staycation.

This is all his fault. If he had never cheated on me then I

would have never in a million years suggested that Mom and I go on a crime spree. Even if the whole Richard thing had still happened, even if Mom said *she* wanted to go on a revenge rampage, I would have been the levelheaded voice of reason. I would have comforted her in all the standard, healthy, non-illegal ways: binge-eating ice cream and watching the Monica Lewinsky documentary and workshopping a Facebook message to send Richard's wife—you know, one that expertly toes the line between "scorned mistress" and "concerned ally to all women."

Bzzz.

I almost kick the couch in front of me in response to the sudden vibration in my sweatpants pocket. Speak of the ~~devil~~ asshole. Luke's calling me.

"Who is it?" Mom asks. *Bzzz.* She's standing next to me. For some reason sitting down while we channel-surfed for evidence of our impending demise didn't feel like an option. "Tell me it's not—"

"It's just Luke." I hit Ignore. He calls back immediately. I hit Ignore again. He calls back immediately again. "He won't stop!"

"Just let it ring!" She grabs it from me with her free hand. "He's obviously gonna know you're ignoring him if it keeps ringing only one time." *Bzzz. Bzzz.* She looks down at the screen. "Now he's texting you."

"Give it to me!" All I can think about is her pulling up my text history with Luke and seeing the suicidal GPS tag I sent him last night. I snag my phone from her hand before she even has a chance to half-swipe. "Thank you."

LUKE: I didn't tell campus security it was you
LUKE: we're even, ok?
LUKE: I just want to talk about everything

"What's he saying?" she asks.

"Uh." His change of tone since yesterday has completely tripped up the wires in my brain. "His car."

"Lord. I almost forgot about *that*. Does he think it was us?"

I give the messages a second read.

Yup. He's definitely trying to trick me into admitting guilt. What a conniving asshole. I run through possible responses in my head—torn between *Go to hell* and *Eat shit*—but my train of thought is interrupted when Mom lets out a bloodcurdling scream.

I peel my eyes off my phone and see her frantically turn the volume up on the TV while a drone camera hovers over what's left of Richard's house. There are rows and rows of blackened wooden beams where the roof used to be. The master bedroom is a pile of ashes and soot. Every bone in the top half of the house is exposed and charred. Which happens to be exactly how all of *my* bones feel right now, too.

Things are slightly less apocalyptic-looking on the bottom half. The front door seems weirdly unaffected. I wonder what the other side of it looks like.

"...the flames broke out overnight at 33 Marble Lane in Short Hills—a home that *just* went on the market yesterday," the anchor proclaims in a straightforward tone that totally undermines our panic. This is just another day for her. I'm so jealous I could die. "We're told the owner is out of town and the home has been vacant for some time, which makes this case all the more perplexing for investigators." More shots of the house cross the screen. "The damage, as you can see, *is* significant." Now she's doing that reporter-y thing where she emphasizes every other word like a calm yet constipated slam poet. "But it could have been *much* worse...if it weren't for a fast-acting neighbor in the *right* place at the *wrong* time."

They cut to a close-up interview with a tired-looking blond woman in a purple Reebok hoodie with a pair of chunky head-phones around her neck, and—oh, fuck. It's the bitch we almost mauled at the crosswalk.

"Oh, fuck," says Mom. "It's the bitch we almost mauled at the crosswalk. Remember—"

"I REMEMBER!"

"I'm a total night owl," Joggy McBitch tells the camera. Her voice sounds more evening gown than athleisure wear—rich, untouchable, self-assured—very Hillary Clinton. As if we didn't have reason enough to resent her already. "So I'm always going for jogs around the neighborhood at odd hours." The camera pans across Richard's idyllic street. "I must have passed that house six, seven times last night before I saw the fire. There was cer-tainly someone there when it started. I saw a strange car in the driveway and the garage door was wide open." Her annoying voice starts to quiver. "You know, you just can't *imagine* some-thing like this would happen in your own neighborhood. Until it does."

And now the camera is on the reporter. She's standing in front of the wreckage in a taupe power suit. Speaking of Hillary.

"The witness says the mysterious car was no longer parked in the driveway when she caught sight of the flames." She cocks her head slightly as the camera angle shifts. "The Essex County Pros-ecutor's Office has confirmed that the origin of the fire *does* appear to be suspicious. Investigators are on the scene in search of clues. The question they are *desperate* to answer"—she raises an eyebrow and looks straight ahead—"is *who* did that car belong to?"

Mom clicks the TV off and drops the remote. Her entire body follows as she collapses into a ball on the floor. My knees are also threatening to buckle. I grip the arm of the couch to catch my bal-

ance. My mind races back through each step we took last night —
desperately recalculating every conclusion I've drawn thus far
with the new knowledge that the jogger wasn't just a jogger but
a *witness*. Does she remember when we almost hit her at the crosswalk? Did she see our faces? Does she remember what kind of car
we were in? The color? She didn't say anything about the make or
model when she talked about it in her interview.

But even if she does remember. *Everyone* has a Nissan Altima.
Right? Surely she didn't take down our license plate. Why would
she do that? She didn't know about the fire until after we were
long gone. But what if she has a freakishly photographic memory?
What if she stopped to take a selfie at some point during her run
and inadvertently captured the plate number in the background?

"We need to go to the police," Mom wails from the floor. "It's
only a matter of time before they put it all together."

"Go to the police *now* that we've fled the scene and it's on the
news?" I shoot back. "They'll never believe it was an accident."

"I wanted to go to them yesterday!"

"If we tell the cops, we're officially turning ourselves in as
criminals." I grab Mom's lifeless hand and pull her back up to a
standing position. "And then Richard becomes the victim. Fuck
that! He's not a victim. He has the money to buy a new house!
Fuck him."

Mom shoves a tuft of hair out of her face. It's holding up
pretty well considering the night we just had.

"Then we need to go somewhere," she says. "That jogger saw
our faces. We can't be in Jersey right now. This apartment is a ticking bomb."

"It sounds like they don't have any leads yet," I say. "Hold on."

I pull out my phone and head to Twitter to scan all the news
accounts. Surely Joggy McBitch talked to more than one reporter.

Maybe there's an interview where she says, "I have no idea what kind of car it was or who might have been driving it. Now that I think about it, the whole car thing was probably just a coincidence. I'm sure it was just an electrical problem or something." Followed by the anchor saying, "The investigators seem to agree with her"—cue dramatic head tilt and constipated-reporter-voice—"they've decided to drop the case entirely."

I type *Short Hills fire* into the search bar and the first thing that comes up is a picture of the house from when it was actively burning overnight, unruly flames sprouting from the top of it like giant, glowing fall leaves. It has nineteen—wait, it just went up to twenty—retweets.

"Oh, no," I say. "Look at thi—"

I'm interrupted by a vigorous knock on our front door.

Our rusty silver chain lock jangles with each bang. Suddenly my throat feels like one of those burnt wooden beams where Richard's roof used to be.

"Shit!" I whisper-scream. "Do you think it's a cop?"

"Don't say anything." Mom wipes a tear from her eye and pulls herself up from the floor. "It was all me. You got that?"

The irony is that I'm sure this was all me. It was the GPS blunder. I know it. I can feel it. Luke's whole "I'm over it" text was just a mind-fuck to keep me off guard. He saw the news or the tweet or an article and thought to himself, "33 Marble Lane? JOEY TEXTED THAT EXACT LOCATION TO MY PHONE YESTERDAY," and immediately called the Essex County Prosecutor's office. He probably cackled as he hung up the phone and pictured me getting arrested. And then he went back to blowing Joshua.

Bang. The knocking continues. *Bang. Bang. Jangle.*

"Do you understand?" Mom's hand trembles as she places it

on my arm and looks up at me with her hopeless, defeated eyes. "You didn't do anything."

She's clearly ready to go to jail for me — like, for real. This realization creates a freezing lump in my throat. She's being irrational, just like she was when she wanted to turn herself in last night, but I don't have any more time to talk sense into her. She's already making her way toward the door.

"Neither of us did anything wrong," is the only thing I can manage to whimper in response.

Bang. Bang. Jangle.

Mom looks back at me and mouths *I love you* before tiptoeing up to look through the peephole. I stay put — basically my only option, given that my limbs are currently stuck in place.

The banging stops.

Total silence.

And then a voice calls out from the other side of the door.

"Gianna? Joseph? Open up!"

nine

My muscles all unclench at once. Mom lets out the heaviest sigh I've ever heard as she unlatches the chain and flips open the dead bolt. The voice behind the door belongs to Nonna.

"Jesus, Ma!" Mom says. "What are you trying to do, give me a heart attack? What happened to your key?"

"It must be in my other purse," Nonna says. "It's hotter than hell itself out there. I can't tell if it's April or August." She throws a white pastry box on the counter and scans the apartment with her knife-sharp eyes. "Not for nothin', but you two look like crap run over twice. What's going on in here?"

"It should be on your keychain," Mom says. "You come here enough, don't you think?"

"Yeah, yeah." Nonna struts over to me "Joey. Your eyes are redder than a tomato. You still cryin' over that *stunad*? Forget about him."

"It's not that," Mom says before I can answer. "We're in trouble."

I shoot her a vigilant look, like, *Don't you dare tell Nonna we set a house on fire last night. It will absolutely ruin her day.*

"What do you mean, trouble?" Nonna pours herself a cup of

coffee and unties the string from the box. "Here. I brought some sfogliatelle from Mozzicato's." She takes one out and dips it in her coffee. I haven't had a real appetite for more than a day at this point, but seeing that delicate chunk of flaky golden perfection is almost enough to make me drool. "They asked about you, Joey. I said you had a change of plans this week and might be able to pick up a shift or two."

"Why would you do that?" I say. "I'm still on spring break. Just because I'm a single loser with no friends doesn't mean I want to spend the whole week filling cannolis."

"Don't be a *googootz*," she says. "You need the money. And it's better than sitting around here sulking with your mother all day." She turns to Mom. "What's this trouble you're talking about?"

"It's nothing," I proclaim before Mom can get a word in. "Just, uh, car problems. Mom's car won't start. Actually. We were gonna ask if we could borrow yours for a couple days."

Mom was right—Jersey is a ticking bomb. It's only a matter of time before the next series of bangs on our door *aren't* coming from Nonna. And we obviously can't be driving around in the car that every cop in the state is probably looking for right now.

"A couple days?" Nonna asks. "Gia, just call AAA and have it towed to Firestones."

"It's *Firestone,* Ma." Mom rolls her eyes. For some reason she hates the way Nonna is always adding *s*'s to things that don't actually have them. Ruby Tuesday is Ruby Tuesday*s*, Rite Aid is Rite Aid*s*, and so on. I think it's hilarious and definitely something I plan to put in my act one day. Eventually. After we get this whole arson situation sorted out. "And Joey." She narrows her eyes at me. "Don't be stupid. We don't need Nonna's car."

"But what about our *trip*?" I ask. "We're already running late.

If we go to Firestone we'll have to wait for, like, five hours. We gotta go now."

"Trip?" Nonna says. "What trip? Gia, you gotta work."

"Actually, Mom took the week off too." I don't even know where these words are coming from, but they feel necessary. I turn to Mom and try to give her a look that says *please go along with this*. Nonna will quickly call bullshit if Mom acts even a little surprised by what I'm saying. "She wanted to help me get my mind off the Luke thing."

"Um..." Mom starts.

I hold my breath so hard it's like I'm ten feet underwater.

"Yeah," she continues. "I don't think Joey should be alone this week. And I feel like a change of scenery will really help him...heal."

And just like that, my head is above water again.

"Madonna mi," Nonna exasperates. "Both of you. Just taking off of work like it's nothing." She gestures around at our run-down living space. "And you wonder why you don't have a pot to piss in."

"Please?" I plead. "I totally get what you're saying, but this is my last spring break from high school ever! In just a few months I'll be in college."

Nonna smiles. "Well, I'm glad you came to your senses with that whole 'maybe I won't go' nonsense." She looks over at Mom. "Where do you two plan on taking my car? When are you gonna be back?"

"It's a surprise," Mom says. "I mean. I want Joey to be surprised. You know, give him some suspense." I could almost laugh. Suspense is the last thing we need more of today. But I am loving that Mom is fully invested in my plan now. Thank God. "I'll call you later and tell you. When Joey's in the bathroom or something."

"Ay yi yi," Nonna says. "Just drive safely, please. Okay? Here." She pulls her car key out of her purse and hands it to Mom. "You're going to have to drop me off at Teresa's. I guess I'll just have her cart my ass around all week. Lord knows she owes me." She takes a swig of her coffee. "Do you want me to take your car in to Firestones while you're awa—"

"No!" Mom and I bark back in unison.

ten

I decide to embrace the illusion that everything will be okay. Maybe it's not even an illusion! Like, right now it's broad daylight outside. We just crossed out of Jersey into New York. And we're in a totally nondescript vehicle that has absolutely no connection to any recent crimes in the tri-state area. As far as we know, at least. I presume Nonna hasn't robbed any banks lately. That would be extremely out of character for her. But—oh, my God—how amazing would it be to randomly discover ten grand in the trunk during our next pee stop?

We still have every reason in the world to be freaking out. We don't even know where we're going other than "in the direction of Canada." And there's this voice in the back of my head that's constantly whispering "you're fucked, you're fucked, you're fucked."

But it's getting easier to drown out with every exit we pass.

I crack open the window and let the spring air flow in. "Ring the Alarm" by Beyoncé comes on, which—just like every other song on the Playlist—has taken on a whole new level of significance since last night. I spend the entire first verse and chorus nodding my head to the beat in anticipation of my favorite line, in which she tells her ex he's never seen a fire like the one she plans on causing. But Mom skips to the next track before Beyoncé can even get the first word out.

"Hey!" I say. "It was just getting to the good part."

"Sorry," she replies. "Just hits a little too close to home right now."

"That's why I was so excited about it."

And then we both laugh.

I'm able to relax even more as I spend the next thirty minutes of our drive obsessively combing social media and the internet for more information on the fire. The results are surprisingly tame.

I'm still a little paranoid about Big Brother (or whoever) tapping into my phone activity, so I've developed a rule of thumb for internet browsing: if it's something about the *news* of the crime ("fire in Short Hills," etc.) it's okay to search. But if it's something about the potential *consequences* of the crime ("jail sentences for arson," etc.), it's off-limits.

So here's what I find out:

Joggy McBitch's real name is Lisa. She was the one who posted the picture to Twitter, but it seems to have peaked at just thirty-five retweets. She gave one other news interview, but it's clear that she basically knows nothing. She doesn't even remember what kind of car she saw.

"It was a sedan," she told Channel Four. "A Camry or a Maxima, maybe. I didn't get a great look at it. But it was definitely there."

Even Luke seems to have simmered down a bit. I sent him a response—We don't need to talk, I'm over it—and he hasn't gotten back to me. He's probably too busy sixty-nine-ing with Joshua. Which, honestly? I couldn't care less about at this point. Being an inadvertent arsonist has totally put things into perspective for me. Fuck our breakup. Fuck worrying about getting in trouble for smashing a windshield. People have those fixed all the time. It'll probably even be covered by his insurance.

My biggest concern right now is just letting the clock run out for the week until the fire investigation blows over and we can resume our lives as if nothing ever happened. I'll even gladly go to Rutgers in the fall. I can deal with seeing Luke and Joshua around campus. I'll find a new boyfriend. I'll force myself to love finance or whatever other bullshit major. I'm sure it will be at least a little better than jail. More food options and the ability to poop in private.

Mom randomly pokes my shoulder.

"Do you think it's weird that I haven't heard from Richard at all?" she asks. "Even if he didn't think it was me, wouldn't he at least reach out? He doesn't know that many people in New Jersey." She pauses. "The fucker. He's probably leaning on Big Tits McGhee for support. I can't believe I was his *side* side bitch."

"Okay, I feel like you're heading toward a dark place. The fact that Richard hasn't reached out is *amazing* for us. It means he thinks you have nothing to do with it."

"I guess." She flicks her signal and merges into a rest stop exit lane. "By the way, I saw that text you sent."

I shift in my seat. "What are you talking about?"

"You know what I'm talking about, Joey."

Shit. She knows. How has she not brought it up until now?

Maybe she doesn't think it's a huge deal. It's not, really. Just a harmless little geolocation tag that Luke probably deleted by now anyway. There's no way he'd even put two and two together! Why would he think to do that?

"I know it was so stupid." I do my best to sound like I'm not actively pissing myself. "I was just in such a messed-up state of

83

mind from the whole night. You know? I figured that if Luke knew we were in Short Hills, he'd stop accusing us of trashing his car and—"

"Wait a minute." Mom widens her eyes at me as we approach the rest stop. "I was talking about the text you sent to Marco from my phone. '*I miss you.*'" She pulls up next to a gas pump. "You told Luke we were in Short Hills last night? Joey! Have you lost your mind?"

I shrink down to Lego-size. I am a Lego-size human now.

"I..."

"What were you thinking?"

"I wasn't thinking!" I say. "Obviously."

"Well, fuck." Mom thoughtlessly grabs a cig out of her purse. "Now we gotta hope *he* doesn't go talking to the cops."

"He won't." I snatch it out of her hand. "And are you trying to get us blown up? We are literally surrounded by gasoline."

She rolls her eyes. We sit in silence for a few seconds before I realize that there is no station attendant coming to assist us.

"We're definitely not in Jersey anymore," Mom says. "Look at all these bitches filling up their own tanks."

I hate them in the same way I hated that news anchor. They're just going about their mistake-free lives. It occurs to me that even if the worst of the worst were to come of this—we get arrested, go to jail, have to somehow figure out a way to pay for a million-dollar house, go to jail *again* for whatever illegal stunt we have to pull to not end up homeless in the midst of all of the above—the rest of the world will just go on.

I guess that's obvious. But it doesn't seem fair.

We both jump out of the car—Mom to pump gas, me to execute a snack run.

"Here." She hands me two twenties and pops open the gas

cap. Her getaway outfit consists of an oversized Victoria's Secret *Pink* tank top, black leggings, and high-heeled suede boots that go all the way up to her knee. The thought of her pumping gas is hilarious. I kind of wanna stay and watch. "Tell them to put thirty dollars on our pump. I took out four hundred before we left Jersey, which has to last us—"

"Got it." I'm not in the mood to think about how we're not only on the run, but we're also broke and incapable of using credit cards (because they're all traceable and shit). "Thanks."

I flash the attendant my best *I'm-definitely-not-running-from-the-law-right-now* smile as I walk into the QuickMart. Scanning through the bottled water selection, I remember that my Luke secret is now out in the open. Was Mom pissed? Or did she actually accept "He won't say anything" as my final answer? Maybe she'll just drop it altogether. Once again, this whole thing could have been avoided if I had just *thought* for, like, two seconds before opening my mouth. Obviously she was talking about the Marco text! I literally sent it from her phone. Honest to God, I'm a dumbass.

Wait a minute.

Marco.

Duh.

That's where we're going.

We're already headed in that direction. It's meant to be! We'll be safe with him. We always were. Even if we do become suspects, the cops would never think to look for us at a random lake in upstate New York. We're Jersey Shore beach people! Total lake virgins.

I run across the pavement and slide back into the car. Mom is in the driver's seat, blotting her face with a Clean & Clear oil-removing wipe in the rearview mirror.

"Maybe this Luke thing isn't so bad," she says. "Even if he does try to say something, you could say you lied to try and save your ass from getting in trouble for the windshield. Then it's just your word against his."

Oh. She's still on this. I consider coming totally clean and telling her that it would actually be my word against the irrefutable geolocational proof I sent to him, but you know what? It's not even important anymore.

"Forget about Luke." I toss the plastic QuickMart bag — full of Combos, Dasani, and Altoids — on the floor. "I figured out where we're going."

"Where's that?"

The seat belt alert dings as Mom zooms back onto the highway.

"Marco's."

She doesn't react to my brilliant idea.

It is a brilliant idea, right? Yes. We can tell Marco we're on a spontaneous spring break vacation — popping our lake cherries — and thought we would stop by since we're in the neighborhood. Then we'll get drunk and pass out on his couch, thereby ensuring we have a place to sleep for the night. Then Mom and Marco will fall back in love and he'll ask us to move in with him! I gotta say: Living on a lake sounds so chill, so peaceful, so *I'm-definitely-not-running-from-the-law*. We'll leave New Jersey behind altogether. I'll drop out of school and find a new bakery to work at during the day while I perfect my act. College would have sucked anyway. I'll save up all my money and move to LA in a couple years, where I'll be discovered and become the next Ali Wong (except less pregnant and more gay). Maybe I'll even talk about this whole story in my debut Netflix special. By then our crime will be two years old and I'll be rich enough to buy us out of whatever potential punishment might still strike us.

"Think about it!" I continue. "Even if we are wanted, no one's gonna find us in some lakeside cabin out in the middle of nowhere. Maybe Marco can even help us —"

"Now I *know* you've lost your mind." Mom scrunches her (perfectly matte) face. "We can't just pop back into his life after eight years without any notice. What would we even say to him?"

"The truth." *Ding.* "Shut up!" I scream at the dashboard. It can be such an asshole with those dings. I hastily jam my buckle in. "Okay. Maybe not the *truth* truth... but. Like, the version of the truth that we told Nonna."

"He's gonna know something's up."

"Yeah, maybe he'll be surprised. But in a good way. And even if he did think it was weird that we're showing up out of the blue, you know he would never tell us to get lost."

She exhales.

This is good. This means she's thinking about it. Granted, I've done enough thinking about it for the both of us, but I guess I can appreciate her need to roll it around in her head before admitting that I'm a genius and this is the perfect solution to all our problems.

"It's not like going to Marco's hasn't already crossed my mind," she finally says. "It just seems a little unfair to get him involved in this. And I don't want to lead him on, you know?"

"He won't *know* that he's harboring two runaway fugitives," I say. "So he'll still be innocent. And I'm sorry, but leading him on is just a risk you're going to have to take to keep us both out of prison. Small price to pay, I think. And who knows. Maybe you'll fall back in love. Maybe we'll be able to move in and live with him permanently... I'm just spitballing, here."

"Did you smoke some crack in that QuickMart?" she says. "He has a life of his own. He's not just sitting around waiting for us to barge back into it."

"Forget the whole falling-back-in-love thing. That's not important. What's important is that we call him and find out his address."

Mom exhales again—this time longer and louder—half defeat and half relief. "All right."

"Yes! Thank you."

I reach for her phone from the cupholder and it immediately starts buzzing.

Shit.

It's a text.

From...

RICHARD: You wouldn't happen to know anything about
        my house burning down, would you?

eleven

"Does Richard know who Marco is?" I ask Mom.

Now that Richard has decided to rise from the dead, I'm starting to question how realistic our plan is. Theoretically, anyone
who knows about Mom's past with Marco could eventually place
"with Marco" on the list of our possible whereabouts.

"No," she says. "Or. Maybe. I don't know?"

"Which is it?!"

"I don't *knooww-ah*. Jesus!" As if Richard's ominous text
weren't enough, there's also a big-ass Amazon Prime truck going
approximately two miles per hour in front of us. "What is this bitch
doing in the left lane? MOVE." Her hair almost slaps me in the face
as she checks her blind spot and jerks the car into the right lane to
pass. "I was with Richard for two years, so yeah. I've probably mentioned Marco. It's not like I told him his life story." She shoots me a
look. "Calm down. He wouldn't know where Marco lives."

I look at Richard's message again to determine exactly how
worried we should be. I guess I should be relieved that he didn't
send a frantic all-caps accusation. But then again, the fact that he
didn't send a frantic all-caps accusation is also kind of weird.
Who the hell in his current position would be so calm?

"What does this text even mean?" I ask. *"You wouldn't happen to know…?* Is it a genuine question? Is he accusing you? Is he, like, assuming that you wouldn't know anything but asking just for good measure?" *Bzzz.* "He's texting again!"

"What now?" she asks.

RICHARD: http://njnews.com/short-hills-house-fire

"It's a link…" I click and recognize the page from my internet-combing session earlier. "…to one of the news stories."

"That's it?" she asks. "A link? No words?"

"No words."

"Good. That's good." She breathes. "Right? He thinks we don't even know about it. Otherwise why else would he send a link?"

"Unless he knows and he's taunting us."

"You think it's a threat?"

"I mean, I don't know."

"Oh, my God, it's a threat!"

"No. No. Let's look at the texts again." I read the first one aloud. "I think you're right. He was probably just like, 'I'm gonna ask Gia if she knows anything about my house burning down.' Then he sent it and thought, 'Oh. Maybe she hasn't heard the news yet. I'll send her a link to fill her in.' He's probably sending those same two texts to literally everyone he knows in Jersey."

"This is some shit." Mom lets out a tiny laugh. "He leaves me, I burn his house down, and I'm *still* over here trying to decode his short-ass texts."

"At least he's not hurling insults at you like Luke did to me," I say. "And to think that was *before* we destroyed his car."

She lets out an even tinier laugh. "What does the link say?"

"I already read it," I tell her. "Same as the other ones. Sounds like they still don't have any leads." I take my phone out to do another news scan. "That picture of the fire still only has like forty retweets. Honestly? I think we should just ignore Richard for now. We gotta call Marco."

Mom indicates her agreement with a shrug and we spend the next few minutes brainstorming the story we're gonna tell him. The mutual consensus is that *less is more.* As long as we get his address and an invite, we can figure out the rest of our story later on.

"I'll do the talking," Mom says. "You just make sure you have your phone out. I'll ask him his address so you can type it into Google Maps."

"Wouldn't that be traceable?"

It's getting exhausting worrying about every little thing we do with our phones that could possibly be used as evidence against us, but it's second nature at this point. I can't tell if we're being way too cautious or not nearly cautious enough, but I feel like anything GPS-related calls for us to err on the side of paranoia.

"Open the glove compartment,' Mom says without missing a beat. "I think Ma has a Garmin in there."

"A what?"

"It's like an old-school electronic thing that does GPS navigation only," Mom says. "From like, before you could do it on your phone."

"Wait. Really? Amazing." I find the ancient device amid a nest of half-stuffed envelopes and used air fresheners. I pull it out of its tiny neoprene case. Good thing we took Nonna's car. "I got it."

Please work, I think as I jam my thumb into the On button. *Please give us accurate directions. Please don't let Marco be lying when he says he misses Mom. Please let him have literally no plans all week. Please make all our problems go away.*

Please, please, please.

Wait.

Shut up, Joey.

It's a Garmin, not the magic fucking lamp from Aladdin.

Mom turns the music off and I hear a faint ring come from inside her phone. She must have called Marco at some point while I was busy berating myself.

"*Hiii*, Marco." Does her voice sound suspect? Oh, my God. Her voice sounds suspect. It's all wobbly and fake-nice. "Yeah. I know, I know. Right? I'm goo—well—I'm not good. Joey and I are in a little bit of trouble . . ."

"What are yo—" I start to whisper before she sticks her shiny hot-pink nails in my face.

"Trouble was a strong word. Joey just broke up with his boyfriend." *Boyfriend?* I'm guessing Marco just asked. "We're in New York. Going upstate. It's spring break, so I wanted to take him on a vacation to get his mind off things." *Pause.* "I think we're close to where you live." Marco's deep voice faintly echoes from the phone, but it's mostly drowned out by the wind whipping through the ash crack in Mom's window. "Really? We'd love to stop by." *Pause.* "Yeah, I know." *Pause.* Awkward chuckle. "That's fine. Joey—get this down."

Finally! Something is going right for us. Marco's gonna take us in and save the day. Everything is going to be okay. It will be like we never burned down a house at all. *Better*, even, because otherwise we wouldn't have our amazing new lakeside lives to look forward to.

My new best friend Garmin tells me we're just two hours away. But I'm sure we can make it in an hour forty-five if Mom speeds a little bit.

twelve

We've been off the highway for at least fifteen minutes. Apparently we're in a town called Putnam, but the word "town" feels generous. Even "village" would be giving it too much credit. That would imply that there are, like, sweater-wearing humans and cozy cottages lining the streets. Maybe even a shoppe or two. Villages have shoppes and not shops, right? I don't know. Really my only point of reference is *Little Women* — the nineties version starring Winona Ryder and Kirsten Dunst.

Anyway! We're out here in the wilderness like a couple of pilgrims. Ever since we took a left onto Marco's "street," pavement has ceased to exist altogether. It's all pebbles, dirt, the occasional tree root. Does Marco live in a house or has he been literally camping for the past eight years? I wonder. And this path is so narrow. If another car approaches us from the opposite direction right now, we'll have to drive straight into the actual woods.

I'm not complaining, though. This is just the kind of environment we need to be in. Even the Garmin doesn't know where we are — it just lost its signal.

We keep driving straight, like Marco said, until the trees clear and we finally approach a driveway.

Phew! It's an actual house and not just a large tent. The look is log-cabin-without-any-actual-logs. Wood siding, hunter-green window panes. I shouldn't be surprised. Marco always gave off an L.L.Bean-y kinda vibe, which was super weird coming from a New Jersey Italian. I guess he finally mustered up the courage to live in his truth.

"Sure as hell ain't Bayonne." Mom is gawking up at the view just like I am. "Look—you can see the lake. Past the porch."

"It's beautiful." I squint and see a slice of glimmering water in the distance, but it's mostly blocked by the house and trees. "We're completely off the map."

"Right?"

Mom turns the car off and we sit in silence absorbing the nature that surrounds us. I think back to what my life was like two days ago and what it's like now, and my brain crashes like an old desktop computer. In the past twenty-four hours alone I've racked up enough life experience to fill, like, five HBO specials' worth of comedy material. I hope I can remember all the random thoughts I've been having. I haven't been writing *any* of this stuff down.

There's a loud knock on the driver's-side window.

Mom and I snap out of our respective daydreams and scream like banshees. We look to the window and see Marco crouched down right in front of it. His short wavy hair is more salt-and-pepper than it was eight years ago, but otherwise he hasn't aged a day. It's almost like seeing a ghost. He's wearing a teal L.L.Bean rugby shirt (I totally called it) and smiling. Wow. I forgot about his smile. It's the kind of smile Mom deserves—approachable, genuine, excited to see her. Nothing like Richard's toilet-seat-shaped fucker-grin.

We eject ourselves from the vehicle. Sex is great, but have you tried stretching after having been seated in a car for several hours? It's euphoric.

"You scared the crap outta me." Mom playfully pats Marco on the chest. She almost sounds flirty! I have a good feeling about all of this. "Good Lord. You didn't tell me you lived out in the middle of Bumblefuck. I thought Lake George was supposed to have, like, restaurants and mini golf and shit."

"We're a forty-five-mile drive away from all that." He laughs. "Lake George is big!" He looks across the car at me. "Speaking of big. Is this the same Joey Rossi from Bayonne, New Jersey? The one I used to have to pick up just so he could reach the Cocoa Puffs at Stop & Shop? Holy mackerel. You're the same height as *me*."

I suddenly remember why Mom got so bored with him. Because he remembers thoughtful little details from forever ago and says things like *holy mackerel*.

"They shouldn't keep the kid cereals on the top shelf," I say. "Whose dumb fuckin' idea was that?"

"Ah." He looks at Mom and then back at me. "I see you've inherited your mother's mastery of the English language." She cocks her head and flips him a lighthearted middle finger. He accepts it with a laugh. "Just like old times."

Marco leads us through the pebbly path to his front door. I consider stopping to get the duffel bags we packed from the trunk, but then remind myself that Marco thinks we're just stopping by to say hello. He doesn't know yet that we'll be spending the night. Let alone the week. Let alone the entire foreseeable future.

His cabin is a rustic oasis with beamy wood ceilings that stretch all the way to the sky. There's a giant pair of windows overlooking the lake. So *this* is where all the breathtaking views have been hiding. I look up and see a loft tucked away in the corner with a big wooden ladder leading up to it. I can already see myself taking ownership of the bed up there, looking down over the open-concept living room and out at the tranquil expanse of water outside. Is Marco rich now? Or is this place just cheap because it's out in the middle of nowhere? I decide the answer lies somewhere in between. *My Lottery Dream Home* meets *Lakefront Bargain Hunt.*

"This place is beautiful." Mom hops onto a stool at a shiny wooden bar counter off the kitchen. "Even if you are living out here in the middle of the woods like the Unabomber."

"I'm going to pretend you didn't just compare me to a deranged domestic terrorist," Marco cracks. It's funny because he's the furthest thing from a deranged terrorist. More like a... sane weatherman. "I just wanted to be closer to nature, that's all." He opens his fridge and hands us two bottles of water. "I mean, look at this place." He gestures toward the window. "It makes Jersey look like hell on earth."

"Can't argue that," I whisper.

"So what's going on with you two?" he asks. "I don't see you for almost a decade and all of a sudden you show up at my house at two o'clock on a Tuesday afternoon."

"Why are you home at two o'clock on a Tuesday afternoon?" Mom totally ignores his question in favor of her own. "How are you paying for this place if you're not working?"

"I am working," he says. "Same job I always had. They just let me do it remotely now."

"Ah." Mom and I nod in unison, even though the concept of doing a job "remotely" couldn't be more foreign to either of us. She can't cut someone's hair via FaceTime. I can't stuff a cannoli over email. I guess that's one of the reasons Nonna has always been so obsessed about getting me to go to college.

"So what about *my* question?" he asks. 'Is everything okay?"

There's a concern in his voice that is already making me feel less guilty of the crimes Mom and I have committed. Like he somehow senses or understands that we're in deep trouble, but it's not because we're criminals—it's because we're victims. It almost makes me feel like we can tell him the truth. Who knows? Maybe he'll have a totally obvious solution that we haven't yet thought of.

"Everything's fine." Mom flips her hair back and takes a sip of water. "Other than Joey's boyfriend cheating on him. But that's why we're on this trip. To forget about that jerk."

The room goes awkwardly quiet for a moment.

"I'm sorry to hear that," Marco offers. "Screw that guy, right? You'll find someone better in no time, I bet." More awkward silence. "Are you—uh—you're eighteen now! You pick a college yet, or what?"

"Rutgers," Mom answers.

"My alma mater." He smiles. "Nice."

"I don't know if I'm gonna actually go," I say. "I mean, it's not like I need college. It's so expensive. Instead, I could spend four years working and saving up for a move to LA."

Marco looks at me like I've just confessed to murder (and/or arson). "But you gotta go to *college*."

"He's going to college." Mom hits me in the arm.

"Have you decided on a major?" Marco asks. "They have a great program for—"

"Do you have a bathroom I could use?" I interrupt. This topic couldn't be more useless right now. "I have to pee so bad."

He motions to a door across the living room. I make a beeline and shut it behind me.

Everything inside this bathroom is bear-themed—the shower

curtain shows a large black bear sitting in a bathtub, scrubbing his pits like a human. The soap dispenser is a ceramic bear with a metal pump sticking out from its head. The hand towels have claw prints embroidered onto them. It's all a bit much. Like, we get it, Marco. You live in the woods!

I turn to the mirror for a reality check. But what even is reality at this point? There's a part of my mind telling me we have to return to Bayonne eventually and deal with the mess we made. But the other part of my mind—the one that daydreamed that whole scenario of moving in here and leaving Jersey behind forever—is starting to actually view that as a possibility. Marco clearly lives alone out here. He was able to just welcome us back into his life on zero notice this afternoon. Why should tomorrow afternoon and all afternoons thereafter be any different?

I take out my phone to see if I've missed anything in the ongoing investigation of the fire. Somewhere between the wooded path to his house and here, I regained two bars of service. So that's good. Or bad, depending on how you think about it.

Nonna called. She'd be delighted to hear that we're with Marco, but I can't tell her. The less she knows, the better. That way if this situation completely blows up in our faces, she can honestly say she had no idea about any of it. As much of a law-abiding citizen as Nonna is, I know she'd lie to the cops if it meant protecting Mom and me. It's bad enough we took her car. I'd never forgive myself if we took her innocence, as well.

I do a quick news scan, but there haven't been any developments. Joggy McBitch's picture has gained a few more retweets, but that's about it. So. Phew. Okay. Everything. Is. Going. To. Be. Fine.

I reach for the doorknob but stop upon hearing traces of a heated discussion between Mom and Marco. I can't tell what about, exactly, because they're whispering. So I glue my ear directly to the door in an attempt to get a better listen. Eavesdropping on Mom's conversations with boyfriends has always been one of my favorite pastimes, but I'm especially curious to hear what they could be talking about right now. It definitely sounds kinda tense. Is she telling him everything? Oh, my God. Why would she do that without me?

My attempt at making out their syllables is ultimately fruitless. Their voices are too deliberately soft. I make a mental note to grill Mom about it the next time we're alone.

"So, Joey!" Marco says as I emerge from the bathroom. "Gia tells me you two haven't eaten all day. You must be starving."

"I had some sfogliatelle this morning." I shoot suspicious looks back and forth to Mom and him. "And some Combos on the way here. But yeah."

"Okay." He scratches the back of his neck. "So I have to wrap up a few things for work in the next couple hours, but once I'm done I can throw some burgers on the grill. Or we can go into town and eat out somewhere. I'll let you two make the call."

"Sounds good."

"It's a beautiful day for April," he adds. "You can go and hang by the dock if you want. The water's freezing...but you can at least try to get some sun or something. Or you can stay here. Whatever you wanna do."

"We'll go to the dock," Mom says. "That sounds nice."

Marco's giant windows make it look like the water is right outside, but there's actually a steep hill you have to walk down to get there. Mom and I take turns almost tripping on it until we're finally at the dock.

The water is even more breathtaking up close—an endless stretch of shimmering metallic blue in all directions. The shore across from us looks like it's at least a mile away. "Shore" isn't even the right word. It's all just trees and mountains. You can see other lakefront houses and docks dotted along the edges — Marco has a couple nearby neighbors to either side of us — but overall this feels like a part of nature that has been mercifully spared from humans and their bullshit. Like something out of a "beautiful places" calendar or stock desktop background.

"We're staying here forever," I tell Mom as we tiptoe onto the dock. Maybe if I say it out loud it will become closer to being reality.

"I don't know about forever." She takes her boots off and pulls her leggings up to her knees. "But we're good for tonight."

"Really? You asked him already?"

"Yeah. While you were in the bathroom."

"So that's what you were being all whisper-y about."

"I told him we're strapped for cash and that I didn't have the money to take you on the vacation I promised. He felt bad and offered to let us stay. He hasn't changed at all." She pulls a cigarette out from her purse and gestures at the scene around us. "Except for the fact that he's now living on the set of *Deliverance*."

"Come on." I grab the cigarette out of her mouth and toss it in the water. "Look where we are. You really wanna destroy all this beauty with your stink sticks?"

"Says the bitch who just threw one into the lake," Mom snaps back. But then she takes a look around, inhales deeply, and seems to agree with me. She points to the other side of the dock. "You think that's his boat?"

"What's his job again?" I ask.

"Something with...computers, right?" Mom says. "He used to try to explain it to me, but it never made any sense."

"He's gotta be rich if he has a *boat*."

The only people with boats in New Jersey are, like, Richard-level yuppies and/or mysteriously wealthy Italian families who almost certainly have mafia ties. (Side note: Why couldn't Nonna and Mom have mafia ties? Life would be so much easier. Not only would we have money, but we'd also probably have a crooked cop on speed dial who we could totally extort to make sure we never get arrested. We wouldn't even have to be on the run right now.)

"I guess he does good for himself out here." Mom shrugs and gestures toward a pair of kayakers gliding across the water heading toward us. "Look at these bitches."

For a quick second I fear they may be cops en route to arrest us, but that's just ridiculous because *one*) as they get closer I see they are just a straight teenage couple, and *two*) in what world would cops make an arrest via kayak? There's no backseat. The suspect could just wiggle around and tip the whole thing over!

"Is it just me, or is the guy insanely hot?" I ask. "Who knew they existed out here in the wild?"

He has this Latin lover thing going on that kinda reminds me of a young A-Rod. He looks like his hands would totally know their way around a baseball bat. (For all the healthy, normal reasons. Definitely not for Mom's and my reasons.) Wait a minute. Is he shirtless under his life vest? He's shirtless under his life vest. His chiseled shoulders and biceps involuntarily flex with every row of his paddle. Shit. I need to think about dead puppies or something. The last thing I need right now is a boner.

I focus my attention on his kayaking partner. She's laughing and paddling with a grace and ease that suggests she's probably a joy to be around. You know what? Fuck it. You only live once. I'm gonna check out the guy some more.

Should I give him a wave and/or a smile? Normally I would never even consider something so brazen. But we're on the run and our lives as we know them could be over any minute now, so I feel like it might be the time to start doing some bucket-list shit. What's the worst that can happen? The hot guy ignores my wave? He returns my smile with a disgusted look? He calls me a faggot? Actually — never mind. Mom and I are dealing with enough right now. I don't need to add rejection and a hate crime to the list.

"They don't exist in the wild," Mom says. "They're visiting from the city. Marco told me when you were in the bathroom." She lowers her feet into the water. "Ow! That's cold. How is that guy not wearing a shirt?"

She stretches her legs out in front of her and flaps her feet around until they adjust to the temperature. "That house over there belongs to some family" — she points at a log cabin at the bottom of the hill across the bay —"they have a daughter your age. She's having friends over for spring break. Marco thought you might wanna hang with them." Oh, my God. It's a sign. I should totally wave. "Don't worry," Mom adds. "I told him you'd rather drink horse piss than randomly introduce yourself to a group of teenagers."

"First of all," I start, "I saw on Wikipedia that Janet Jackson used to get horse piss injected into her veins because it helps with weight loss. So I don't know why this has to be an either/or situation." I laugh at my own joke. "And secondly, maybe I *should* say hi!"

Right as I finish talking, the hot guy smiles and waves at us.

He's totally gay! Right? Straight guys are never that friendly. Waving isn't even in their vocabulary. The best they can do is constipated head nods. The girl he's with must be, like, his cousin or best friend or something.

I try to imitate his smile — carefree, casual, chill — and reciprocate the wave. And then he keeps on paddling until they reach the rocky shore across the bay. He wobbles out of his kayak and helps his platonic bestie out of hers. I hope he'll come running over and introduce himself to me, like, "Hi I waved at you because I think you're perfect and I would like to make out with you immediately." But no. He and the girl just disappear into the house.

"Earth to Joey." Mom waves her hand in my face. "Hello?"

"Sorry," I say.

"You can gawk at Ricky Martin later." She reclines back onto the dock and is basically just talking to the sky at this point. "I was just thinking. Should we throw our phones into the lake?"

thirteen

"You still like your burgers well done?" Marco asks through the screen door. "Or are you finally ready to try a real one?"

He's outside on his wraparound porch playing grillmaster while Mom and I sit on his brown leather couch drinking wine that makes the bargain stuff we usually consume seem like horse piss. (Listen, I never actually said horse piss would taste *good*. I just said there are reasons one might want to drink it anyway.) We decided to stay put for dinner, just in case we happen to be suspects in the Short Hills investigation and somehow a random upstate bumpkin goes all MacGyver and cracks the case on us while we're just trying to enjoy some fried calamari. I know we're being paranoid, but you know what they say: better safe than ~~sorry~~ indicted.

"Well done!" Mom yells back at Marco. "I'm not trying to get salmonella up in this bitch."

"That's a chicken disease," I remind her. "How many times have we been through this?"

"Whatever," she says. "I'm not trying to get mad cow disease, either."

"I mean, same." I take a sip of wine and curl up with a flannel throw blanket on the couch. Everything about this scene is so chill. Marco has a soft classic rock playlist tinkling through his Bose sound system as the moonlight softly illuminates the lake view before us. I wish I could freeze time. "Think we should finally call Nonna back? I feel bad. She's been blowing us up."

We ultimately decided not to commit phone suicide down at the dock earlier. I get why Mom suggested it — with no phones in our possession, we'd be able to just go about life in blissful ignorance of whatever was unfolding in the aftermath of our wreckage. Are the cops and/or our disgruntled exes trying to get a hold of us? Long hair, don't care! Phone-free, can't see! We're off the grid.

But then we realized that chucking our phones might create more problems than solutions. For one thing, I find great comfort in being able to check the news at any time and reconfirm the fact that we're not actual suspects. I've been monitoring the coverage every hour or so, and it seems like the story is already starting to die down. Did you know there are bad things happening *all* the damn time? Since the fire was first reported — barely even twelve hours ago — there have been car crashes, kidnappings, shootings, drug busts, and political scandals galore. And that's just in Jersey! I never thought I'd say this, but I'm kinda glad we live in such a fucked-up world.

"We should call her," Mom says. "You *know* she's been freaking out all day."

"I think we should tell her we're here with Marco," I say. "She would be so happy to know that you guys are getting back together!" Oops. I didn't mean to say that out loud. Am I drunk already? I guess that's what happens when the only thing you've eaten all day is one Italian pastry and two mini-bags of Combos. "We should, uh — we should tell her we're here so she knows we're safe."

"Hold the phone." Mom does a sassy little hand movement. "What are you talking about, 'getting back together'?"

"Nothing. Just. I don't know. You seem like you're back in a groove with him. And when he was telling us which beds we could sleep in, he totally did this, like, *pause* where I swear he was about to say you're welcome to stay with him in his room." I give a forced half-laugh, which is met with silence. "You mean to tell me you haven't been flirting with him, even a little bit?"

"That's just how I talk." She's trying to be coy, but I see through it. She's totally remembering why she loved him back in the day. "We can call her and tell her we're safe, but we can't tell her where we are exactly. God forbid the cops question her or something."

Well. That killed my buzz.

Marco comes in with a platter of burger patties in his hand and looks at us on the couch.

"Hey," he says to me in a goofy dad-joke voice as I take a swig of wine. I already know where this is going. "Does your mother know you're drinking?"

"Ha," I deadpan. "I guess she does now."

"It's not like he's guzzling rum," she says. "Wine has antioxidants. It's basically salad."

"Thanks for the nutritional wisdom, Dr. Rossi." Marco flashes an amused smile. He is so adorably into her. "I was gonna grab a beer from the fridge, but you've sold me on the Chianti."

"I'm gonna go call Nonna," I say. "I'll be right back."

Mom looks relieved. I could tell she liked the idea of Nonna knowing that we're safe more than the idea of actually talking to her herself.

"Tell her I said hello!" Marco says. "How is she doing?"

"She's fine," Mom and I respond in unison.

"Good." Marco pours himself a glass of wine. "I'll pop your burger in the oven so it's still warm when you get back."

I slide out onto the porch and walk down the hill to have a modicum of privacy for this conversation. I have no idea if things are gonna escalate into yelling or crying and I'd rather not do anything to arouse suspicion in Marco.

"Madonna mia." Nonna picks up on the first ring. "You and your mother take off with my car and then you ignore me for hours on end. Real nice. Do you have any idea how worried I've been? All day I've had *agita*—"

"I'm sorry." I try to sound as calm as possible as I cut her off. It helps that I'm standing before a moonlit lakefront oasis. I look up and there are actual stars in the sky. Lots of them. "Whoa," I mindlessly marvel out loud.

"What *'whoa'*?" Nonna asks. "Are you okay? Tell me what's going on before I have a heart attack."

"We're fine. Mom was driving all day and I fell asleep in the car. And then by the time we got—uh—here, she fell asleep. And then my phone died. And then *I* fell asleep...again. It's been a long day." I take a breath. "But we're fine. Your car is fine. We're excited for this vacation! I've already forgotten about Luke." Huh. My nonsensical rant has culminated in an actually true statement. "So it's working."

"Good," she says. "But where the hell are you?"

"I..." —*am an idiot who really should have figured out how the hell I was gonna answer this extremely predictable question before I called you*—"don't know exactly. A few hours away. It's like, a vacation place on a beach somewhere. We're renting an Airbnb for cheap. Since it's the off-season and all. It's super nice."

"How many nights do you have this *Air-bean-bean* for?"

"Until...Friday?" It feels so dishonest to say something definitive about the future, but I need to at least get Nonna off our back for a few days. "We'll be home Friday."

"Something's not right about this. I have a bad feeling." She stops talking. The silence is thick with disappointment. "Have you seen the news? That *medigan* your mother's been seeing was on Channel Five today." It occurs to me that Nonna doesn't even know Mom and Richard broke up. Just when I thought she couldn't be more clueless about our situation. "His house burned down. You believe that?"

"No way! Really? That's crazy." I am definitely trying too hard. "Did he tell the reporters how it happened? Was it an unattended candle? I bet it was an unattended candle." Shit. I'm not sounding surprised enough. "Oh, my God. I can't believe his house caught *fire*."

"*Oh, mio Dio!* Joey." She sounds like she's ready to have that heart attack she was talking about a minute ago. "Joey, Joey, Joey."

Was I really *that* unconvincing?

"What?" I ask.

"I knew it," she says. "I knew it the second I saw him on that screen."

"Nonna, don't be crazy! What do you think you know?"

"You think I don't know how your mother operates?" she says. "This was all Gia. And now she's gotten you mixed up in it. How could she do this to you?" Her breathing gets heavier and heavier. "I need to sit down."

"Please stop." I should have never walked out here and called her. Everything was so great five minutes ago. I had wine. I had a burger. Now I have a melodramatic Italian grandmother in the throes of a total breakdown. "You're jumping to an insane conclusion. Mom and I had nothing to do with this! You think we're criminals? Calm down." I hear her attempt to inhale on the other end. I don't care how convinced Nonna is of her theory, there's no way I'm going to admit anything to her. If we confirm her suspicion, we implicate her as an accomplice. At least now all she has is a feeling. I need to convince her that her feeling is wrong. "What did Richard say to the reporters?"

"He had that same guilty smile as always," she says. "Said he just got off a plane from California. There was a neighbor who saw a car in the driveway, but the dumb *putan'* can't even remember what kind it was."

"See? It couldn't have been us." As if Nonna is a one-woman jury and the lack of evidence on Channel Five is proof of our innocence. "You saw us this morning. Did we look like we just burned a house down?"

"Yes!" she responds. "And then you ran off with my car."

Mom was right. We should have just thrown our phones into the lake.

"We didn't do anything, okay? Please chill. We'll be back Friday and everything is going to be fine. Stop acting like a crazy person."

"I hope to God that I *am* crazy," Nonna says. "Put your mother on the phone."

"She's still sleeping." I force a laugh. "Imagine: Mom and me burning down a *house*. Nonna! That is nuts. You're just looking for things to worry about."

"Tell her to call me when she wakes up." She sounds a little less frantic right now. Hopefully she's at least questioning her theory. As she should. It's really an insane conclusion to jump to. Even if it happens to be completely accurate in this case. "I don't like being ignored."

"She'll call you tomorrow. I love you, Nonna."

"Mhm," she says. "Love you, too."

I swear to God. Marco better have at least three more bottles of wine in his kitchen. And then another three if he and Mom want to have any for themselves.

As I turn around to make my way back up the hill, I catch sight of the neighbor's house. It has a giant lake-view window just like Marco's, and I can see right through it. A blur of bodies wades through the living room with red Solo cups in their hands. I wonder which one of them belongs to Kayak Guy.

I'm feeling expertly capable of improvised deception after that phone call, so I consider going over there and crashing the party. How hard would it be to just slip in and introduce myself to him? "Hi! We waved at each other earlier! Is this beer? I love beer." And then he'll whisk me away to a bedroom and make all my problems go away.

But then I remember that I look like shit and Mom and Marco are waiting for me.

When I get back onto the porch, I peer through the window and see them sitting very closely next to each other on the couch. They're talking and laughing between sips of wine. I can't remember the last time I've seen her like this with a guy.

"There you are!" Marco says as I slip through the screen door and slide it shut behind me. "I was starting to worry you'd fallen into the lake."

"So?" Mom asks. "Nonna?"

"All good!" I decide not to ruin her mood by telling her how the conversation really went. I'd rather just obliterate it from my memory entirely. I zip over to the counter where I left my wineglass and fill it all the way up. "Nonna's just peachy."

"Easy, tiger." Marco chuckles at my heavy pour. "You gotta give it room to breathe!"

"Right." I take an extreme guzzle until the glass is only half-full. "There we go."

"You sure you're okay?" Mom asks.

I ignore the question and turn toward Marco. "So are your neighbors having a party or something?"

"Oh, yeah. They let their kids have the house to themselves for the week. I actually promised I'd keep an eye on things." He laughs to himself. "I'm clearly not doing a great job."

"They expected you to babysit all week?" I ask. "Do they think you don't have a life of your own?"

"No, no, it's fine," he says. "They're good kids. The daughter especially — Shayla. Straight-A student. Going to NYU in the fall. They're probably just playing board games." He sits up straighter. "Why? What did you see out there? Did it look like a wild rager?"

"Uh..." I consider telling him about how they are most definitely *not* playing board games, but then I remind myself that a normal eighteen-year-old probably wouldn't just feed an adult that kind of information. It would be like "ratting them out" or whatever. So for the sake of my relationship with Kayak Guy, I keep my mouth shut. "Yeah, no. It totally looked like a Scrabble situation."

"You should go over there," he says. "You were always great at that game."

Was I? I remember the *vibe* of our Scrabble nights back at the town house — sitting around the ottoman, laughing at Marco's dumb jokes, him putting his arm around Mom (before she started to recoil at the gesture) — but I don't remember actually playing. I was probably too busy dreading going back to school on Monday and facing my bullies.

"We've had a long day," Mom explains on my behalf. "I don't know if Joey is up for crashing a party full of people he doesn't know."

"Sure he is." Marco is clearly trying to work this as an angle to get Mom all to himself for the rest of the night. He's giving off a very distinct *I-live-in-total-seclusion-and-haven't-gotten-laid-in-months* energy. "I know Shayla. Joey, you're gonna love her. And I'm sure her friends are great."

"I'll totally go," I respond—much to my own astonishment. "Why not?"

"Really?" Mom asks.

"Sure." I take a breath and start brainstorming ways to make Kayak Guy fall in love with me. "After another glass of wine." I catch a glimpse of my reflection in the big lake window. "And a shower."

fourteen

Have you ever taken a scalding hot shower while drunk? It's a strange sensation. I think it actually kind of enhanced my buzz? Or maybe that's just the adrenaline pumping through my veins as I walk down the hill to mingle with a house full of strangers.

I didn't think to pack any decent clothes when we spontaneously fled Bayonne, so I'm rolling up to this shindig in khaki jogger pants and an old Nike quarter-zip. I look like an errand-running soccer dad, but whatever. Who has time for things like self-consciousness and social anxiety? Not me! I'm a runaway fugitive.

I shove my thumb against the glowing doorbell.

"Hiiii!" I'm greeted at the big oak door by Kayak *Girl* from earlier. She's wearing ripped jean shorts and a white crop top, looking like a young Blake Lively. "Joey, right? I'm Shayla. Marco just texted and told me you were coming." She lowers her voice so that I can barely hear it over the EDM humming from the nearby living room. "Thank God you showed up today. I was worried he'd be all up in our business this week."

"He says hi." I peer past her and see a young couple hunched over the kitchen counter smoking pot out of one of those little glass pipe-y things people use. "He thinks you're having a Scrabble tournament."

"Shut up! That's hilarious. I love Marco. He's adorable." Shayla sees me staring at the smokers and giggles. "Want some?"

"Nah." The smell of it wafts toward me and triggers an unpleasant memory. I deliberately shift my glance to the stainless steel refrigerator. "I'm good, thanks."

"Oh — come inside!" She grabs my arm and drags me into the dimly lit kitchen. "Do you want a bev? What are you drinking?"

"I've been having wine, but —"

"Wine?" She covers her mouth and stifles a laugh. "Who *are* you?"

"I'm Italia —"

"He's the chef from *Ratatouille*!" One of the stoners interjects from his perch at the counter. He pokes his girlfriend. "Right, babe? That's totally who this dude looks like."

"Which chef?" I ask, unsure if he's making fun of me with his random-ass Pixar reference or if I truly bear resemblance to one of the characters from *Rata*-fucking-*touille*. I haven't seen that movie since I was nine years old. "Because if memory serves, the primary chef from *Ratatouille* was a literal rat. So." I shift my weight uncomfortably against the dishwasher, and it instantly makes a series of high-pitched beeps. And then it clicks shut and the *whoosh* of the motor kicks in. Oh, my God. I've activated the dishwasher with my ass. I flinch and step away from the appliance. Yep. Definitely drunk! "Sorry."

Smokey Magoo just looks at me and bursts into spontaneous laughter. "This guy's hilarious!" he says to Shayla. "Where'd you find him?"

"Don't worry about it." Shayla pats my arm and rolls her eyes. "Derek is a total dweeb. Don't listen to him." She grabs a red Solo cup, fills it with ice, and pours me a concoction of half Tito's vodka, half La Croix seltzer. "Pamplemousse," she explains. "You will *love*."

I take a generous sip — as if I need it — and take a look around. The space is open-concept with various wooden accents, a giant lake window, and a few strategically placed fur rugs. Your standard lumberjack chic scenario.

But then I notice an enormous contraption hanging from the high vaulted ceiling above the living room. What the fuck is that thing? I tilt my head and squint as hard as I can to un-blur my vision. It's . . . a wagon. Like, out of a horse-drawn carriage type of situation. (The *Little Women* moments are piling up out here, truly.) It's got these giant wooden wheels and seating for at least four (human-sized) passengers. And it's just dangling up there! Maybe about two feet from everyone's heads, connected only by four rusty chain links secured to the ceiling. I thought I'd seen some weird rich-people décor on HGTV before, but this is some next-level shit.

I take a sip from my red Solo cup and continue to take it all in. I do a quickie headcount and estimate there are maybe twelve people here in total. There's a group of six coeds huddled over a phone in the corner by a stone fireplace. A few couples on couches. Not exactly a "wild rager," but still . . . it may be the biggest party I've ever been to.

"This tastes like grapefruit," I tell Shayla. She looks at me blankly, like, *duh*. The vodka instantly upgrades my buzz, so I decide to put feelers out on my future husband. "So that guy you were kayaking with earlier today . . ."

"Robbie. He's straight." Shayla smiles. "And *mine*. Sorry. I totally saw you checking him out by the dock."

"What? Me? No." I down the rest of my drink and help myself

to a refill. Is that rude? Whatever. "I wasn't checking him out. That's absurd!"

"It's totally fine. All the gay boys love my Robbie." She pauses. "You are gay, right?"

"I mean, yeah. But." You know what? I need to leave. If it's a no-go with Kayak Guy, then what am I even doing here? I could be drinking wine and stalking Twitter coverage of the fire from the comfort of that super-inviting loft above Marco's living room. "I just remembered, I can't stay. I have—"

"You must stay! I have another boy for you." She looks me up and down. "You're *so* his type." She slams her drink down on the counter, tops us both off with vodka, and scans the area. "I don't know where he went, though."

I can't tell if I should be flattered or offended. On the one hand, I'm intrigued by the prospect of a replacement for Kayak Guy as my lake-boyfriend. On the other hand, it's a little presumptuous on Shayla's part to assume I'd automatically be interested in talking to whatever gay guy happens to be in attendance at her little spring break retreat. (The fact that her assumption is totally correct is beside the point.)

She grabs my hand and drags me into the living room.

We are now standing directly beneath the wagon. I reach up as high as I can and tap the bottom of one of the wheels with the tip of my finger, for some goddamn reason. The wheel does a half-hearted attempt at spinning while the rest of the vessel makes an ominous creak. Okay! So these chains are rickety as a bitch. The phrase *death trap* might be a little overdramatic, but . . . there is no way I will be caught dead standing under this thing for longer than the fifteen seconds that I already have.

"My dad has an Oregon Trail fetish," Shayla explains as I take several messy steps to the left, comfortably outside of the zone that would be impacted if the wagon were to spontaneously fall and crush the humans/furniture it so menacingly hovers above. "Don't ask."

It's funny she says that, because I definitely want to ask.

But before I can, the group that's huddled over a phone in the corner erupts into a mix of shouting and laughter. And then they disperse. I must have missed something while I was wagon-gawking. Within seconds, Kayak Guy appears and wraps his big man-hands around Shayla's tight little waist. I have no choice but to take yet another giant swig of my beverage in response. Because fuck. He's so hot. She's so lucky. I'm so wasted. Shayla's mouth morphs into a *totally-loving-this-attention-from-my-boyfriend* smile. I know that smile all too well. I used to wear it every weekend with Luke.

"Babe," she says to him and then points at me. "This is Joey. A...friend?...of Marco's."

"Hey, man." Robbie flashes that same handsome smile that tricked me into thinking he was gay before. Frankly, it's rude. "You were down at the dock earlier, right?"

I give him an emotionless head nod and reply directly to Shayla. "Marco is my mom's ex," I explain. "They—"

"Wait a sec," Shayla sloppily blurts. It occurs to me that I'm not the only one who's drunk right now—so is she. Along with probably this entire household. "That was your *mom*? With you at the dock today?"

"It was."

Robbie laughs. "Don't take this the wrong way, man. But she's freakin' hot."

Shayla slaps his arm in disapproval.

"Gross." I really hate it when guys my age call Mom hot. Luke used to do it all the time, but I gave him a pass because he was gay.

I never told him that it reminded me of my middle school bullies. If they weren't calling me a cocksucker they were probably calling her a slut. As if *their* moms were all…what? Virgins? "I'm gonna pretend you didn't say that."

"She seems so young!" Shayla hiccups. "Am I being rude? Sorry. I'm just saying. My mom is like fifty."

"We get that a lot," I say. "She's thirty-four." I try to look directly at Shayla and *not* at Robbie's bicep, which happens to be peeking out of his fitted black T-shirt like an overstuffed meatball hero. There's evidence of a tattoo I can't quite make out, which isn't helping. "I'm eighteen."

Shayla doesn't respond right away, probably because she's doing the mental calculation everyone does when they hear about the age difference between Mom and me. Filling in the gaps of our story with whatever pop culture references of teenage motherhood they have on hand. Usually MTV's *Teen Mom* is involved.

Shayla smirks at me. "You're doing it again."

"Doing what?" I ask and then realize she just caught me checking Robbie out. "No! I'm not." My face burns with embarrassment and my heart thumps with the need to change the subject ASAP before she says it out loud and I'm completely humiliated. "Weren't you looking for someone?"

"Oh, my God, right." She slaps Robbie right on his tattoo. "Do you know where Will is?"

"Where do you think?" Robbie says as I once again undress him with my eyes. I can't help it! You know what? Alcohol should be illegal. "He's probably in the bear bedroom, reading one of his little history books."

Did he just say *bear* bedroom? Also, is he low-key reciprocating my eye-fucking right now? Oh, my God. He totally is! No, he's not. Yes! He is. Okay—I need to snap out of this. This man's girl-friend is literally right in front of me, and I'm not a homewrecker. I'm the one who gets homewrecked.

"Come!" Shayla drags me into a hallway lined with old-timey wagon pictures and various wagon-related artifacts. Random dis-membered spokes, a wire basket, half a seat. It's basically a Cracker Barrel up in this bitch.

"What do your parents do for a living?" I ask her in an attempt to figure out exactly what kind of New York City rich people have such tacky taste.

"My dad's a surgeon and my mom doesn't work." She skips ahead of me and waits at the end of the hallway until I catch up. "Here!" She opens the door to her left, grabs my arm—aggressively!—and thrusts me through it with all her might. Half my drink cascades onto the hardwood floor in the process. She twirls back out into the hallway before I can even regain my balance and absorb my new sur-roundings. "You boys have fun."

"Wait," I start. "Shayla!"

She slams the door shut behind her.

fifteen

I can't believe I thought Marco's bathroom was over-the-top with the bear theme. Because *this* room is bear-ier than anything I've ever seen. Bedspread, pillows, wall art, curtains...all bear!

But there's also a human in the room.

"I presume you're Will?" I ask him in an attempt to break the awkward silence between us. Did I really just say *presume* out loud? This vodka-pamplemousse has truly transformed me. I make an inverted-lip monkey face and rock back on the heels of my sneakers. "I'm Joey."

"I'm gonna kill her," he replies from his corduroy love seat nook by the window. He doesn't even bother looking up from his giant-ass book. *Grand Expectations: The United States, 1945–1974.* Seriously! This is what he's reading.

"Yeah." I make an uncomfortable chuckle and reach for the doorknob. "I can go..."

"Sorry. I didn't mean to sound rude." Will closes his book and looks at me for a second before relaxing his shoulders a little. He laughs quietly to himself. I can't tell if I should be flattered or offended. "Leave it to my sister."

"So Shayla is your sister," I say—half to Will and half to

myself. I've been trying to figure out how they could be friends despite clearly having so little in common. "That explains it."

He scrunches his face up and tilts his head slightly. "Explains what?"

"Why she's getting high in the kitchen and you're in here reading a book about —"

"She's smoking out there? I'll kill her."

"Sorry — kidding!" No need to insert myself in family drama. "It wasn't actually Shayla. Just two of her friends."

Will does another face scrunch, this time in numerous directions. I'll admit he's kinda cute — short brown hair, hipster glasses, slightly larger-than-normal ears that give him this quirky intelligent look — but his energy is more thoughtful nerd than tattooed heartthrob. No need to worry about accidental eye-fuckage here.

"Her friends. Right." He cracks a low-key smile that almost makes me think he might be trying to flirt. Oh, no. "Now I'm gonna have to go out there and be a dick. I swear to God. She's literally my twin but sometimes I feel like I'm her parent." He sighs and looks back at me before taking any action. "Do you have any siblings? Or — whoa! Hey! You okay?"

Apparently I just lost my balance standing here listening to him. This might be the drunkest I've ever been? I don't know! All I know is that I'm currently shoulder-to-wall, with my entire body weight just daring me to embrace a total collapse. Will runs over and grabs my arms, moves me to a sitting position on the bed. He plops down next to me. I notice that he's wearing these light khaki shorts that stop at about the halfway point of his tan, thick, hairy thighs.

Okay, so his thighs are hot. (Did you hear that in a *Shania-Twain-That-Don't-Impress-Me-Much* voice just now? Because that's fully how I intended it.)

"I'm fine," I say. "Just lost my balance."

Will's hand is on my back, which seems like a bold choice for someone who literally just met me two minutes ago. But I'd be lying if I said it didn't feel kinda nice to have a guy in here with me exhibiting signs of concern for my well-being, so I'll take it. Even if he's clearly a total Nice Guy.

"Here." He grabs a large bottle of room temperature Evian from the nightstand. "Drink this."

"Thanks." I take a sip. "I'm really not that drunk."

"Of course not," Will says in a tone that conveys he means the opposite of what he just said. "So are you a friend of Shayla's or something? She's never mentioned you. Did you just come up from the city tonight? How come I've never seen you before?"

I put my hand up and finish my current swig of water. "Just met her tonight." I explain the whole Marco–Mom connection and try to make it extra clear that coming up to the lake was a spontaneous last-minute decision and certainly *not* the result of being on the run from the police. "This is all extremely random for me. I had no idea when I woke up in New Jersey this morning that I'd be going to a party with a bunch of rich kids in the middle of nowhere." Will narrows his light-brown eyes at me. "No offense."

"Where in New Jersey are you from?" he asks. "My uncle has a house in Short Hills."

It takes a second to register. And then I'm like, *of course*. Of course this guy would have family in the same town where Mom and I recently deep fried a McMansion! Naturally!

It's probably just a coincidence, right? But still. Hearing the words "short" and "hills" out loud in sequential order right now feels a little too close for comfort. If I were sober I'd probably be having a full-on meltdown.

"Short Hills? I have never been there." I enunciate every sylla-ble in an attempt to make it as clear as possible that I am com-pletely unaware of any hypothetical fires his uncle may or may not have seen on the local news within the past twenty-four hours. "We live in Bayonne."

"I know where that is," Will replies. "My dad's a member of Liberty National Golf Club in Jersey City. Right down the road."

"Fuck golf," I blurt. Just hearing that word reminds me of Luke. "No offense."

"None taken." Will laughs. "I'm not a huge fan myself." I'll admit his laugh is endearing. It conveys genuine amusement — basically the opposite of the Luke-laugh I'd become accustomed to during our relationship, which usually came off as cocky and somehow mean. "Are you okay?"

"Yeah, totally." I'm still drunk but the water is making my head feel at least a little less...*spinny.* "Sorry I interrupted your history lesson. I should probably get back —"

"Are you sure?" he asks. "You're welcome to...uh." He stops himself as he seems to have a realization. "Yeah, no. You seem tired."

"I am."

"How long are you gonna be up here? Maybe we can hang out...on purpose...tomorrow?" Yep. He's definitely hitting on me. Except he's doing it in a way that sounds like he's asking for my permission — which basically nails the coffin shut on any chance we might have had for a potential lake-romance. I need a man who's going to *tell* me we're hanging out tomorrow. You know? An aggressor. "Do you have your phone?" he continues. "I can put my number in it —"

"I'm sorry." I let out a wildly uncomfortable defense-mechanism laugh. "I'm way too fucked up for you."

"No, yeah, I know — obviously," he fumbles. "I'm talking about tomorrow. When you're sober —"

"I don't mean fucked up from drinking." Ugh. I feel bad for this dude. He deserves an emotionally healthy surprise party guest to hit on! Not someone like me. "I mean I'm *fucked up,* like...you know. In general." I flop my hands out in the air. "Overall."

"Oh." Will lowers his head slightly. "Gotcha."

He scratches his leg, which momentarily draws my attention back to his manly-beyond-his-years thighs They almost look like they could belong to a totally different guy.

You know what? Fuck it.

"Here." I pull my phone out of my pocket and gently toss it in his direction after touching the fingerprint lock. It lands on the bed, right between his legs, and — oh. Okay. He's sitting in such a way that his shorts display a rather intriguing bulge. "Send yourself a text."

He gives a confused chuckle — like he's maybe about to be like, *just forget about it* — but then he shrugs and picks it up.

"Whoa," he says. "What's this?"

His baffled tone sends a shockwave to my brain.

Shit! How did I not think to check the phone myself first before tossing it to him? There could be any number of nightmares on that screen right now. I don't *think* I've felt any notable vibrations since I got to this party, but what the hell do I know? I've been stumbling around and crashing into walls this whole time. I could have easily missed a call from the police notifying me of an arrest warrant. Or a text from Luke saying that he cracked the Short Hills fire case with the GPS tag I sent him. Or a —

My chest plummets down to my balls as I reach over to grab the phone out of Will's hand.

"Wait!" He swats me away and continues staring at the screen. He's laughing, which seems like kind of a rude response to whatever electronic proof of my imminent demise he's looking at. I try again, this time basically getting halfway on top of him. "Okay!" he finally relents. "Sorry. I wasn't trying to snoop. It was open when you gave me the phone."

Turns out I didn't miss any nightmare texts.

He was just looking at my Notes app.

I exhale in relief. But then I tense back up in panic. *Another human has just glimpsed my list of mediocre half-baked jokes.*

I close out of the screen immediately and just ask Will to recite his number aloud. I enter it myself and shoot him a text with a jumble of letters that autocorrect miraculously changes to Joey before I hit send.

"Were those your jokes?" Will asks. "Are you a comedian or—"

"No," I say reflexively. "I mean. I want to be."

"Why?"

"*Why?* My jokes are really that unfunny?"

"I didn't say that!" he says. "You freaked out and snatched the phone away before I could even get to a punchline. I just meant, like...I've never met anyone who wants to be a comedian. I was curious how you got into it. That's all."

"I don't know." I've just always loved the feeling of making people laugh. Isn't that why anybody gets into comedy? And lately I've been obsessed with the structure of jokes—cracking them open and dissecting their words, investigating what makes them work (or not work), trying to replicate the magic of my favorite stand-up specials in my head. "It's just a dream I've had since I was a kid, I guess. It's dumb."

Will puts his hand on my knee. "It's not dumb."

Apparently that's all it takes for me to throw myself at him. I lean over and sloppily attach my mouth to his. Which is crazy! I never make the first move. I'm going to blame this on a combination of pamplemousse, wine, sleep deprivation, and a desperate need to change the subject from my nonexistent comedy career.

Will jerks his head away. "I'm sorry." He straightens his posture. "You're still super drunk."

"Right." So now I've been rejected by a Nice Guy who I *swear* I didn't even want to kiss in the first place. Who even am I? "My bad."

"Here." He grabs the now-empty Evian bottle. "I'll go get you some more water."

"Don't worry about it," I say. "I should leave anyway."

His face falls for a second, but then he nods in agreement. "Want me to walk you back to Marco's?" he asks.

"Nope!" I say, a little too defensively, as I lift myself off the bed and head for the door. "I'm fine."

"At least let me walk you out." He gets up and grabs my shoulder, which helps to steady my wobbly steps. He guides me through the Cracker Barrel hallway and back toward the living room, which is empty. The party is now concentrated in the kitchen. "Here. I'll let you out the back way so we don't have to deal with everyone."

That Evian really didn't help as much as I'd thought it did. I'm definitely still spinny. My legs feel like a pair of silicone stilts. If it weren't for Will's support, I'd have totally toppled over by now. Which is why it's quite inconvenient when he lets go of me.

"Whoa." I hobble to the nearest wall and lean against it.

"I'll be right back," he says. "If you're not gonna let me walk you home, then you should at least have another bottle of water. Wait here."

He heads toward the kitchen. I stare at him for a moment

before shifting my gaze back up toward the looming wagon. I still can't get over this thing. It's ridiculous! I steady myself as best I can and meander my way back to the center of the living room so I can get another up-close look at it. I stare at the giant wheel hovering above my head and wonder if this monstrosity has ever actually been a functioning wagon, or if it was created purely as a piece of décor meant to *look* like it was once a functioning wagon. For reasons only the vodka can explain at this point, the wheel beckons me to spin it again.

Right as my finger makes contact, I'm interrupted by Will's voice calling my name from behind. This startles me and causes my wobbly legs to lose their balance yet again. So in a split second, without thinking, my hand grips onto the wheel for dear life. I know! This thing could barely withstand a tentative little tap earlier, let alone the full body weight of a drunken gay arsonist. But it's my knee-jerk reaction and I can't take it back.

A splinter of wood digs into my hand as the wagon immediately jerks downward from the ceiling above. I have the distinct feeling that I'm yanking out a tooth. And yet I can't let go, because drunk-logic is telling me that if I do then I'll fall face down on the floor. Never mind the fact that a giant antique is about to crush me from above.

"Joey!" Will repeats as he runs toward me. There's a piercing *snap* sound in the air, and for a moment it's raining wood chips on my head. Will grabs me by the waist and drags me to the wall. "What the hell are you doing?"

"I...uh." I blink aggressively and open my eyes to see that every single party guest is now scattered across the perimeter of the living room—frozen like a group of rubberneckers at the scene of a car crash. It's almost enough to jolt me into instant sobriety. "I'm sorr—"

Before I can finish my apology, Shayla storms forward from the crowd and slams her hands into my chest.

"What the hell is wrong with you?" she barks. "Look what you did!"

Every nerve ending in my body trembles with shame and embarrassment as I follow her instructions and survey the damage I've just caused. One of the four chains that was holding the wagon up has popped off entirely—taking a literal chunk of the wooden beam it was attached to with it—and the one next to it looks like it's ready to snap any second now. A small pile of wooden debris from the ceiling has pooled on the area rug directly below it, which is almost as disturbing as the sight of the partially unhinged wagon itself.

"I don't understand," Will says. He sounds more disappointed than pissed, which makes me feel even worse. "I left you alone for two seconds."

"I'm seriously so, so, so sorry." I dig my knuckles into my eyes and blink some more. "I lost my balance, and then I don't know—"

"You're gonna have to pay for this," Shayla and the vein popping out of her head tell me. "I hope you know that."

Robbie steps in and starts rubbing her back. "It was an accident," he says. I should mention that he is still extremely fuckable—perhaps even more so now that he's defending me with that strong, masculine voice of his. "Dude lost his balance. Calm down, babe."

"Calm down?" She slaps his hand away and shoots her furious eyes over at Will. "Dad is gonna kill us!"

Will opens his mouth to respond, but he's interrupted by a loud crack from above.

The room explodes into a cacophony of gasps and screams as

131

another chain rips itself from the ceiling right before our eyes. More wood chips sprinkle down as the wagon jerks and flips into a lopsided position—like a stalled amusement park ride. The seats, which were previously facing the ceiling, are now facing the wall. Two of the side wheels are lodged against the ceiling, and the two wheels on the other side are parallel to the floor— taunting the room like a pair of circular wooden storm clouds.

I'm positive the other two chains are going to snap any second now. The entire wagon is gonna come crashing down. I can already see the shrapnel flying, the furniture destroyed, the party guests stunned. And it's all my fault.

But somehow this doesn't happen. I narrow my gaze and notice that the remaining chains are attached to a different wooden beam than the other two were. And this one seems like it might be able to sustain the extra weight.

For now, at least.

"Please don't hate me," I whisper—to everyone and no one— and tiptoe my way to the back door.

sixteen

I wake up to a relentless ray of sunshine pounding me right in the eyes. It's aggressive! And I'm delirious. For a few seconds, I'm even blissfully clueless about my current set of circumstances. Am I hungover because Luke and I downed too many Bud Lights in his buddy's dorm room last night? Or did Mom and I drain a magnum of Luna di Luna at home?

I slowly absorb my surroundings — I'm all the way up on Marco's loft, the lake-view window sprawled out below me — and it all comes rushing back. The breakup, the fire, the lake. Shayla, Will, the wagon. Oh, God — the wagon.

There's a shuffling sound downstairs.

"Joey?" Marco's voice from below startles me. "How you feeling, bud?"

"I'm . . . not sure yet."

"Fresh coffee down here if you want it."

"Yes," I croak, "please."

Marco holds the ladder in place while my shaky hands and feet climb down like a slow monkey with arthritis. He's got two Advil waiting for me at the kitchen table. I've never been so happy to see a couple of little brown pills.

"I guess I shouldn't be surprised." Marco's fresh stubble makes way for a smirk. It's almost like he grew a literal beard overnight. Between that and his flannel pajama pants, he's really committed to this whole lumberjack-in-the-woods motif. "Gia and her wine. You didn't stand a chance."

"Ha," I mumble. "Yeah."

"Pretty crazy to see you all grown up." Marco clearly hasn't been told about the havoc I wreaked at his neighbor's house last night. So that's a (very mild) relief. "Up until yesterday I still pictured you as a chubby little kid."

"Please don't remind me." I cringe. "Well. You haven't changed at all." I take a sip of coffee and imagine it traveling up into my brain rather than down into my stomach. My brain needs it more. "I mean"—I gesture around the room—"except for all this."

"Not bad, huh? I love it. Even if sometimes I do get a little stir-crazy." He shifts in his seat and runs his hand through his hair. I wonder if what he really means is *lonely*. "I'm glad you and your mom surprised me."

"Thanks again for letting us crash."

I'm about to ask him for some details about how the hell I found my way to his loft (and up that ladder) last night, but I'm interrupted by the creaking open of his bedroom door across from us. Mom tiptoes out of it, draped all the way down to her knees in one of Marco's oversized shirts. "Bedhead" doesn't even begin to describe her current hair situation. She shoots me a half-surprised-half-guilty look, as if she has no idea how she ended up in there but also *totally* knows how she ended up in there. I knew she was full of shit when she said she didn't feel anything for him!

"Oh, my God. Ew!" I shift my eyes back and forth from her to Marco. "I...really don't wanna know."

"What?" Mom's voice sounds way too Jersey for our current setting.

Marco just laughs. "Morning, Sunshine." He pops the Advil back open and grabs her a bottle of water from the fridge. "Here." There's a very long, very awkward pause until Marco finally breaks the silence and says, "Okay. I gotta jump on a conference call and then get some work done this morning. You guys can feel free to hang around, though."

"How about a walk?" Mom asks me.

"There's an awesome trail starting about a quarter-mile up the road," Marco suggests. "If you make it to the top you'll see some incredible views."

"Let's do it." I'd much rather zipper my eyes shut until this hangover wears off, but I feel like Mom and I have some major catching up to do. And maybe the mountain-slash-lake air will be healing.

I climb back up to the loft to change clothes and check my phone before we go. Jesus. I have five missed calls. Two from Nonna and...three from...ugh. Luke. Why won't he go away? He's also sent a bunch of texts.

LUKE: Open the door Joey

LUKE: I'm at your apartment

LUKE: Come on, I told you I just want to talk

LUKE: I know you're here, I'm looking right at your mom's car

Seriously? Showing up unannounced at eight o'clock on a Wednesday morning? Who *does* that?

ME: What are you even doing???

ME: I told you I wasn't mad anymore

ME: we're not home

ME: her car is broken

ME: Please leave immediately

These are the first texts I've sent in more than twenty-four hours and it feels wrong. Like I'm betraying the whole "off the grid" ethos of the lake. But I also feel like I can't just sit around while Luke bangs down our front door like a delusional psychopath.

He starts typing and then stops. I have no idea what his deal is. If he wanted to talk so badly, why didn't he call or text me yesterday? If he was pissed off enough about his car to drive all the way to Bayonne to confront me in person, it seems weird that he'd wait more than twenty-four hours to do it. Then again, maybe that's how long it took for the car to be operational again.

Bzzz. Luke's replies come in all at once. It must have taken them extra-long to make the journey out here to Bumblefuck. *Bzzz.*

LUKE: I'm really sorry, ok?

LUKE: I don't even care about my car anymore

LUKE: I miss you

LUKE: you've never ignored me like this

LUKE: I hate it

LUKE: Joshua and I don't do that shit anymore, I swear

I guess he's right. I've never ignored him like this. Fleeing the state in a post-crime panic has really been great at forcing closure! Otherwise I'm sure I would've had at least one conversation with him by now. If only to bite his head off and/or interrogate him on the extent of his sexual history with Joshua. It must be killing him to think I didn't even care enough to bother. Good. He deserves to miss me.

Oh, my God. Wait.

What if he doesn't miss me at all? What if he's just trying to throw me off guard? What if this is all just a tightly organized sting operation? Luke saw the news, connected the dots to the GPS signal I sent him, and is now serving as the prosecution's key witness in the arson investigation. What if the cops are hiding out in an unmarked van across the street from our apartment, just waiting for Luke to utter the secret code word into the wire that's taped to his chest? What if his phone is totally bugged?

No.

That's silly! Even if he did report us for the crime, that's not how it would play out at all. He wouldn't just *text* me. They wouldn't do a *sting* operation. This might be New Jersey we're talking about, but it's not the *Sopranos*. The cops would show up themselves to arrest us. And I'm sure Mom's phone would be blowing up just as much — if not more — than mine.

Shit. Has she even looked at her phone since last night?

I'm jolted out of my thoughts by the sound of her voice from downstairs.

"Joey? You ready?" she calls out. Does she sound nervous and frantic? Fuck. She sounds nervous and frantic. "Let's go!"

seventeen

I spend the entire walk up Marco's gravelly road bombarding Mom with a rapid-fire round of *are-we-fucked-or-are-we-fine?* questions.

"Have you gotten any texts from Richard?" I ask.

"Nothing," she says. "The prick—"

"Anything from Luke?"

"Luke? Why would he—"

"The cops?"

"No." She laughs grimly. "Joey—"

"What about Nonna?"

"I thought you talked to her last night."

"Yeah," I say. "But she keeps calling me."

"She's called me a couple times, too."

"And you've been ignoring her?"

"What's with the third degree? Jesus."

"I'm freaking out!" I finally admit as we approach the trail entrance—all giant trees and rocks and dirt. "Luke sent me some insane texts. He showed up at our apartment."

"What? Why?"

"He says he just wants to talk," I answer. "But I'm scared there's more to it than that."

"Don't be crazy." Mom marches ahead in her knockoff Lululemons. She sounds calmer than I'd expected her to, especially given the tone of her voice at the house a few minutes ago. Maybe I was just projecting when I thought she sounded frantic. "Did he say anything else?" she asks.

"Nothing important." I take a giant step over a veiny cluster of roots in my path. "He said he's sorry again."

"See?" she says. "I told you he'd come crawling back."

"Whatever." I shake my head. I couldn't care less about that right now. "You really think we're safe out here? Off the grid?"

"Seems like it." She pauses in thought for a moment. "But what the hell do I know?" Her calmness seems to crack a little bit, like one of these dead leaves out here on the ground. Didn't take much. "In the long run... I have no idea what we're gonna do."

"Maybe the answer is that we just stay here," I suggest. "Like forev— for a long time. At least long enough for the fire investigation to blow over."

"I don't know." Mom sighs. "Being around Marco last night did make me feel better. He's so safe, you know? I didn't realize how much I missed that." She pauses. "You missed him, too. I can tell."

"Not really," I lie. "But I mean. He is so much better than Richard."

"Ha." She clicks her tongue. "There were moments last night when I totally forgot who I am — the mess we're in — but then it would all come rushing back to me. And I'd just think, *God. I shouldn't be here. I don't deserve him. He doesn't deserve this.* He's such a good guy —"

"Stop that! You're being way too hard on yourself."

"You do wish I stayed with him," Mom says. "Don't you?"

"I think you have me confused with Nonna," I tell her. "You did what you had to do! At the time. You weren't happy toward the end. I remember. You guys fought so much."

She groans as we approach a steep incline. "I guess I still haven't really forgiven myself. Even if he has."

"Forgiven yourself for what? You just grew apart." I wipe a bead of sweat off my eyebrow. "And now"—I grin—"you're growing back together."

She takes a breath like she's about to say something, but swallows it back instead. "You still haven't told me about the party. How'd that go? You must've stayed late. We didn't even hear you come back in."

"Oh, my God—the party." A boulder of shame forms in my stomach as I sort through all my mental snapshots from last night. They're fuzzy as hell, but I remember more than I probably should, given my level of intoxication. "It was all rich kids from the city. I mostly just talked to this one guy..." I give her a synopsis of my interactions with Will, and finish with a retelling of the hell I raised on my way out. "I feel so horrible. Like a total piece of human garbage."

It's true. I feel worse about this stupid wagon than I do about Luke's car or even Richard's house. Will seemed like a decent guy, you know?

"Holy shit," Mom says breathlessly. "So that big-ass wagon is still just dangling there?"

"I don't know!" I tell her. "It totally could've fallen by now." The shame-boulder in my stomach presses into my rib cage. "Do you think they'll tell Marco? Shayla said I'm gonna have to pay for it. How much do antique ceiling-hanging wagons even cost? This is such a nightmare."

"Accidents happen," she says — not necessarily calmly — more like she's just given up on caring about things. Like we're already in such deep shit with the car and the house, what's a wagon on top of it all? "Don't be so hard on yourself."

"Thanks." I give myself permission to take a breath. "Who even hangs a *wagon* from their ceiling in the first place?"

"Who knows with these rich bitches?" Mom says. "I used to be friends with this girl Brittany in high school. Her parents had a mansion in Montclair. All kinds of weird-ass family heirlooms." She lets out a breathy chuckle. "No wagons, though."

Huh. This is the first I've ever heard of a Brittany from high school.

"How'd you become friends with a rich girl from Montclair?" I ask.

"Cheerleading camp."

"Come again." My eyebrows float up in surprise. "How have you never told me you went to *cheer camp*?" I stifle a laugh at the thought of Mom in full *Bring It On* regalia. Something about the image doesn't fit — maybe because cheerleaders aren't typically known for drinking wine and saying the word *fuck* twenty times per sentence — I don't know. "How has *Nonna* never told me about this?"

"It was just one summer, okay?" Mom clarifies. "And I don't know, because it was obviously Nonna's idea. She saved up for an entire year to afford it."

"Of course she did."

"Anyway," Mom continues. "We only got along because her mom also forced her to go. But we stayed friends after the summer ended. I slept over her house some weekends — oh, my God, it was unbelievable. This house they lived in. Everything was so perfect and clean and *comfortable*. Her family would go out to eat at *nice* restaurants. They weren't eating at Da Vinci's Pizza only for special occasions, you know what I mean? They just had a totally different way of life — never had to worry. Sometimes when I slept with her in her queen-size bed, I would close my eyes and pretend it was *my* bed. Just for a second, before falling asleep." She stops to lean against a tree. "Jesus. It's hotter than a bitch out here."

"So what happened?" I ask. "Did you have a falling-out or something?"

"To say the least," Mom says. "Her parents, like, *forbade* her from being friends with me after I got knocked up. I think a pregnant sixteen-year-old from Bayonne was a little too much of a blemish on their perfect little existence."

Though I've never heard this particular story before, I have heard versions of it about other people from her past. Pretty much everyone in Mom's life flipped on her that year. She's told me it felt similar to what happened to Monica in the nineties: a total public shaming. One in which the man took absolutely no responsibility for his (significant!) role in the whole thing.

"That's really unfair." I look down and see that my arms have a shattered-glass glow from the rays of sunshine sneaking through the thick ceiling of leaves above us. It's kind of stunning. "I'm sorry."

"Whatever, I was used to it. It's not like they were the only ones." She sighs. "I don't recommend being a pregnant teenager. It's the worst."

"Yeah."

We continue hiking in silence for a while. Partially because it really *is* hotter than a bitch out here and breathing is becoming a challenge, and partially because I'm not sure what to say after that last story. This is why we don't usually talk about Mom's high school years. It was such a dark time for her — and yet I'm the direct result of that darkness. So it always ends up making us feel shitty. Like, I know she loves me more than anything in the world. But also, what if I'm the worst thing that's ever happened to her?

Finally we make it to the top, where the ground levels out. The fragmented rays of light on my arm disappear as we emerge from under the brush. Sunshine blankets us from every direction. You can see miles and miles of lake and mountain from up here. It's the type of perfect scene that you can't even bother taking a picture of, because you know your phone could never do it justice.

Mom and I sit down on opposite sides of a giant rock.

"So what about this Will guy from the party last night?" she asks. "You like him?"

"I don't think so." I flash back to the sloppy kiss I tried to give him. That was a mistake. The thought of someone like Will knowing what to do with someone like *me* is akin to the thought of a kindergarten teacher knowing how to operate a machine gun. "But even if I did, I'm sure he never wants to talk to me again."

"You don't know that!" Mom says. "They have enough money to fix their wagon. Life's easy when you can afford it."

"Even if he doesn't hate me, it would never work. He's a total Nice Guy."

"And that's a bad thing?" Mom asks and then throws her hands up, like, *duh, why did I even ask?* She shakes her head and laughs in what I'd estimate is a fifty-fifty combo of amusement and disappointment. "Jesus. We need therapy."

eighteen

Our hike was so effective at helping me escape the prison of my own mind. After enough time weaving between trees, it almost started to feel like the story we fed Marco and Nonna was true all along—we just came here on a spontaneous spring break(up) whim. To experience nature! That's all.

But now we're headed back to Marco's, and there's a police siren in the distance.

Our feet freeze in place. Mom grabs my vibrating wrist with her similarly shaky hand and squeezes it into paralysis.

"No way," she says. "There's no way."

"What do we do?" I crane my neck and look around. Behind us is the entrance to the trail we just came out of, and branching in both directions is the gravelly road that leads from Marco's house to the main road. Nothing but trees and bushes everywhere else. "Should we go back into the woods?"

"And do what?" Mom asks.

"Hide! Obviously!"

"You know what? We're being silly." She collects herself with a breath and starts walking in the direction of Marco's—which is exactly where I imagine the police are headed as well. My wrist is still clutched in her hand. "The odds of that siren being for *us* are so slim."

"Who else would it be for?" I ask. "I assume the pool of potential fugitives would be kinda shallow out here in the middle of Bumblefuck! Don't you think?"

"Why hasn't anyone called us, then?" she asks.

Just as she says this, my phone vibrates several times.

"My phone is buzzing!" I shriek. "Oh, my God, Mom."

We freeze in place again as I reach into my pocket and unlock the screen.

WILL: Nice meeting you yesterday. Hope you made it
    back up the hill safely.
WILL: And sorry about my sister at the end. I know it was
    an accident.
WILL: I've always hated that dumb wagon anyway!
WILL: How you feeling? Up for a hang later?

"What is it?" Mom asks.

"Will." My pulse descends back to a slightly less life-threatening rate. I can't believe he's willing to forgive me just like that. "The guy from yesterday."

"Oh." Mom resumes walking. "See? We're fine."

The siren gradually fades from earshot as we get to Marco's. It's gone by the time we step inside. The only thing we can hear is the fuzzy echo of Marco's conference call droning on speakerphone from behind his closed office door. The emotional roller coaster of the past few minutes still has me on edge, though. How exactly does one adapt to a lifestyle where every siren we hear is a potential death threat?

"Maybe we should shave our heads," I whisper. "We're eventually gonna have to go out in public—"

"Bitch. If you think I'm about to pull a *G.I. Jane* on myself because of a random police siren, you're insane." Mom grabs onto a clump of hair, as if to protect it from the suggestion. "No one is looking for us. It was nothing. A speeding ticket, probably. Or an ambulance."

"Can you at least do me?" I know I'm being ridiculous. Even if that siren was looking for us, what the hell is a fresh cut gonna do? It's not like a cop is gonna take one look at me and be like, *Oops, my bad. The guy I'm searching for has an unkempt mop of greasy dark-brown curls. Carry on!* But still. At the very least, I need a reinvention of some kind. Maybe by cutting off all this extra hair, my constant worrying habit will fall onto the tile floor along with it. "Do you think Marco has a clipper set?"

She shrugs. "I'm sure he does."

We find it under the bathroom sink in a toolbox-looking case with the words CONAIR imprinted on it in big nineties-looking letters. Mom recognizes it as the one she got him for Christmas a zillion years ago.

"Go as short as you can without making me totally bald." I plop myself down on the closed toilet seat and prepare myself for a new identity. "But higher on top. You know — make me look like a cool soccer player."

"You do realize you're just going to look like *you* but with a skin-tight fade, right?" Mom drapes a towel over my shoulders and chest. "Your face is your face, hon."

"I don't care," I say. "Just do it, please?"

She purses her lips and appeases me. The electric sound of clippers fills the room.

"Remember how I used to bring you with me to the salon on Saturdays?" Mom says over the buzz. "When you were a kid."

"Of course."

I can still smell the burning hair tools and Paul Mitchell styling products. I loved that scent combination! Dreamed about it all week at school, actually. Screw math and science — I wanted to be on that big leather couch in the waiting area, watching Mom work miracles for her customers. She was a superhero in that place. I remember one time this lady came in with a frizzy-ass rat's nest on her head and an equally tragic story coming out of her mouth about how some dickhead had recently ghosted her. Within a couple hours, Mom had blessed her with the smooth hair of a runway model and the sassy advice of an Instagram life coach.

"You always know how to fix me," the lady had told her on her way out. Then she looked and pointed at me, my head buried in the latest *Allure* and/or *Glamour*. You know! The usual eight-year-old boy mags. "Is he yours?"

"That's my Joey." Mom beamed from behind the register. "He's a real comedian."

"Oh, is he *fresh*?" the lady asked.

"No, I mean he's actually funny!" Mom said. "You should hear him. Always making up these little jokes. Joey, tell her a joke."

I shook my head like a frightened monkey and giggled into my magazine in embarrassment. Basically the same reaction I would have nowadays if someone were to put me on the spot like that. Rude! But the memory brings a smile to my face nonetheless.

"I always loved when you came to work with me." Mom digs into the toolbox for a shorter clipper attachment. "Even if my boss was a twat about it sometimes."

148

"Really? But she was always so nice to my face!"

"I know, right?" She pauses. "I mean, I probably should've just left you at Nonna's those days. But I liked having you there."

"Yeah," I say. "I liked being there."

Our conversation falls into a serene lull, both of us lost in our own versions of the memory. I look down at the thick collection of discarded hair clippings on the towel before me and somehow feel better already.

"I think you should take that guy up on his invitation," Mom finally says. "He clearly still likes you."

"For some reason," I say.

"Hey!" She smacks my arm. "There are a million reasons he could like you. Don't be stupid. And maybe it will take your mind off everything. What else are you gonna do all day?"

"I don't know. What else are *you* gonna do all day?"

"I'll figure it out," she says. "Maybe go into town with Marco. Yesterday he said he wanted to take me out to this—"

"In public?" I ask.

"Keep your head still." She presses down on the top of my scalp and runs the clippers up the back of my neck. "Yes, in public."

"You need to be careful." I think back to the sound of that siren slicing through the mountain air and feel my heart quicken. But Mom's right. Right? She has to be. It was nothing. A speeding ticket. An ambulance. A false alarm. "Please."

nineteen

Somehow the wagon is still dangling up there.

"We thought about moving all the furniture out of the room," Will explains. He's clean and preppy in a pair of Nantucket Red shorts and a white linen button-down with the sleeves rolled up. There's a whisper of light-brown chest hair showing, which — was that there last night? Because damn. It's hot. "But it seems too risky to stand under that thing for even a second."

"I'm so sorry." I bury my idiot face in my hands. "I feel like such a piece of shit."

"I'm telling you, it's fine. It was only a matter of time before something like this happened. That thing has always made me nervous. My mom, too. She'll probably be relieved that she finally has an excuse to make Dad get rid of it."

The energy in this space has transformed overnight. There's emptiness where all the drunk bodies used to be. Silence in place of music. And I no longer have that liberating buzz. Without it, I have to wonder if coming here was a mistake. Somehow I feel like I'm actively telling a giant lie just by existing around Will.

"Nice cut, by the way!" he says. "When did you —"

"My mom," I tell him. "She's a hairdresser."

"She does good work. You look handsome."

"No, I don't." Of course my kneejerk reaction to receiving a compliment of any kind would be to immediately invalidate it. "I mean...thanks."

Will tilts his head and gives me one of those scrunch-faced looks of his.

I clear my throat. "So where is everyone?" I ask. "This place feels like a ghost town compared to last night."

"I'm surprised you remember last night." He playfully grabs my shoulder. His hand has a better grip than I would've expected. I don't hate it. "Pretty much everyone went home this morning. I think *Wagongate* freaked them out. Robbie's the only one who stayed. He and Shayla are down at the dock. They convinced our dad's maintenance guy to dewinterize his boat early because of the weather."

"Oh." I almost forgot I was dealing with a rich person. No wonder he's not stressing out more about the wagon. His dad has a *maintenance guy*, for Christ's sake. "That's cool."

We stand around in silence for a few seconds. I take a moment to observe all the kitchen finishes — hickory wood cabinets, stone tile backsplash, butcher block island. And so much open counter space! Nonna would kill for a kitchen like this.

"You seem uncomfortable," Will finally says. "Is this weird? Do you want a drink or something?" He looks at the clock display on the stove. "I guess it's only one o'clock, but you know. Spring break." His eyes wander for a moment. "Unless you're too hungover."

"I'm not an amateur," I say. "I'd love a drink."

He smirks and pulls out two tall cans of Goose Island IPA. I've never heard of this beer, but I have to assume it's fancy. (Is it actually not fancy and in fact totally plain? Listen, I'm not a beer aficionado and Luke was a Basic Budweiser Bitch.) "Here." He pours the cans one at a time into two separate pint glasses. "Cheers."

"*Salut.*" I clink my glass to his and take a swig as we both settle onto barstools at the oversized granite counter. "Whoa. This is different."

"Nice, right?" he says. "I love a hoppy brew."

I cock my head and look at him in an attempt to process the fact that I'm drinking with someone who just (a) poured our beers into actual pint glasses, and (b) used the phrase "hoppy brew." He shoots me a dimply half-smile, which I'll admit looks adorable alongside his stubbly facial hair. Shit! You know what? I misjudged this guy. He can *get it*. There's an easy confidence about him that I somehow didn't pick up on last night. It's more welcoming than it is intimidating—which is new to me—but it's still confidence.

"What?" he asks.

"What?" I repeat.

"Do I have something on my face?"

"No."

"Oh." He smiles again. "Okay." He takes a big sip and intentionally gets a thick layer of beer foam on his mustache. "What about now?"

Any other guy would lose major fuckability points for this goofy-ass maneuver (it's Marco-esque!) but somehow Will doesn't. He actually gets a laugh out of me.

"You're funny," I say.

"Well…I'm no *comedian*."

The sneaky way he says it makes the memory come crashing back into me like a benign tsunami. He saw my Notes app last night. "Oh. Right."

He pokes my arm. "Tell me a joke."

Every organ in my body winces at once. "You didn't actually *see* anything on my phone last night, right? I will fully die of embarrassment."

"Just that one joke about…frozen vegetable medleys, I think it was?" He snickers to himself as my organs wince all over again. "What? I thought it was cute!"

"Cute is the opposite of funny!"

"Not to me," he says. "Come on. Tell me a joke."

I almost want to sputter out something stupid — quickly and ironically — just so we can move on from this subject. But I can't think of any material off the top of my head that doesn't make me want to punch myself in the face. And pulling out my Notes app would just look pathetic. What kind of comic can't ad lib a fun little zinger on the spot?

"We're in a kitchen!" I tell him instead, as if that explains everything. "I can't just randomly pull a joke out of my ass in a kitchen. That's not how stand-up works."

"Fair enough." He leans back on his stool and takes another sip of IPA. My eyes pick up on a hint of muscle definition as he lifts the pint glass. My mind responds by trying to calculate the shortest possible route from *this-painful-conversation-about-my-nonexistent-comedy-career* to *us-just-getting-naked-and-hooking-up-already.* "Do you ever perform at any clubs?" he asks. "I'd love to see you in action."

I almost choke on my beer. "You're kidding, right? No. Never."

"What are you scared of?"

"Bombing!" I say. "Comedy audiences are ruthless."

"Who cares what they think?"

"Me!"

Will chuckles and brushes off my hysterics. "I'm sure you'd be great. After a few drinks, especially."

"What's that supposed to mean?"

"You just seem like you're a little more comfortable in your skin when you have some lubrication."

Ding! My mental GPS just found a shortcut.

"Are you trying to tell me you wanna fuck right now?" I fake-gasp. "Because I might be okay with that."

"Uh." Will's face turns completely red. "This took a turn."

"Was that too far?" I ask. Even though I know the answer is unequivocally yes. "That was too far."

"No, let's do it!" Will digs into his pocket. "I know I've got a condom in here somewhere. Might be expired, but..."

"Ha ha—"

"You're okay with bottoming, right?"

Oh, my God. I think he might be serious? Okay! So I'm fully about to hook up with this guy I barely know. On a Wednesday morning in the middle of the woods. Whilst hiding out from the police after committing arson not even forty-eight hours ago. Who says you can't have it all?

My face flushes with heat as I fumble to formulate a sexy response.

"I'm kidding!" Will says and then pauses. "Did you think I was serious?"

Before I can figure out my answer, the front door swings open and Shayla floats into the kitchen like a fairy princess. Her eyes widen when she sees me.

"It's you." She flashes a bitchy look at Will. "Please don't tell me you invited him onto the boat with us. He might break that, too."

"Why do you have to be like that?" Will asks her. "I already told you I'm taking the fall for the wagon. It's not even your problem at this point."

"Hi, Shayla." I swallow my embarrassment and try to sound as sane as possible to counter the image of unhinged chaos I presented her with yesterday. "Listen, I seriously am *so*—"

"Whatever." She adjusts the strap on her sundress and seems to thaw out a little bit. "Just don't go getting all sloppy again. I *won't* hesitate to throw your ass overboard."

"Oh — I actually wasn't planning on joining you guys."

"You have to!" Will says.

"Yes." Shayla flips her hair. "You just *have to* save my tragic brother from being the third wheel he was born to be."

"Ouch, sis." Will rubs fake tears from his eyes. "Very ouch."

Shayla purses her lips.

Seeing them in the same room again reminds me of just how different they are — in both looks and personality. "Are you sure you're twins?" I ask.

"Oh, yeah, no — we're not," Shayla zings. "Will was a last-minute pickup at the hospital."

Will pinches her arm. "Now you're just being mean."

"I'm obviously kidding!" She pinches his arm back. "Listen, Robbie's out there and ready to go. I'm gonna change real quick. If you're not out at the dock in five, we're leaving without you."

twenty

This is wild. I'm on a boat!

Can you *even*? Because I can't. The only "boat" I've ever been on was a dilapidated ferry in the nasty-ass Hudson River, going from Jersey to New York for the San Gennaro Festival in Little Italy. Nonna paid seven dollars each for us to experience twelve windy minutes on the water, cramped into a pair of ice-cold metal seats, surrounded on all sides by tourists and commuters. "We really shoulda taken the train," she'd said as we floated past the Statue of Liberty. "But I was feeling *fancy*."

If she could only see me now — reclining on the cushy ledge of a sleek, modern speedboat as it careens through the endless royal-blue ripples of Lake George. Surrounded on all sides by mountains draped in lush fir trees.

"Babe, slow down!" Shayla's shimmery platinum hair blows in a thousand different directions. She's curled up on a seat in front of Robbie's captain perch. "I basically forced my dad to let us do this. We need to *not* crash."

Tank top–clad Robbie cracks a sly grin and revs up the speed. My balls rocket up to my throat in response to the acceleration.

Colliding with another boat seems unlikely—we appear to be the only ones out here so far—but still.

I try to relax. What's the worst that could happen? Robbie knows what he's doing. I watch his shoulder muscle flex slightly as he cranks the speed control even further up. It turns out his bicep tattoo is of an angry-looking tiger. Goddamnit. I almost forgot about how hot he is. And now that he's actively putting our lives in danger, he's only getting hotter. Is there any greater turn-on?

Stop! There's an actual gay guy on this boat who likes you. Focus on him!

I make eye contact with Will—seated directly to my left—and he tosses me a silly wink. I think back to our banter in the kitchen and smile. It's not like I'm *not* attracted to him. But putting these two guys right next to each other on a little boat is just cruel. Will is cute. But Robbie is...Luke, basically.

"Dude!" Will yells at Robbie. "Look out!"

My balls shoot back up to my throat (a.k.a. their new permanent home) as Robbie swerves the boat away from a giant buoy directly in our path.

The turn is so sharp that the boat goes full-force directly into one of the waves it had just created a few seconds ago. I'm not even exaggerating, the whole thing jerks sideways and almost tips over!

Will's Yeti beer cooler slides across the floor and crashes into my feet. Robbie grips the wheel. Shayla digs her nails into her seat cushion. Will throws his arm over my shoulders. I clutch my fingers around one of those steel rope-holder things on the boat's rim. There's a loud *thump* underneath us. For a moment the boat is completely airborne—dolphin-esque—and then it's rapidly skipping over a series of mini-waves—until another *thump* finally plunks it back into position on the water.

I haven't pissed my pants, but the extreme terror followed by extreme relief I've just gone through has definitely taken my bladder — and every other organ in my body — on a journey.

Will squeezes my arm. "You okay?"

I nod.

"Yo!" Robbie slows the boat to a crawl. "That was so dope."

"You know there are speed limits," Shayla barks at him. "My dad would kill you if he knew what just happened!"

"He's already gonna kill *you* for the wagon, sweet tits," he cracks. "I might as well join you in the afterlife."

"Correction: He's gonna kill *Will*." She pauses. "And what did you just call me?"

"I'd love it if you didn't fling misogynistic epithets at my sister," Will chimes in. "And also if you didn't crash our dad's boat. That'd be awesome."

"Relax. I'm just messing around." Robbie flashes an unapologetic smile. "Don't worry. Alistair's precious little speedboat is fine." He taps the steering wheel proudly. "These things are built for speed. It's literally in the name."

"Don't do it again." Shayla blinks and takes a breath. "Let's just anchor down somewhere. I wanna stay still for a minute."

"Wait," I interject. "Your dad's name is *Alistair*? That might be the WASP-iest name I've ever heard."

Robbie cracks up. "It really is."

"What's *your* dad's name?" Shayla grabs a Twisted Tea from the cooler and plops back down on her cushion. "Let me guess. Um. Super Mario."

"I have no idea what his name is, actually." My statement stuns everyone into uncomfortable silence. Not my intention! It just came out. And now I don't know how to reverse it. "I could probably ask my mom," I continue. "But I don't really care."

Shayla and Robbie look at me like they don't know whether I'm serious or just trying (and failing) to make some kind of weird joke. Will must think it's the former. He looks at me like I'm one of those ASPCA Sarah McLachlan–commercial orphan puppies. Like he's never heard of someone not having a dad before.

"*Okay*...so." Shayla's eyes dart back and forth between me and her brother and boyfriend. "Let's go in the water!"

"You crazy?" Robbie says. "You don't remember how cold it was yesterday? My nuts were practically frozen to the bottom of my kayak."

I process and immediately delete a mental image of Robbie's frozen kayak-nuts. It's somehow wildly enticing despite the grossly non-sexual context of the statement.

"Don't be a bitch, Robbie." Shayla pulls her hair into a pony-tail. "It can't be any worse than the Polar Bear Plunge we did at Lake Louise last year."

He does a sarcastic military salute. "Yes ma'am."

"Too bad I didn't bring any swim trunks," I say. "Who knew it would be eighty degrees in April?"

"The weather people called it last week," Shayla says. "That's why we came up here. Otherwise my ass would have been on the first flight down to Miami."

"Miami was an option?" Robbie says. "What are we doing here again?"

"It's sentimental!" Shayla says. "And I mean, look at this." She motions around at the idyllic scenery as Robbie pulls us into a secluded cove. "It's so pure."

"Thomas Jefferson used to love this lake," Will offers. "He once described it as the most beautiful water he'd ever seen. Rockefeller had a mansion on it, too. This place was *the* summer hot spot for New York elite back in the day."

"Thanks, loser." She looks over at me. "Is this the kind of talk Will was boring you with that whole time you were sitting in the kitchen not making out?"

Will ignores Shayla and looks at me. "I'm majoring in history at Yale next year."

"That's fun!" I lie.

"Is it?" Shayla asks.

Robbie jolts the boat into stillness at a centralized location in the bay. He digs an anchor out from a latch in the floor and throws it overboard. I watch in awe as the water gulps down the rope attached to it. This is all so surreal. I've always associated anchors with, like, summer-themed décor at Home Goods. (The *bears* of beach houses, if you will.) Turns out they're real and people use them!

"Here we go." Shayla stands up and strips down to the navy-blue bikini she's been hiding beneath her outfit. Robbie follows suit and throws his tank top into the corner of the boat. I scratch a nonexistent itch on my forehead and look in literally every other direction.

Will taps my leg. "I'll stay here with you."

"Wusses!" Shayla takes a giant breath and hurls herself overboard.

"Why do I listen to her?" Robbie asks himself before making a jump of his own.

Two seconds later they're wailing in pain from what I assume is extreme temperature shock. Shayla's high-pitched scream combined with Robbie's deep-voiced groan creates a striking dissonance.

"I gotta take a piss," Robbie finally says.

"Babe, gross!" Shayla yelps. "But same."

They swim in opposite directions away from the boat until it finally feels like Will and I are alone. I can breathe easily again now that it's just us. Having Robbie around was making me more self-conscious than I realized—like his hotness was too blinding for me to fully let my guard down.

"So what was that thing about your dad?" Will says. "If you don't mind my asking?"

"Oh." I shrug. "It's not a big deal. I just never knew him. He was a twenty-year-old dirtbag who knocked up my mom when she was sixteen. It was all very 'Papa Don't Preach.'"

"Whoa." He gives me that dogs-on-death-row look again. "That's some heavy stuff. I'm sorry."

"I honestly don't care!" I say. "Fuck that guy."

This is so not a conversation I'm in the mood to have.

"Fair enough." Will unbuttons a few more buttons on his white linen shirt. His chest hair catches my eye again. Good! I managed to survive being on this boat with Robbie all that time and still have the ability to find Will attractive. "Wait," he adds. "What's 'Papa Don't Preach'?"

"Shut up!" I say. "You seriously don't know that song? Madonna?"

"I'm sorry?" He shakes his head and laughs. A dimple emerges at the corner of his mouth; it makes me want to kiss him. "I feel like I just offended you."

"Of course you did," I say. "I didn't realize this whole time I've been flirting with a guy who doesn't understand the iconic cultural impact of Italian-American icon Madonna Louise Ciccone."

Will raises an eyebrow. "This is you flirting?"

Okay, he just negged me. Now I'm *really* attracted to him.

"It *was* me flirting," I correct him. "But that's definitely over now."

"Well, damn." He takes his glasses off and places them in a

cupholder on the inside edge of the boat, which I interpret as an invitation to kiss him any minute now. "I guess we'll have to start over from the beginning."

You *know* I wouldn't normally make the first move, but something comes over me again. Like I need to redeem myself after last night's rejection. So I lean into him and press my lips against his before he has a chance to say anything else. He seems caught off guard, but then his mouth relaxes and he kisses me back. We slip into a groove. For about...ten seconds. Then he comes up for air and squints at me.

"I think we should stop," he says.

"What?" I ask. "You're not into me?"

"That's not it." He uses his hand to wipe a smear of saliva off his lip. Was I kissing sloppily? Oh, my God. "I've been wanting to kiss you ever since the moment you barged in on me last night. But—"

"Then shut up," I reply—sounding about a zillion times meaner than intended. But maybe this is just how it goes with Nice Guys. You have to be the one to move things forward.

Will's neck stiffens for a second, like he wants to question my aggression. But I kiss him harder and force him to relax back into it before he can say anything. I let my hands roam all around him—thighs, arms, neck, chest, back. He's not touching me in quite the same way—his hands are mostly just stationed around my hips—which makes me wonder if maybe he's truly not into this.

But then he kisses me back and his stubble scratches against my face and I decide that he most definitely is. I just wish he was being more of a leader about it. I'd love nothing more than to sit back and give myself entirely to him right now. *Here.* I close my eyes and think about the entire set of circumstances Mom and I are currently running away from. *Fix me.*

I lose myself in a daydream of Will making it all better some-how. *The fire investigation dies out. We dive headfirst into a serious relationship. I visit him every weekend at Yale and work on my act while he's in school. In four years, we move to LA together. My past is rendered irrelevant—burned to the ground just like that stupid house.*

"Listen." Will takes my hand, which I didn't even realize had crept down to the waistband of his shorts. "This is getting a little hot and heavy for broad daylight."

"Is it, though?" I ask. "We're literally the only people out here."

I crane my neck and scan our surroundings for evidence of life. I peer through the sunlight and see Robbie crawling out of the water to join Shayla on a rocky island jutting out of the water in the distance. His back is strong and his ass is perfect. No. I'm not looking!

"Shayla and Robbie," Will says.

"They're all the way over there." I point at the rock-island on which they're currently having a make-out session of their own. Completely unconcerned with us. "See?"

"We're still out in the open." He pulls away and sits back. "And we were starting to have a good conversation before. I was hoping we could continue it. Get to know each other a little bet-ter, you know? I'm sorry if I gave you the wrong idea."

This is uncharted territory for me. I've been rejected and/or ghosted by dudes more times than I can count—but that's always a blow reserved for *after* we hook up. Not that Will is rejecting me altogether; he does sound serious about wanting to get to know me better. But still. What better way is there to get to know some-one than by shmooshing your bodies together?

I don't know what to do, so I decide to try kissing him one last time to see if I can change his mind. Will moans, which I interpret as a sign that I've achieved success. Good! I bring my hands back down to his thighs and sneak one of them up his shorts until I can feel the elastic trim of his boxer briefs. His leg flinches a little but I don't care. I wiggle my hand up further — and further — and further — until my fingers are fully wrapped around his junk. This time his leg flinches a lot. He pulls away.

"Dude!" he whisper-shouts. "What the hell are you doing?"

The boat rocks as I roll myself off him and we detach entirely.

"I thought you liked me..." is the only thing I can think to say. Which sounds extremely pathetic, because it is. This is humiliating. "It's not like you're not hard."

"Of course I do," he says. "And I am. But Joey — I mean, you're going from zero to a hundred here." He adjusts his shorts. "I *just* told you all I wanted to do is hang out and talk."

"I know," I stammer. "I didn't think you actually meant that."

"Why would I say something I don't mean?" he asks.

"I don't know, I'm sorry." I can't help but think about my first date with Luke. My head was buried in his crotch not even two hours into it. And that was in the backseat of his Subaru — on land! In a Houlihan's parking lot! Way riskier than being out here in the middle of a deserted lake. "God. You must think I'm such a mess. First I break your wagon and then I grab your —"

He interrupts me and tells me *it's not a big deal, let's just start over, it's fine.* But I know it is a big deal, it's too late to start over, and it's not fine. Because my first impression was right after all. I'm way too fucked up for this guy.

twenty-one

It's past nine and Mom and Marco still aren't back.

It was still light out when I got here and I didn't bother turning any lights on, so right now I'm sitting on the bed up in the loft. Scrolling through my Notes app in the dark. I've been trying to come up with some new jokes, but so far all I could think of is this:

Rich people make no sense. Their lives are so easy, they have to invent ways to feel pain — like jumping into freezing lake water and calling it a "Polar Bear Plunge."

Meanwhile, actual polar bears are out here dying at the hands of global warming. And rich kids are just trolling them, like, "Ha ha, bitch! Our species wasn't even built to withstand this level of frigidity but we're doing it for fun because we're bored. Anyway, have fun with extinction."

Lame. Needs work.

But I can't focus. Mom hasn't answered any of my texts since I got back here. And my calls keep going straight to voicemail. I'm trying not to freak out, but also: I'm freaking out. It was a stupid idea for us to split up. Like, yeah, that spontaneous boat adventure was a cute little reprieve from reality — but it didn't change the fact that my phone is no longer a phone—it's a tiny dread machine just waiting to explode with news of our tragic fate. Mom *needs* to be here with me when that happens.

Bzzz.

I get a text but it's not from her.

WILL: hey
WILL: I still feel weird about what happened today
WILL: wanna come over and make me feel un-weird?

I groan with residual embarrassment from earlier. Why is he still trying to talk to me? He should hate me so much right now.

ME: sorry—tired

His typing bubble pops up but then disappears. Now I feel bad. I start to write a follow-up text about how maybe we can hang out tomorrow, but then I hear the front door swing wide open and see a glow of light flicker on from the kitchen.

"This is why I couldn't stand being with you, Marco." Mom's voice whooshes into the house like a tornado. "This right here!"

I sigh in relief at the sense of her presence. But then my chest tightens back up as I realize she is literally mid-battle.

"Calm down," Marco says.

"Fuck you, calm down!"

"Joey?" he calls out. I close my screen and bury myself under the blanket, keeping my muscles as still as possible so as not to induce any creaks from the bed's weathered wooden frame. "He must still be next door."

All I hear is shuffling—the fridge door opens and closes and someone pours a drink—until the fight starts back up again.

"You *always* talked down to me like you were better than me," Mom says. "You think I don't know how to raise my son? I've been doing it for eighteen years."

This fight is about *me*? Seriously? What the hell did I do?

"Gia, you're drunk." He sounds frustrated but not quite as manic as she does. "All I was saying is that you should be a better influence. I wasn't trying to start a fight, but come on. You said he's been down at Rutgers every weekend this year sleeping over with some college guy. Then the poor kid gets his heart broken and your solution is to trash the guy's car? What kind of example are you setting?"

She told him about the car! Is she insane? What the hell has she been drinking all night? *Honesty Potion? Truth Juice?*

"Why do you care so much?" Mom asks. "You lived with him for a few years and you think he's your son or something. Newsflash, asshole. He's not your son!"

"But he *is* yours!" Marco yells back. "Instead of acting like his mother, you act like some kind of friend — and not even a good one. You're like the bad influence who smokes in the bathroom and gets expelled."

Okay, you know what? Fuck Marco. We've been here for two days and he thinks he knows everything about our current relationship. Mom has literally devoted her entire life to me. Sure, she can be messy sometimes. But same goes for all humans. I don't need a mom who's a "good influence." I need a mom who loves me unconditionally. And she always has.

"And you were a saint in high school?" Mom spews. "I can't believe you. The whole time we were together, you always tried to act like you're so holier than thou, so much better than all the other assholes I dated. Meanwhile, you're just like them. You're worse!"

"Worse? Joey's scumbag father pushes you down the stairs when you're pregnant, every guy you get with after that treats you like dirt . . . but *I'm* the worst." Marco does one of those pissed-off sarcastic laughs. "I did everything for you. We had a good life together. And then *you* cheated on me. Remember?"

So now he's straight-up lying. Marco knows that Mom is always the one who gets cheated *on*. She would never do that to him. Or anyone. Ever.

"How could I forget?" she says—not denying it. What? No. That's not possible. "You only reminded me every fucking day until the end."

This bed suddenly feels like it's made of razor blades. It takes all the strength I have not to jump out of it and confront them both about the bomb that was just dropped.

"Because I gave you the best life you've ever had!" Marco says. "And it still wasn't enough for you. You couldn't stand being with someone who actually gave a shit about you."

"What the fuck is that supposed to mean?"

"It means love is *wasted* on you, Gia!" he fumes. "Love is wasted on you because you hate men. You love Joey, and that's it. Fuck everyone else. You've always been that way."

"So now I love my son?" she asks. "Two minutes ago you were telling me I was the world's worst mother."

"Just because you love him doesn't mean you know what's best for him."

"And you do?" Mom yells back. "You're a fucking weird, sad freak, Marco! You live in isolation in the middle of the woods!"

She lets out a furious scream and slams . . . something . . . on . . . something. I can't see anything from up here in my dark cocoon. But there's a loud noise. Followed by crying. And then she sighs in that way people sigh after they realize they just said the most damaging thing they could think of and now have to figure out how to undo it.

My body is still frozen in place, but my mind is an explosion of questions and emotions. Each one is like a piece of shrapnel with the power to cause fatal destruction if it moves even a millimeter. I don't know who I feel more betrayed by. On the one hand, Mom has been a secret cheater this whole time. How could I even begin to process that fact? I thought Luke was horrible for lying to me every day for ten months. Meanwhile, my own mother has been lying to me every day for eight years. At least. Who else has she cheated on? Our entire shared identity as the victims of shitty men is now a giant question mark.

And then there's Marco. I had no idea he could be so mean.

Objectively, I understand he's the one who was cheated on in this scenario and so of course he must hate her. If the roles were reversed, we'd be saying all bets are off—this lake house may not even exist, because we'd have burned it down by now. But still. It's Mom he was yelling at. Hearing him verbally eviscerate her felt like a bullet to the heart. *Love is wasted on you.* Who says that to someone?

My thoughts are interrupted by another loud *slam*. This time it's the very recognizable sound of a door being kicked shut. The vibration echoes throughout the open structure. The kitchen lights turn off before I hear the slamming of another door in the opposite direction. I guess that answers the question of whether they'll be spending the night together again.

Now that they're gone, I take my phone back out and check my texts.

WILL: ???

It takes all the strength I can muster just to reply with maybe tomorrow before placing my phone on the little table next to the bed. This day has been a damn marathon.

My mind continues to race and race until it's finally so burnt out that it starts to collapse into itself from sheer exhaustion. My eyelids eventually follow suit.

My subconscious keeps going, though.

Suddenly I'm sitting in the passenger seat of Luke's car as he speeds down the turnpike. He's wearing his New Jersey Devils hat and Rutgers hoodie, smirking. It's one of those dark, twisted, scary smirks that subtly sets the tone for an all-out nightmare.

I look behind me and see Nonna in the backseat. She's mouthing at me to "get out" but not actually saying it out loud.

"I'm fine," I assure her. "I'm fine."

She slaps me on the arm in response—a gesture that means *Don't be stupid!* in Nonna—but still won't speak a word. She doesn't have a voice. I refocus my attention on Luke's side profile and feel safe.

"I love you," he says.

"I love you, too," I reply.

There's this unspoken understanding between us that bygones are bygones—the cheating is forgiven, the windshield doesn't matter, we're back to normal.

"Joey," Luke says.

"Yeah?"

His serial killer smile returns. "Tell me a joke."

My face burns up and I can't breathe.

Now I'm standing in the middle of Marco's living room with Will. We're looking up at the loft for some reason, as if we're expecting something. And then—all at once—it bursts into flames. Not the house. Just the loft.

"Good," Will says. "It's contained."

The flames are small and delicate. Calm. The reds, oranges, yellows artfully spread themselves onto the bedskirt, nightstand, lamp, carpet, railing—in perfectly contoured patterns, almost like an invisible painter is applying them with a brush.

I stand there, transfixed, feeling safe again.

And then one of the flames catches the chunky wooden ladder that leads down to the living room.

An outbreak of new flames follows—growing more and more intense with each rung of the ladder consumed. The fire is no longer delicate. It's raging. The ladder has become nothing more than a flaming tower of chaos. Smoke fills the entire space around us. I blink and Will is gone.

Mom appears out of nowhere.

She wraps her arms around me as the flames spread down to the hardwood floor and engulf the worn-out area rug directly below our feet.

"We're fine," she says. "We're fine."

twenty-two

LUKE: YOU BURNED DOWN THAT GUY'S HOUSE??

LUKE: JOEY WHAT THE FUCK

LUKE: THE COPS SHOWED UP AT MY DORM

LUKE: Where are you???

LUKE: I showed them our text history

LUKE: I'm so sorry

LUKE: I didn't have a choice

LUKE: seemed like they already knew it was you anyway

LUKE: there was a witness

LUKE: WHERE ARE YOU

It's seven in the morning and I just woke up to a relentless *tap, tap, tap* on the roof directly above my head. My brain barely had time to register they were raindrops before I swiped into my screen and saw that these texts have been burning a hole in my phone unanswered — along with an endless log of missed calls — for the past eight hours.

The nightmare I had overnight comes rushing back to me. A five-ton pit in my stomach tells me Luke's texts are just the tip of the iceberg.

I gain control of my fingers just enough to tab out of the conversation and into Twitter.

The fire tweet blew up overnight. Thousands of retweets and replies drawing a giant spotlight on the destruction Mom and I have spent the past three days running from. Within moments of digging through the #ShortHillsFire hashtag, I find an updated Channel Four New Jersey story posted just an hour ago.

"Investigators have a lead in the mysterious Short Hills fire case..." the same reporter from Tuesday morning says; a selfie of Mom and me in her car flashes onto the screen. Mom's Facebook profile picture. We took it on a random afternoon last fall when she was having an amazing hair day. "Police have issued a warrant for the arrest of thirty-four-year-old Gianna Rossi and her eighteen-year-old son, Joseph, both of Bayonne, who have been missing since Tuesday morning."

My fingers go limp and my wrists turn to stone. My phone makes a muffled thud as it drops onto the carpeted floor of the loft.

Breathing? Nope. My lungs don't know what that is. There's not a single cell or organ in my body that knows what *anything* is. I'm just a frozen black hole of numbness—a frozen black hole of numbness *who doesn't know what the fuck to do next.* I have to gasp for air.

This moment has been inevitable all along, I know. And yet I still can't believe it's happening.

How could our picture show up on the news without our knowledge? I think about all the pictures of everyday people— suspects, victims, whatever—I've ever seen flash in those little boxes on the screen over the years. I guess I've always just assumed it wasn't a surprise to them. As if producers give a heads-up before the segment goes live or something. *Hi there, we're emailing to inform you that your mom's profile picture will be used in tonight's broadcast, in which you'll both be identified as the primary suspects in an ongoing arson investigation. Tune in at ten o'clock!*

I'm also thinking about all the pieces that must have come together over the past two days for the cops to figure this out. While Mom and I were driving up here blasting "Ring the Alarm," they were searching for answers. While I was unsuccessfully making out with Will on the boat, they were searching for answers. While Mom and Marco were ripping each other's heads off in the kitchen last night, they were searching for answers.

And now they've found them.

I almost fall several times on my way down to the living room. Climbing down a ladder in my current state is more difficult than riding a mechanical bull. Everything shakes and I can't get a grip. It's a miracle I don't crack my head open.

The *tap, tap, tap* of the raindrops is the only sound in the house. There's a certain peace in the air that totally betrays the chaos pounding and twisting and churning throughout my body. If it weren't for my phone, this would be an extraordinarily chill Thursday morning. The view out the giant lake window is breathtaking in a whole new, dark way—an endless stream of water splashing into an endless puddle, a sky-consuming dark cloud where the sun used to be.

I barge into the guest bedroom and find Mom curled up on the floor. She's weeping as the *tap, tap, tap* continues to assault the walls from all directions. Her face is buried in her hands, shrouded under her blanket of dark, dark hair. I can only imagine what *her* phone looks like right now.

"We're on the news," I say through a tear.

"I saw." She looks and sounds like a ghost. "Richard texted."

"Where's Marco?" I ask. "Does he know?"

"No." She stares straight ahead, out the window, as she answers. Her monotone is freaking me out. Shouldn't she be hysterical? We should both be hysterical. "He left twenty minutes ago. Ran out of coffee."

"We need to think of something!" I say. "Come on."

She peels herself off the floor and messily folds herself into my arms. I brace for her to start sobbing harder — probably while yelling some variation of "I'm sorry" over and over again — but she doesn't. We just stand there hugging as the windows continue to collect drops of rain. *Tap, tap, tap.* Minutes pass before either of us comes back to life.

And then she yells.

"How could you do that, Joey?" She pulls away and hits me on the chest. It's like a switch has been flicked. "GPS coordinates? What were you *thinking*?"

"What are you talking about?" I ask. Mostly as a reflex. It really doesn't matter anymore. "I don't kno —"

She throws her phone at me.

RICHARD: You psychotic bitch
RICHARD: Your kid sent his boyfriend a location tag from
  my house
RICHARD: WHERE THE FUCK ARE YOU?

"I'm sorry." I break into tears until my face is indistinguishable from the rain-soaked windows that surround us. "I'm sorry."

"And you lied to me about it!" she weeps. "How could you keep a secret like that from me this whole time?"

I'm reminded of *her* secrets…but I can't even think about those right now.

"I wasn't thinking," I stammer. "I mean, at the time I thought it was smart. I was showing him we weren't at Rutgers. As proof that we didn't trash his car." I bite my lip and force a breath. "How was I supposed to know we'd end up burning the house down? That wasn't a part of the plan!"

"We're fucked," Mom says. "We need to go back to Jersey and deal with this."

"What? Why?" I ask. "Nobody knows we're here."

"There are warrants out for our *arrest*, Joey." She pulls her hair back so hard I'm surprised it's not coming out in clumps. "Do you know what that means? They're looking for us. Marco and I have a history. It's only a matter of time before they question him."

"Maybe we can tell him the truth," I say. "Maybe he'll cover for us."

"Then he becomes an accomplice! We're not dragging him into this."

"We're not turning ourselves in." I can't believe she's even suggesting something so extreme. After everything we've been through. "That would be insane."

"Our faces are out there," Mom says. "You sent Luke *proof.* It's over. Maybe if we just tell the truth, we can make it out of this with a punishment that won't completely destroy our lives." She wipes her eyes. "No one got hurt. That has to count for something."

"Mom." I grab her by the shoulders. "We're not the guilty ones here. Luke cheated on me. Richard lied to you about getting divorced—for *two years*. How is it fair that we're the ones who should get arrested? We're victims."

This logic isn't quite as comforting now that I know Mom is also a cheater—or at least has been, in the past. But it's still enough for me to feel like turning ourselves in is not an option. We still have time to get back on the road. We haven't spent any of the cash we came with—that can keep us afloat for a while until we figure out where we're going.

"We have to go home," Mom cries. "We have no choice."

"We can get back in Nonna's car!" I say. "And just keep driving."

"Let's be real. If we leave here, where are we going? We have four hundred dollars. We don't have credit cards or passports. We don't have another Marco living out in the wilderness somewhere who can take us in. We've run out of options. We'll be living out of Nonna's car."

Maybe that's true. But giving up? Driving down the highway, directly toward our own demise? It feels wrong on every level. I'm not ready to leave the lake. I'm not ready to stop believing this could all be nothing more than a bad dream. I'm not ready to let Luke and Richard—and every other man who's ever treated us like we're worthless—win.

I pace back and forth for a few seconds, as if the movement will somehow inspire a solution. The rain intensifies.

I look out the window and see Will's house across the way—it's about the size of a small jewelry box from this distance. I wonder what the three of them are doing right now. Probably sleeping, unaware it's the end of the world. It kills me to think that up until just a few minutes ago, I was like them: unconscious, totally oblivious to the cancer lurking in my phone.

Actually? Maybe *that* should be our next move.

Sleep.

Denial.

Avoidance.

The end of the world is only happening digitally—on our phones, on Twitter, on local New Jersey news channels. Here in the physical realm, it's just raining. I lean against the chunky wooden dresser in the corner and roll this idea around in my head.

The worst case scenario is that they track us down today and we get arrested. The best case scenario is... I don't even know. I'm not delusional enough to believe that any of my starting-a-brand-new-life fantasies could actually come true now. But maybe we can at least steal another day, week, month of the lakeside illusion that everything is going to be okay. If we go back to Jersey right now, that illusion officially dies. Everything will stop being okay *immediately*.

"So then what if we just stay here?" I finally ask Mom. "Let them find us."

She looks up from the floor and rubs her GIA necklace between her fingers for a moment. This means she's absorbing the idea. Good.

"Our phones," she finally says.

We exchange intense stares for a few seconds before coming to a nonverbal understanding. We know what we need to do next.

It's anybody's guess how much digital evidence we've already emitted with our phone activity thus far. Was my call to Nonna traceable to a nearby cell tower? Can they just track our GPS coordinates even if we don't have GPS turned on? Maybe they can only do any of this shit if the phone actually exists. If it's destroyed, how can anyone trace it? Mom had the right idea the day we got here. Our phones are nothing but liabilities — not to mention constant reminders of how fucked we are. Our eyes stay locked until we finally just mutter "the lake" in unison.

She springs into action — running into the living room, through the back sliding door, out onto the porch. She races barefoot down the steps without even looking back to see if I'm keeping up. Which I'm not. My feet are moving carefully — too intimidated by the slickness of the porch, the steps, the ground to really launch into a sprint.

She zooms down the hill toward the dock. I'm doing my best to catch up, but it's kinda hard to run with water continuously assaulting my senses from all directions. It's like I'm in the center of an endless waterfall that follows me around like a spotlight.

Mom seems to be unfazed. She glides over the swampy ground like some kind of Olympic relay star — except with a black spaghetti-strap tank top instead of a uniform and a soaking-wet cell phone clutched in her hand instead of a baton. And also with a flailing posture than I'm guessing any real Olympian would have addressed several training sessions ago.

I finally get into a groove by running on the balls of my feet, using the slipperiness of the grass to launch into each new step.

My anticipation builds as I look ahead. I think about the way we're going to hurl our phones out into the vastness of the water — with all our might — never to deal with any of that bullshit again. A few days ago, the thought of losing my phone would have been on par with the thought of losing some kind of essential organ. Now I can't think of anything more freeing.

My speed increases just enough to make it out onto the dock at just the same time as Mom. The wooden surface is slimy against my feet but a very welcome change of texture. It almost feels like solid ground.

"We should have worn shoes for this!" I yell through the panoramic sound of rain beating against lake.

"You think?" Mom sarcastically yells back.

We both start laughing at the absurdity of this entire situation. There's no turning back now. Even if we don't throw our phones in the lake, they've probably suffered enough water damage from the run alone to stop functioning properly. But I'm not even close to having a change of heart. The more we stand out here like drenched lunatics, the more I realize just how much hatred I have for this stupid little device in my hand. I know the real root of this entire problem is the pain Luke and Richard caused us—but it's our phones that set everything into motion. Our entire breakup saga took place over text message. Mom found out about Richard's house being on the market through her god-damn Zillow app. The angry text messages, the retweets, the news reports—none of this would have existed without a network connection.

Good fucking riddance.

I look at Mom and realize that at some point our laughing fit has evolved into a crying one. Our tears are impossible to differ-entiate from the rain, but the look on her face and the feeling of mine give it away. We wipe our eyes simultaneously—more as a reflex than anything—and swap knowing nods.

Good fucking riddance.

The dock unfurls like an airplane runway ahead of us. We do a final death sprint toward the water and, upon reaching the dock's edge, wind our arms up. One, two, three—*throw*. Our phones are airborne. We've hurled them with enough force that there's actually a decent shape to the way they arch up before nosediving down and sinking into the water like a pair of bombs. Between this and my batting skills from the other night, we should probably just join a softball league.

"Holy shit," I say breathlessly through a zillion raindrops.

The magnitude of what we've just done hits me all at once.

We're...free. We're also lost, disconnected, unreachable, and fucked—totally out of touch with reality from here on out. But then again, isn't *this* reality? Mom and I standing out here in the rain—no one around to witness us but each other—soaking, sobbing, surrendering. Giving in to the unknown. No more tweets or articles to keep us informed on the status of our impending demise. No more *bzzz*-es from Luke or Richard. No more *anything* — other than what's directly in front of us. All we have is each other.

"Yeah." Mom looks at me with equal parts relief and terror. "Holy shit."

twenty-three

My sweatpants are muddy and my face is all cry-snotty when we get back to the house. Even after all that rain, I'm still not clean.

It doesn't help that Marco is here, drinking a Dunkin' Donuts coffee and reading a newspaper at the kitchen table as if it's just another morning.

"You two all right?" he asks. Hearing his voice makes last night's fight come rushing back to me all at once. "It's really coming down hard out there."

"We're fine," Mom lies.

"Just a little wet." I motion toward the bathroom door. "I'm gonna go take a shower."

"And get more wet?" Marco jokes.

I force the fakest closed-lipped smile in the history of fake closed-lipped smiles and excuse myself to the bathroom. I wanna be scalded.

My hand cranks the faucet all the way to the hot side. I wait until the air outside the curtain is clouded with steam before stepping in. The fiberglass surface of the tub transports me back to the scene at Richard's house on Monday night. Why did his stupid-ass bathtub have to *melt* the second it was exposed to a little bit of fire? Why couldn't he have just had a combination shower-tub like everyone else in the world? If there had been a showerhead to turn on, Mom and I could have easily drowned the flames out with cold water like we did at Leo's. Richard would have come home to find the ashes of a few dress shirts and the charred under-wire of Big Tits McGhee's bra — nothing a trip to the mall couldn't fix. But no. He just *had* to have a five-piece master bathroom — and now Mom and I have warrants out for our arrest because of it.

By the time I step back out onto the damp bath rug, I instinctively reach for a towel so I can dry my hands and check my ph — oh. Right. This is probably gonna happen a lot today.

I try not to think about all the texts and calls — many of which probably contain clues of our fate — that are just floating around in the ether right now without a destination. Where do those even go? What happens after a phone drowns and a new one isn't activated in its place?

I miss Nonna. I wanted to call her from Marco's landline phone to at least let her know we're alive, but Mom shot the idea down during our death march back up to the house. The cops could have bugged her phone by now. They do stuff like that, right? Still. I want to assure her we're okay. Even if it's a lie. She's already been through so much just raising Mom and then me for the past thirty-four years. The last thing she needs is to be seeing our picture on the news and fielding questions from the cops about why she lent her car to two outlaws. She deserves a quiet, peaceful life filled with espresso and sfogliatelle! Not this trainwreck.

I throw on some jeans and a wrinkled graphic tee from my bag and step out into the living room. The weather took a complete turn — the big window now displays an idyllic sunny day on the water. If the porch and leaves and grass didn't all have a thick sheen of moisture on them, you might not even know it rained.

Marco is still at the table.

"Where's Mom?" I ask him.

"Shower." He looks up and gestures toward the master bedroom. "What the heck were you two doing out there?"

"You know." I scratch the almost-bald back of my head. "Admiring nature." I chuckle awkwardly and lean against the kitchen sink. "We wanted to know what fresh lake rain feels like."

"Right." He furrows his bushy eyebrows at me. "Your mother said it was because you were looking for a pair of sandals she left down by the dock."

If you already had the answer, why'd you ask? I want to say but of course don't.

"Oh, yeah." I nod. Mom's excuse was so much better than mine. "That, too."

Marco squints skeptically but moves on.

"Late night yesterday? I didn't hear you get in. Guess I don't have to ask whether you and the kids hit it off."

"I guess we did." My chest sinks thinking about how I ended things with Will. "Maybe I'll go back over there today."

"I'm glad they could take your mind off the breakup." Marco flashes his pure, innocent, friendly smile. I try to remind myself that he said horrible things to Mom last night and I should be mad at him, but I also feel bad. How could she cheat on *him*? Of all people. He's the last guy who deserves that. Is this why she's since been cursed with an endless supply of Richards and Leos? Did she totally ruin her man-karma? "Sounds like this trip has been a success."

I almost forgot how much of a gap there is between why Marco thinks we're here and why we're actually here. Now I feel even worse for him. I hope he doesn't get in trouble for harboring us. Between him and Nonna, I'm starting to wonder if we ultimately hit the wrong targets on our revenge streak. The only people who should be feeling like shit right now are Luke and Richard. Not Mom and me and the two people who care about us the most.

"It's amazing." Marco grins. "It still feels like yesterday you were an awkward fourth-grader who couldn't even look at the other kids at school. Let alone make friends with any of them."

"That wasn't my fault," I interrupt. "It's kind of hard to make friends when you're being terrorized by—"

"Brooks." Marco shakes his head. "I remember."

"It only got a million times worse in middle school," I share. "In case you were wondering."

"Damn, really?" His face falls. "I wanted to kill that kid and his stupid little cronies. I went to school with guys just like that. Punks." He forces a quiet laugh. "Lucky your mom was there to put him in his place, right?"

"Lucky?" I recall that Marco and Mom used to fight about how she needed to be more mature when dealing with my bullying situation. *Two wrongs don't make a right*, he used to say. (Clearly the wisdom didn't stick.) "You hated when she yelled at my bullies."

"She could have been a little more…composed. Sometimes your mother doesn't think before she—" he stops himself as if he isn't sure where the sentence is going. "In retrospect, I'm glad she stood up for you. Someone had to put that little jerk in his place."

"That she did." I laugh as I remember this one time she made a whole scene in the parking lot by telling Brooks that his sideburns looked like "a pair of fucking merkins." I was in sixth grade and learned something new that day: a merkin is a pubic wig. It's a shame Marco wasn't around for that one. It was some of her best work.

"I'm rooting for you, Joey." His tone veers into earnestness. He randomly taps the counter. "Always have been."

Something about this statement nearly triggers a breakdown. It floods me with a longing for the adolescence I might have had if he and Mom had never broken up. We would have had such a normal life. We would have moved to a new house in a new town where I might have been able to make friends. I would have ended up with a boyfriend ten times better than Luke. I would have had this father figure *rooting* for me the entire time.

"I heard you guys fighting last night," I mumble. "I was up in the loft the whole time."

Marco's typically relaxed face tenses up and he rubs his forehead, presumably trying to remember all the details, insults, and bombshells flung between them in battle. The air between us is uncomfortably stale. All I can hear is the muffled sound of water rushing through the shower pipes to the master bathroom.

"Why didn't you say anything?" he asks. "How did we not hear you?"

"You guys were kinda loud."

"I'm sorry—"

"Did she really cheat on you?" I ask. "She never told me."

"Joey—"

"You said she's a bad mother. Do you really believe that?"

"That's enough." He stands up. We exchange depressing looks for a few beats of silence until he finally breaks. "Of course I don't. You know how she gets. She likes to pick fights when she drinks."

"You didn't answer my first question. Did she cheat?" I need to hear him say it. Even if they made it painfully clear last night, there's a sick part of me that wants all the twisted details. I need to know if it was just a drunken mistake that she confessed to immediately. Or if she was living a full-on double life just like all the men we've ever hated. "Did she? How many times? How did you find out?"

"Jesus, Joey. Don't you realize how fucked up this conversation is?"

I don't respond.

Once again all we can hear is the sound of the pipes. I make a mental note to keep paying attention to it so I know when to end this conversation. Lest we risk her getting out of the shower and hearing us.

"This is exactly what I was trying to say to her last night," Marco continues. "You shouldn't care about these things! You've always been so *invested* in her relationships. That's not healthy. How she and I broke up is more complicated and adult than you—"

"Spare me the maturity lecture, please." My cheeks flush with anger. It's not surprising to hear *him* claim that their breakup was too "adult" for me to understand, but what kills me is that Mom has apparently felt the same way all along. She kept this from me like I was just a kid—all while pretending we were equals. "I *am* an adult."

"You were ten when I left." He's already contradicting the version of events I've heard my entire life. It was supposed to be Mom who left. She no longer felt the spark. "For what it's worth, I am surprised she didn't tell you." He pauses and then scoffs. "But of course she wouldn't tell the one story that doesn't end with *poor Gia, helpless victim.*"

"I deserve to know what really happened," I assert. "I don't know why you think that just because I was ten, I shouldn't have known what was going on in my own mom's life."

"Because I know what it was like to have an actual child-hood!" he says. "And it always killed me to think you couldn't."

"Well that ship has fucking sailed, hasn't it? So you might as well just give me the courtesy of the truth."

"This is what I'm talking about," he says. "What kind of kid talks like this? You sound exactly like her."

Now I'm the one who's scoffing.

"Maybe because I'm not a kid!"

"You wanna know?" He throws his hands up. "Fine. I was gonna ask her to marry me. She didn't tell you that? I had a ring. Your nonna gave me her blessing. I left work early to go surprise Gia at the salon — and I get there and they tell me it's her day off. She told me she was working a double." Now he's tearing up. "So I go home and the first thing I see is some guy's SUV in the drive-way." He wipes off the two and a half teardrops he just let himself cry and composes himself. "And I just knew.'

My heart races as the blanks fill themselves in. Leo drove an SUV. Mom started dating him shortly after breaking up with Marco. A year later, she caught *him* cheating. I remember it all so vividly — how we trashed his condo and burned his jerseys. How the glow of the flames was no match for the aura of Mom's pain.

I had no idea that Marco was in just as much — if not more — pain of his own. How did she feel entitled to any semblance of rage after what she did to him?

"You couldn't just *know*," I attempt. "It could have been any-body's truck. It could have been —"

"I went inside," he solemnly finishes. "I saw them."

So much for that theory. Not that I believed it or anything.

"I don't get it. Why have you been telling her you miss her all this time? Why are you even letting us stay here right now?"

"I don't know, Joey. Because I love her." He lowers his head in shame. "I never stopped loving her."

"You said last night that love is *wasted* on her."

"I didn't mean that." He sighs. "I really think she's a good person. She's just been through a lot. Our relationship is complicated."

Jesus. He sounds like...*her*. All those times she's held on for too long while whatever dirtbag she'd been seeing repeatedly fucked her over. Making excuses for inexcusable behavior while we drown ourselves in tears and wine on the couch. It occurs to me that Nonna was absolutely right the other day. Men *are* weak. They're just better at not admitting it.

"Cheating is still cheating," I mutter. The shower pipes come to an abrupt stop, whooshing the room into total silence. "And you deserve better."

twenty-four

I feel like such a creepy stalker walking down to Will and Shayla's without having first given a heads-up. But I had to leave Marco's before Mom got dressed and came out of the bedroom. Can you imagine if I had to face her right now? There's a ten out of ten chance I'd start the biggest fight of our lives. And I can't be fighting with her — not now. We're all either of us has left. I'm furious with her, but I can't lose her.

I look out at the lake — calm and blue and sparkling — as I trudge my way down the damp ground to Shayla's yard. There's a pair of flat red boards meandering around in the water. Shayla and Robbie, kayaking again. Shit. I hope Will is still at the house. I hope he didn't give up on me and go back home to the city or something. Even though I couldn't blame him if he did.

"Joey!" Mom yells. I turn around and see her arms waving at me from Marco's back porch. "Wait!"

Dammit. I told him not to say anything.

"What?" I motion toward the house. "I'm just going to hang out next door."

Mom runs down to me — re-muddying her freshly showered bare feet — as I try not to scream and/or cry and/or both.

"I'm sorry." She's now standing directly in front of me, clutching my forearms. I'm slightly lower on the hill than she is, so we're the same height. For the first time since probably fifth grade. "Listen. I never lied to you, okay? It was complicated and—"

"You most definitely lied to me," I correct her. "And there's nothing complicated about *not cheating on someone*. What did you say Sunday after I found out about Luke? It's not the 'Riddle of the fuckin' Sphinx'? Yeah. That." Her eyes are pleading for me to stop. So of course I keep going. "He was going to propose to you! How could you keep that from me all this time?"

"Joey, please—"

"He bought a ring, Mom. It was literally *in his pocket* when he found you and Leo at the town house." My voice shakes as I realize that I don't even need to use insults to fight with her. Simply stating the facts is bad enough. "Our lives could have gone in a totally different direction. I could be, like, ninety-five-percent less damaged right now! So thanks a lot." I'm being meaner than I have to be. But I can't help it. "I'm so lucky I had a mom like *you* steering the ship."

Her eyes remind me of Richard's house as it started to fall apart—begging, screaming for help. But she's not crying. Which feels like a wasted opportunity, really. She came barreling out here before her face was finished. This would've been the first time all week her tears could fall without the interference of makeup.

"I was sixteen when you were born," she pleads. "I was twenty-six when Marco and I broke up. What the hell did I know about... 'steering the ship'?"

"Being young isn't an excuse—"

"I did the best I could with what I had," she interrupts. "Every choice I've ever made over the past eighteen years has been for *you,* first and foremost. If that wasn't enough for you" — she lets go of my arms and throws her hands up — "then I'm sorry, Joey. I really am."

"Oh, I see." It's clear I've succeeded at making her feel like shit. But I'm still so fired up that I can't stop trying to make her feel even worse. "So messing around with Leo behind Marco's back — you did that for *me.*"

"I'm human," she says. "I had so much pain back then. I loved Marco so much it *terrified* me." She pauses. "I didn't want him to hurt me like every other man in the history of my life, but I also figured it was inevitable that he would, eventually. So I guess I thought I was beating him to the punch." Her voice quivers as she tries to find more words. "How was I supposed to know he was the *one* good man in the world?" She rubs a few tears out of her eyes. "I don't know what else to say. Hurt people *hurt people.*"

"You're gonna throw a cliché at me right now?" I say. "Really?"

"I'm just saying I made a mistake."

"Cheating is not a mistake!" I yell. "How many times have you been on the other end of it? All these assholes — they just made *mistakes*? Then why did I smash Luke's windshield? Why did we burn Richard's clothes in his bathtub? You're such a hypocrite."

"Joey?" a male voice calls out from behind me.

Mom wipes her eyes and pulls her hair behind her ears, forcing composure now that there's a distant witness to our madness. *Is that him?* she delicately mouths at me. I almost forgot that I told her about Will yesterday. If we weren't fighting I'd have so much to catch her up on.

I turn around and see him standing outside his front door in cotton pajama bottoms and a Yale T-shirt.

"Hey!" My voice sounds way croak-ier than it should. I clear my throat and give my best attempt at a friendly wave. "I'm coming down—"

And now he's galloping toward us.

"Hey there," he says directly to Mom. "I'm Will."

"G—" she stammers. "Gia."

"So you're Joey's—"

"Mom," I finish. Then I look at her. "Will and I are just gonna hang out next door. Okay?"

She exhales in defeat.

Is it weird that I want to hug her? I don't know. I'm still pissed, but I also feel bad about everything I just said. Especially because I didn't fully mean it. I know how much she's been through. And I definitely know how much she's done for me. It's one thing for her to be called a bad mom by other people. But now that *I've* called her a bad mom...I'm afraid she might actually start to believe it.

"Nice to meet you," Will offers through the tension.

"You, too." She turns around to go back up the hill without even saying bye to me. Her hair trails behind her in the wind.

twenty-five

"She seems upset," Will says as we make our way to the house. "Everything okay with you guys?"

My emotions are like a two-sided coin spinning around on a flat surface. One side feels like a weight has been lifted. Now that she's gone, I can focus on Will and block everything else out of my mind. But the other side wants to chase after her and tell her that I'm sorry. That she is a good mom. That love is *not* wasted on her.

"We're fine." Fuck it. The coin lands on Will. I'm going to run from Mom's begging, screaming eyes just like we ran from Richard's begging, screaming house. "So how was last night?"

"It was fun." He chuckles to himself. "Actually, no. It wasn't. I just read my book while Shayla and Robbie had quality 'couple time' in the other room. And I kept thinking about what happened on the boat. I'm sorry I freaked out. I didn't mean to make you feel weird."

"It's fine," I say. "I should be the one apologizing."

"I do feel a connection with you," he offers. "If we had been in...you know...a more private setting...I might have been totally into it."

He opens his big wooden door and motions me inside the house. My gaze immediately zeroes in on the wagon — still hanging on its two remaining chains like an ICU patient who somehow manages to cling to life despite their vitals being irreversibly down.

"I still can't believe I turned your wagon into a death trap," I say. "God. I'm such a worthless piece of shit."

"Dude, it was an accident." Will grips his hand around the back of his neck. "Even Shayla has gotten over it by now. Last night we came up with a new plan where neither of us will have to get in trouble." He smiles. "We're going to leave it as is and not say anything . . . and then act totally surprised when we come back up with my dad in the summer. Like it mysteriously happened when no one was here."

"Or you could tell him the truth now," I say. "Before you become so entangled in a web of lies that your every waking moment is infected with the debilitating fear of being caught." Am I projecting right now? Perhaps. "Just kidding. That would be insane."

He crinkles his brow and smiles. "Yeah, I'm not sure the situation is quite that serious."

"Of course not." I turn my attention away from the wagon and directly to Will's messy bedhead and dimply stubble. I came here for a distraction, not a reality check. "So . . . I really want to make out with you. For real this time."

"Well, then." He moves in closer. "Now that we have some privacy, I might be open to that."

I lower my face to his and start kissing him — softly at first, and then furiously. He matches my energy and digs his hands into my lower back. I gently bite his lower lip in response. Our mouths and tongues are going at it like a pair of pro wrestlers. His mouth is minty — it's very clear he just brushed his teeth — and I love it. This is exactly what I need.

We ride the wings of our sexual chemistry straight to the nearby couch, where I straddle him and feel him get excited through the thin cotton fabric of his pajama bottoms. There is a zero-percent chance we're not hooking up today.

"Wait, Joey." He jerks his head away. "Stop."

This shit again. Seriously?

"What?" I ask.

He points up and across the room. I can feel his heart thumping through his shirt. Mine starts doing the same as I realize we've now placed ourselves closer to the wagon. It looks massive from this angle — all thick wooden planks and spokes. The spot where the two remaining chains attach to the ceiling seems ready to explode — one of them is half-detached already.

"Let's go to the bedroom," Will squeaks.

I peel myself off of him — carefully, so as not to inadvertently stumble into the area directly below the dangling beast. "Yes, please."

We evacuate the danger zone and make our way through the wagon-themed hallway into the bear-themed bedroom. (This fucking place.) I notice Will's book on the nightstand and have the distinct feeling that decades have passed since the last time we were locked in here together.

"That was a close call." He locks the door behind him and I jump onto the king-size bed in the middle of the room. The décor might be all woodsy and bear-filled, but this is the most comfortable bed I've ever had the privilege of laying on. It makes the twin-size bed up in Marco's loft feel like a giant slab of uncooked lasagna.

"This is what you've been sleeping on all week?" I ask. "No wonder you always look so well-rested and pretty."

"Pretty? Take it back." He walks from window to window and adjusts the blinds until they emit nothing more than a few thin lines of diagonal light. "How's this?"

"Dark," I say. "Perfect."

"Isn't life crazy?" Will plops down onto the bed with me. "Shayla just dragged you in here the other day — totally out of the blue — and I haven't been able to think about anyone or anything else since. It's almost like..."

Don't say fate. That would be so corny and Nice Guy–ish.

"...fate."

I force what I hope is a sweet, non-disgusted smile.

"Or we're just two horny gay guys who happen to be stuck in the woods together surrounded by straight people," I blurt and immediately regret.

"How romantic." He forces a small laugh but it's not like his other ones. "Who *hurt* you?"

"I'll write you up a list," I blurt, and regret my words once again. "Oh, God." I flinch and cover my face with my hands. "This is coming out weird and sarcastic. I'm sorry."

"It's cool." He leans back against a pillow. "I was just trying to say that I like you, Joey. I think I would still like you even if we weren't stuck in the woods together surrounded by straight people."

"Thanks." I need to get this back on track, so I slide across the bed and position myself directly on top of him.

"I like you, too. Genuinely." I kiss his mouth. "I mean it."

He kisses me back.

Now we're getting somewhere.

It doesn't take long before Will and I trade positions and *he's* the one taking the lead. He must have finally realized that I like it better that way. I close my eyes and center my mind on the sensation of his touch. Our clothes disappear within seconds.

Ever since I saw that piece of flaming wood expose itself through Richard's melting bathtub, I've had this omnipresent sense of dread lurking in my body. When I saw the selfie of Mom and me on the news earlier, it became malignant—spreading through my every pore, hair follicle, and nerve ending. But Will's hands on my bare skin are like magic erasers.

I kiss him harder. Something comes over me. I decide to get back on top. Fuck it. There's a first time for everything.

Will lets out a long, heavy sigh as he adjusts to my weight on top of him. His hands stretch out behind his head. I'm not sure why, but I grab his wrists and pin him down. Who even am I right now? Eventually he moans in pleasure—I hope it's pleasure—so I take it further and further until there's nowhere left to take it. I'm going hard, fast, feral.

Soon he protests and tells me he'd feel more comfortable if we traded places. I oblige and try to relax into his touch, which is quite literally the opposite of mine. Soft, slow, gentle. It's nice at first, but something about his tenderness makes me feel hyper-aware of the fact that we have nothing in common. He's an emotionally healthy rich kid from Manhattan; I'm a severely damaged felon from New Jersey. No amount of fucking can make me deserve a guy like him.

twenty-six

"Wow! Damn." Will wipes a blur of sweat off his forehead and rests his back against the thick mahogany headboard behind us. He's beaming. "That was incredible."

Was it? I already don't remember. I'm sure things went smoothly enough once we traded roles, but my mind was on several different planets. The magic eraser effect of his hands on my skin could only last so long. "It was, yeah."

Apparently I'm not convincing.

He scrunches his nose. "You all right?"

I reply with a forced smile and hope he doesn't look in my eyes. I don't trust them not to give me away.

He wraps an arm around me. "You don't think we moved too fast, do you?" he asks. His armpit is warm against my neck. "I've never actually done this kind of thing."

"Are you trying to tell me I just took your virginity?" I deadpan.

"God, no. I'm just saying this is the first time I've ever done... that... with someone I'm not in lov—uh, in a serious relationship with."

"Oh." I wince at the way he cuts himself off when saying *love*.

Almost like he's ashamed of how casual this hookup was. I pull the covers up all the way to my chest. "Right. Me, too."

It's scary how easily this lie rolls off my tongue. Sex is something I've pretty much *only* ever done with people I'm not in love with. The road to Luke was paved with nothing but dead-end hookups — starting with that old-ass finance bro with the scented candle and Under Armour gym shorts.

My mind flashes back to what Mom said to me the next day at the beach. *You deserve a guy who will love you.* Ha. It's something, isn't it? Will is exactly the type of guy she was talking about. But instead of letting him fall in love with me, I've rushed him into what is apparently his first-ever meaningless sexual encounter.

"What's wrong?" he asks.

"Nothing."

"Just so you know." He squeezes my shoulder. "I like you a lot."

"Really?" I ask. "So you'd actually want to know me in real life?"

"Of course — I told you that already." He squirms a little. "And isn't *this* real life? Right now?"

The earnestness of his response brings me back to that same awareness I had when I was on top of him before. It must be so nice inside his head. Money? Not an issue. Sexual history? Healthy and normal. Parents? Two of them. Criminal record? As if! His real life is perfectly charmed. My presence in it would be nothing more than a nasty stain.

"Maybe it is for you." My voice cracks. Shit. My tear ducts are gearing up. I can feel a wave forming behind my eyelids. "But not for me."

"Come on." Will's face falls. "Tell me what's going on."

"Nothing!" Aside from the fact that I'm having a spontaneous meltdown. "I'm sorry."

"Is there something I can do?" He rubs my back as I try (and fail) to construct a dam behind my eyes. "You're kinda freaking me out here."

I just realized something. I've never cried in front of a guy before. The whole ten months I was with Luke? Nary a tear. I screamed at him on several occasions, sure. But crying? That would have been too vulnerable. I've always held back *that* level of emotional expression for where it's safe — on the couch with Mom.

"Fuck." I squeeze my eyes shut and dig my knuckles into them until they're sore. "I'm so sorry."

"You wanna talk about it?" he asks.

"I don't even know what *it* is." Obviously it could be any number of the fucked-up things that have been swirling around my head this whole time — but how could I mention any of them to Will? I've already said too much just by crying. "I don't know what's wrong with me."

"Nothing is."

He takes a breath, like he's about to continue, but stops — probably realizing he doesn't know enough about me to back up the statement he just made. So instead he continues to massage my shoulder blades in silence. His hand gently makes its way down my spine, then all the way up to the back of my head. I relax my neck into the feeling of his fingertips bristling against the tight cut Mom gave me yesterday.

It's such a simple gesture, but I can feel it calming me. Luke would have never done this, just sit here and comfort me. Which strikes me as funny. I always thought I loved Luke *because* of the comfort he gave me. But really I just self-generated that comfort based on the *idea* of him. You know? The fact that he was my boyfriend gave me a sense of approval I'd craved so desperately for so long, just to prove I could be worth it. But it was a lie. *Boyfriend* was just a word to Luke. A label on an empty box.

Will's hand on my back is something else entirely.

It feels like acceptance. I don't have to self-generate anything. It's a level of intimacy so enlightening that it actually starts to pull me out of the emotional black hole I've slipped into.

Maybe I wouldn't be a stain in his real life. He already said he likes me. Maybe he could grow to love me. Maybe if Mom and I somehow make it out of this arrest warrant situation with our lives intact, Will and I can be a thing. For real. The label *and* the box.

"Sorry." I wipe my eyes one last time and blink before forcing a self-deprecating laugh to clear the air. "You must think I'm such a nutcase."

"We all have our moments." Will exhales in relief and smiles. "Hey! I have a brilliant idea to switch up the mood. How about you finally share some of your comedy with me?"

I shake my head. "You won't give up on that, will you?"

"Nope." He straightens his posture and bends his mouth into a goofy grin. "Come on!"

"I'm not asking *you* to give me an American History lecture," I say. "It's not fair."

"I'll totally give you an American History lecture." He reaches for his big book on the nightstand. "What do you wanna learn about?"

"On second thought, I'm good." I playfully hit his arm. "But you're crazy if you think I'm about to stand up in front of you and tell jokes."

"Oh, come on. Isn't that what *stand-up* comedy is all about?"

"Well, yeah." I have to admit he has a point. "But—"

"Fine." He rolls his eyes. "You may remain seated as you tell me a joke."

You know what? Fine. I can trust him. I've already let myself strip and cry in front of him. What's the big deal if I add bombing to the list? Let's just get this over with.

I scan the room and quickly decide to riff on all the bear-themed accents in here.

"Have you ever wondered how *bears* have managed to become, like, the official mascots of rustic décor?" I ask him in my best imitating-all-my-comedy-heroes-at-once voice. "Everyone is so willing to ignore the fact that these are wild animals who *will* maul and/or murder you if given the chance." I grab one of the accent pillows from the corner of the bed. "Why not just embroider a picture of the ghostface killer from *Scream* on your sherpa throw pillows?"

Oh, my God. I hate me.

"Was that supposed to be funny?" Will asks.

"No—I was just—"

"I'm kidding!" Will interjects and offers me a chuckle.

I have to cringe. What the hell was I thinking, ad-libbing some dumbass bear observation on the spot? Obviously bears are included in rustic décor because they're ... creatures of the woods. And they can be cute in theory. Teddy bears! Everybody loves those. Winnie-the-fucking-Pooh is a bear.

Will looks at me—then at the pillow I'm still clutching in my hands, then back at me—and starts laughing harder.

"Oh, my God." I bury my face in my hands. It doesn't help that I'm also naked underneath these covers. "Stop. That joke was lame. It wasn't even a joke."

"I know." He wipes his eyes and steadies his voice. "I mean. I thought it was funny. But I was more so laughing because you called it a 'sherpa throw pillow' before."

"What?" I hold it back out in front of me. "That's exactly what it is."

"Right," he says. "It's just a very detailed description." He leans in closer and smirks. "Most people would probably just call it a 'pillow.'"

"Oh." I don't know how to respond to that. "Right. Listen, I swear I'm not a total fraud." My Notes app is filled with material way better than the half-baked disaster I just lobbed at him. "I have many actual jokes. Where's my—"

And then it hits me. Throwing my phone in the lake this morning meant throwing all my jokes into the lake as well. I can't even remember the last time I backed them up to the cloud. It's been at least a couple months. A couple months' worth of material. Gone.

"—phone," I finish in a somber whisper.

This is so not the reality check I needed right now.

"So..." Will starts. I can tell he's trying to steer the conversation away from another emotional breakdown. "I just realized! You never told me what college you're going to."

"Oh." Great. Another reality check. "I don't know."

"You haven't decided yet? It's almost May." His voice curves up in confusion. "What schools did you get into?"

"I mean, I was gonna go to Rutgers." I tug at the sheet on top of me. Where are my clothes? I have a very strong urge to put them back on right now. "But that was only because my ex goes there. So I guess now I'm kinda rethinking the whole college thing altogether. I didn't apply anywhere else."

His jaw drops down to the bottom of the mattress.

"You didn't apply anywhere else?" he asks. "For real?"

"It's complicated."

"It's one of the biggest life decisions you'll ever make," he says. "And you made it based on someone else?"

This doesn't bode well for my plan to follow him to New Haven and work on my act while he studies history for four years before we take off for LA, does it?

"I didn't." I squirm. "I never wanted to go anyway. It's not like there are any schools that offer a 'stand-up' major. You know what I mean?"

"Aren't there comedy classes, though? Or like, improv schools?"

"You've clearly never met my Nonna," I say. "There's no way in hell she would take out loans for me to go to an *improv* school."

"Loans?" A confused look flashes across Will's face like an error message on a computer screen. Then he remembers what a loan is. "Oh. Right. To pay for it."

"Yeah. So I might as well just not go."

He clears his throat. "I guess I just never realized that not going to college was an option for some people. My dad would *kill* me if I said I didn't —"

"Well, I don't have a dad to kill me, so." I have no idea why I blurted this out. I don't even care about any of this! I need to put my clothes on and change the subject. "Anyway. Are you excited about Yale?"

This is so awkward.

He ignores my question. "So you would just live at home until you started making money as a comedian?"

"Sure. That." I dig my hand under the sheets in search of my boxer briefs. I slide them up my legs while my mouth continues to mindlessly spit out words. "Or maybe I'll just, like, move to New Haven and get a job around there or something."

What the fuck did I just do? That was not supposed to be an out-loud statement! I force an inept laugh. It's too late to take it back, so I try to play it off. Will obviously likes me. Maybe he won't be repulsed. "Then we'd be in the same city and all," I finish.

Will looks at me and then away from me and then back at me.

"You're kidding, right?" he asks in a wary tone laced with shock and revulsion. Inside he's asking what he just got himself into by sleeping with someone as crazy and desperate as me. I'm sure of it.

"Obviously." I shoot out of the bed and pick my jeans up from the floor. "I gotta pee."

The reality of my current situation storms back into my head like a tornado as I walk through the hallway to the bathroom. Will can't save me. Everything I needed to know was answered with that one simple statement. *You're kidding, right?* Yes. Of course I was. It was insane of me to think that Will — or anyone — would be anything but disgusted by the prospect of me latching onto his life like some kind of six-foot-tall locust.

Will doesn't need me. He doesn't even want me. We had sex. He put his hand on my back after I randomly broke down in tears. Big deal. He was just being nice. That's what *nice* guys do. It doesn't mean they wanna get married tomorrow.

I slam the bathroom door behind me and turn the faucet on. My back presses itself against the door and slides down until my body is folded in half on the cold tile floor.

I remain in this broken state for just about a minute.

Then I peel myself up, rub my eyes with cold water, and prepare to go back into the bedroom and tell Will I have to leave. I'll say I have to get back to Marco's, and then I'll just take a really long walk through the woods alone. That seems like a reasonable next step. I'll be off in my own world of tree roots and dirt when the cops show up at the house. Hopefully Mom will find an equally effective hiding place by then as well.

"Thanks again for letting me hang," I say as I reenter the bear bedroom. The air is stale and sad. "I'm gonna take off."

Will's pajama bottoms are back on but he's still shirtless. He sighs, probably annoyed. I'm sure he was hoping I'd come out and be chill again, as if that whole loaded moment never happened.

"Listen, Joey..."

"Nah." I shake my head. "It's cool."

"You sure? I didn't mean to—" His voice is interrupted by a creaky, crunchy, snapping noise shrieking out from the other room. "Shit! What was that?"

Creeeak. Crunch. Snap.

"Sounds like—"

"Fuck!"

He springs out into the hallway. I chase after him. We come to a screeching halt at the edge of the living room. Will looks up, trembling.

The wagon is down to its last chain. Instead of dangling ominously from above, it's now almost vertical, filling the center of the living room, digging into several pieces of nearby furniture. The one remaining chain is already half-ripped from its wooden beam on the ceiling. *Crunch.* Another wood chip flies off and hits the wall across from us. This four-hundred-pound monstrosity is absolutely going to crash down within seconds. I knew it was inevitable—but I really didn't think I'd be around to see it.

Will puts his arm in front of my chest and we step backward in slow motion.

And then it finally happens.

A loud chorus of cracks and bangs rattles my eardrums as the wagon's parts all crush into separate targets. A ceramic lamp shatters, an ottoman folds into itself, a coffee table buckles under the pressure of the wagon's angular oak ass. Scraps of wood burst into the air like confetti.

And then — all at once — it's quiet again. A thick cloud of dust sparkles in the rays of sunlight that slice through the big lake window. The chocolate-brown sofa is pierced in twenty different places from stray wheel spokes.

Will is frozen in shock, but I'm barely even fazed.

Because of course it would end this way.

Like it always does with me.

In destruction.

twenty-seven

I'm such a shit person. Will was so patient and understanding when I spontaneously broke down in front of him before — but what did I do after we watched his parents' living room fall apart? Said *I gotta go* and barreled outside to the dock for a self-pity session.

But whatever. It's not like he bothered to chase after me.

The dock is dry and warm against the back of my shirt. It's strange to think this is the same surface Mom and I sprinted across during the monsoon this morning. I close my eyes as hard as I can and position my face directly into the sun. The heat permeates every pore, but it still doesn't feel hot enough. I just want something to fucking burn me already.

Why does this hurt so much? I barely even knew the guy.

Maybe it's not him I'm mourning as much as it is the distraction he gave me each time we were together. That magic eraser effect. Now I'm left to reckon with the fact that Mom and I have officially been busted and are just waiting around here for the cops to show. Because that's the inevitable outcome of this whole thing, isn't it? We were never going to *not* be found out. We just chose to delude ourselves with hope and lies.

Our revenge on Luke and Richard wasn't revenge at all—it was suicide. At the end of the day, all they did was break our hearts. And in the eyes of the law, a heart isn't a real thing. Not in the way that a house is a real thing. Break a heart, you're just another asshole. Burn down a house, you're a felon. These are basic facts. Maybe they're not *fair* facts—but they are facts nonetheless.

My sun-drenched depression spiral is interrupted by the faint sound of footsteps on the far end of the dock.

I sit up and peel my eyes open, blocking out as much light as possible with my hand. Shayla saunters her way into my blurry field of vision, coming more into focus with each step forward. She's wearing that same navy bikini from yesterday.

"Hey!" She sounds normal—clearly unaware of the crime scene in her living room. Otherwise I'm sure she'd be greeting me with a death threat right now. "What's up?"

She plunks herself down next to me and leans back with her arms stretched out behind her. Her long, tan torso reminds me of a Kylie Jenner Instagram ad for Flat Tummy Tea.

"Not much." I dip my feet in the translucent lake water. It's freezing, but I'm numb anyway, so: perfect. "Just sitting."

"Are you okay?"

"I'm fine," I snap. "Shouldn't you be making out with your big masculine boyfriend on a canoe or something right now?"

"Easy there, Sparky." She makes a face. "Robbie went for a run. I saw you out here and thought I'd say hi before going back to the house. Maybe see if you and my brother have impregnated each other yet. Guessing the answer to that one is a *no...*"

"Why'd you throw me into the room with him that night, anyway?" I ask. "He and I clearly have nothing in common. Like, seriously? You thought he'd like me?"

"He does like you!"

"How? Why?"

"Will is like the Japanese lady from that Netflix show about decluttering," she jokes. "He loves mess."

All right. That was actually kind of funny. Too bad I'm incapable of laughter — and/or any expression of any human emotion whatsoever — right now.

"It's that obvious, huh? That I'm a mess."

"I'm kidding!" she says. "Damn. What the hell happened between you two? I thought you totally hit it off. Will was gushing about you all night last night. Seriously. He wouldn't shut up."

Fuck. That stings.

"He was? I don't — whatever." I kick my foot out and make a bitchy little splash. "It's not like we were ever going to see each other again, anyway."

"He didn't ask you about this weekend?" she says. "When we're back in the city and you're back in Jersey?"

I heave a sigh in response.

She shrugs. "Well, he said he was gonna invite you to some comedy club in the West Village. He was Googling all night looking for the perfect spot. He got so excited when he finally found one. Apparently it's hard to find an open mic night on a Saturday."

This information hits me like a sucker punch to the rib cage. As if I didn't regret the way I ended things with Will enough, now I have to hear evidence that he actually did want us to be in each other's lives. Before I went all psycho and invited myself to move in with him.

"That's nice" is all I can say.

For a few moments we don't say anything allowing the sound of water crashing against the dock to take the place of words.

Shayla finally breaks the silence. "That's not even why I asked if you're okay. I was talking about your mom."

My legs tense up and my feet freeze in the water. Did I miss something?

"Robbie and I saw you throw your phones in the lake," she says. "In the middle of the torrential downpour this morning. What the hell was that about?"

"Oh." I try to come up with a list of reasons why two normal people might feel compelled to hurl their phones into a large body of water during a rainstorm, but can't think of a single excuse that would make sense. "We needed to unplug."

She seems to find this hilarious. "You ever hear of airplane mode?"

"I...don't want to talk about it."

"Sorry if I'm prying." Shayla sits up and teases her hair. "Honestly? I'm jealous."

"Of what?"

"You and your mom."

This has to be a joke—a rich girl trying to act as though Mom and I have anything she could possibly be envious of. "Has it not been made painfully clear to you by now that we are poor?"

"Why does everything always have to be about money with you?" she asks.

Gee. I don't know. Why don't you and your perfect brother try *not having any* for once in your lives and then ask me again?

"I'm just saying," Shayla continues before I can respond. "I wish I had a fun young mom. Or even a mom that was, like, ten percent more human." She sighs. "I was basically raised by a rotating selection of nannies. I could never imagine going on a one-on-one trip with my mom. We'd run out of things to talk about within the first half hour of the car ride up."

I crinkle my eyebrows at her. "Why are you telling me this?"

"Who knows." Her voice drifts and then comes back. "I'm just saying you're lucky is all."

Lucky seems like a bit of a stretch. Sure, Mom and I have always had a close relationship. But that's literally *all* we've ever had. It's a lot—but it's not enough. The events of this week have made that abundantly clear.

"At least you have a dad," I offer.

"He's just as bad," Shayla adds. "I mean. I don't hate my parents. They obviously give me whatever I want"—she gestures toward the prematurely dewinterized boat rocking on the other side of the dock behind us—"but I'm just saying. Gia seems so *cool*."

In the immortal words of Lady Gaga: I have to laugh. I've been called many things before, but cool is not one of them. Not that Shayla just called me cool, but saying something about Mom is basically the same as saying it about me. Has being criminals given us some kind of hip new aura we weren't aware of?

"Even watching you two go psycho down here in the rain earlier," Shayla continues. "I was like, 'Damn. That looks *fun*. I wanna be friends with her.'" She pauses. "Oh, my God. Can I be friends with her? Can you make that happen?"

"We're fighting right now."

"Why?" she asks.

"It's stupid." I barely even know Shayla, but her question feels like an opportunity to get so many things off my chest. Maybe if I say it all out loud, I'll feel better by the time I go back up to the house and am in Mom's actual presence again. "I found out she's been keeping this huge secret from me."

"Yeah?"

"She cheated on"—I stop myself from saying *Marco* out loud, given their lake-house-neighbor status and all—"an ex that she used to be with when I was younger."

"And..." Shayla's voice takes the shape of a question mark. "I don't get it."

"We've always told each other everything," I explain. "And she kept that from me. Also, we're the ones who always get cheated *on* in our relationships. It's kind of our thing." I feel compelled to go further, but I rein myself in. "So now I feel like I can't trust her."

Shayla absorbs my speech for a moment. "I don't mean to play devil's advocate, but is it even any of your business who she does or doesn't cheat on? It was her relationship. It's not like she did anything to you personally."

What the fuck do you know? I ask her in my head. *You and your robot mom don't even talk to each other.*

"She might as well have," I say. "Her relationships are also my relationships. Wait. That came out weird." I pause and try to figure out how to articulate the complexity of my feelings. "I've just always been so invested in my mom's emotional state." This is still coming out weird. And also kinda Norman Bates–y? I need to wrap this up. "I don't know what I'm trying to say." Maybe Shayla's right. I'm not saying I'm over the fact that Mom lied to me, but...I guess I'm not so *under* it that I'm willing to let it totally ruin what we have. Maybe it only has to alter it slightly. "I guess you might have a point."

She smiles and pats my arm. "I always do."

And I know Mom wasn't purposely trying to destroy our lives when she cheated on Marco. She just assumed he would do the same to her anyway, because believing otherwise would mean believing that she was actually worthy of a guy like him. Kind of like me believing I could be worthy of a guy like Will. Given our histories, it's a difficult concept to grasp.

"Thanks for this little chat." I pull my feet out of the water and stand up. "I'm gonna go back up to Marco's. I should probably check on her."

Shayla follows my lead down the dock until we get to the point where her house is on the left and Marco's is up the hill.

"I still think you should give Will a chance," she says. "At least say you'll think about going with him to that comedy club this weekend."

As if it's my choice whether he decides to give *me* a chance. As if he even has a way to reach me now that my phone is submerged in mushy sand at the bottom of the lake. As if Mom and I won't very possibly be in jail by the time Saturday rolls around.

"I'll text him." I muster the strength to give one last fake smile. "Once I get a new phone activated and whatnot."

"Good." Shayla flips her hair and reciprocates with a fake smile of her own. "If not this weekend, then at least another time."

"Def." I'm already facing the other direction. "Bye, Shayla."

I'm positive I'll never see this girl again.

twenty-eight

I press my nose against the glass of Marco's porch door and squint into the living room, but there are no signs of life. I walk around to the front of the house and discover that Nonna's car — which hasn't moved from the side of the lawn ever since we got here on Tuesday — is gone. Along with Marco's truck.

So they definitely went somewhere. But not together.

My hand shakes as I attempt to open the front door and discover it's also locked. Marco's house has been wide open all damn week — I barely even noticed he *had* locks — and now all of a sudden the place is Fort Knox. What the fuck?

Panic engulfs me as I reach into my pocket and remember — for the ten thousandth time today — that I don't have a phone. Fear rockets into my chest as I realize just how alone I am. I have a sour gut feeling that Mom didn't leave willingly. She knows we can't text each other. If she was gonna take off for even a few minutes, she would have found me at Will's house or down at the dock and given me a heads-up.

I drop down onto the splintery wood of the front porch and bury my face in my hands. I have nothing. All I can do is sit here. Waiting. Dreading. Assuming the worst.

The back of my throat constricts as I try to take a brea—oh. Okay. So now breathing is a whole ordeal. Every time I think I have a good inhale going, my heart skips and my chest tightens. All I can manage are these shallow, unsatisfying half-breaths. My eyes feel like bombs waiting to explode. But they won't. The muscles around them just keep contracting. It's like the dry-heaving version of crying.

I try to calm down by dreaming up possible non-nuclear explanations for their disappearance. They just went to run some errands. Separately. He's buying groceries for dinner tonight and she's . . . getting an impromptu pedicure or something.

You know what? I can't do this anymore.

My ability to appease myself by imagining wildly improbable best-case scenarios is officially on its deathbed. I have to accept that this entire situation is and has always been a brakeless freight train headed directly toward a five-thousand-foot cliff.

It was a stupid idea to come here. People can't just start brand new lives as if their old ones never existed. It was a stupid idea to hook up with Will. Arrest warrants don't just go away after you fuck someone new. It was a stupid idea to throw our phones in the lake. It might have bought us a little more time off the grid, but we're not safe. We never have been.

Every minute on this porch-shaped electric chair feels like an hour. I don't even know what I'm waiting for. I almost just want the cops to show up—with Mom already in the backseat—and haul us off to jail. At least then I'd know how this is all going to turn out. At least then we'd be together.

An impossible amount of these excruciating minute-hours go by before the silence is finally interrupted by the sound of a car engine in the distance.

Please be Mom.

I pull myself up and look out at the wooded car path.

Please be Mom. Please be Mom. Please be Mom.

It's Marco.

He pulls his black Chevy pickup into the gravelly driveway as I keep looking out ahead, hoping she's right behind him. I'm praying for a miracle I don't deserve.

"I don't know where she is," Marco says as he steps out of the truck. There's a plague of worry all over his face. "I lost her."

"What happened?"

"She got in the car and sped off. She was driving so erratically. I don't know. I followed her until I got stuck at a stoplight." He throws his hands up in resignation. "She snapped."

"You just let her drive off?" I scream. "You should've run the light!"

"I've been driving around town looking for her for the past two hours." He fumbles for his key and walks around me toward the door. "For all I know she jumped on the highway. She could be halfway to Bayonne right now."

This suggestion knocks the wind out of me. Why does he think she would head home without me?

"She left you a note," he answers before I even ask.

"She—" is the only syllable I can squeeze out of my rapidly constricting throat before it closes in entirely. I can't even take any of those crappy shallow breaths anymore. My knees buckle, which soon gives way to full-body paralysis.

"Whoa. Joey." Marco pushes the door open and slides his arm under mine in an effort to prevent me from collapsing. "Here."

He helps me wobble inside, sits me down at the kitchen counter, and forces me to drink a glass of water. The feeling of hydration illuminates every organ it touches on its way down to my stomach. It brings me about ten percent back to life—not

223

quite enough to regain feeling in my extremities, but more than I expected from a few ounces of Brita.

"Where's the note?" I ask.

He grabs a folded piece of paper from the counter and slides it to me.

Joey,

I'm so sorry for not saying good-bye, but I knew you'd try to stop me.

You were right. I should have steered the ship. You deserve so much more than what I've given you. If I could go back in time and fix the past, I would. But I can't. I can only try to give you a better future. So I have to do this. I'll tell Nonna to come get you as soon as it's safe.

I love you so much!!!

Mom

What was she even trying to do with that last line? There is nothing "I love you so much!!!" about any of this. I could maybe understand "I love you so much . . ." or even "I love you so much." But three exclamation points? The enthusiasm is entirely uncalled for.

"I keep thinking about all the horrible things I said to her last night," Marco says. "I didn't mean any of it. Obviously she's been a great mother to you. One of a kind." He pauses. "You don't think she's gonna hurt herself, do you?"

"She would never," I say with certainty.

I can see how Marco could interpret the note that way. I mean, who writes notes in the first place? But this is very clearly an *I'm-going-to-jail-for-both-of-us-and-I-can't-text-you-so-here's-a-note* note. She's been wanting to take the fall for this from the beginning. She thinks she's doing the right thing. She thinks she's saving me.

I just don't understand how she deluded herself into believing her confession will somehow undo all the evidence that points to *my* guilt. There are warrants out for both of us. It was my phone that sent the GPS signal to Luke. The cops aren't just going to shrug it off. *Well, his mom says it was all her, so . . . case closed!*

I wish I could scream some sense into her.

But it's too late.

"Something's been off with her," Marco stammers. "I was in my office working all day, and every time I came out here she was just quiet and dead-eyed on the couch. Wouldn't even talk to me."

It's clear she hasn't told Marco anything about why we came here, and now that I think about it — now that she's not here — I wish she did. I wish we did. I wish we told him everything the second we pulled into his gravelly driveway. How did we expect him to be able to help us if we weren't even going to tell him the truth about why we were barging back into his life?

"She didn't say where she was going?" I ask.

"No," he responds. "I don't know what the hell is going on. I saw you two fighting down on the hill earlier."

Of all the mistakes I've made this week, that fight might've been the worst. If I had just stayed with her instead of running off with Will, I could have talked her out of this. Or at least gone with her. We could have decided on a path together.

"I'm not stupid," Marco says. "I've known something was up this whole time. You two just show up out of nowhere on Tuesday. You've been acting —"

"We burned a house down," I blurt. It feels like I've just ripped off a full-body Band-Aid. My skin can finally breathe again. "Monday night. It was an accident."

Marco's eyes widen with shock. This clearly wasn't the "something" he thought he knew was "up."

"Are you serious?" he asks. "What house?"

"Richard's. Her ex. Did she tell you about him?" I don't even give him time to answer. "There are warrants out for both of us in Jersey." Everything in me shudders. This is the first time I've acknowledged the truth to anyone other than Mom. It suddenly feels realer than it has all week. Even realer than when I saw our picture on the news this morning. "That's what this note is about. She's going to turn herself in." I slide it back toward him and break open all over his wooden butcher block countertop. "I'm so scared. I don't know how we let it get this far."

Marco looks at me like I just told him . . . well, the truth.

"Jesus Christ, Joey. So that's why you came here. To go on the lam." His face is clouded with the smog of a million sad revelations. "I'm so stupid. She never wanted to be here. She needed a place to hide. If you didn't burn" — his voice slides down into a manic drawl —"a *house* down . . . this week would have never even happened."

"That's not true." I honestly believe that Mom loves Marco. She just doesn't think she deserves him. But either way — that was so not the point of me making this confession. I did it so that he could help me figure out what to do next. "What am I gonna do?" I ask. "I have to just go home and turn myself in. Don't I?"

"You can't keep hiding from a warrant. That will only make it worse." He rubs his eyes and blinks really hard until his system stabilizes. "How bad was the damage? How did they find out it was you?"

My chest thumps as I fill him in on each tiny detail that carried us from "drunk on the couch crying over our cheating boyfriends" to "rain-drenched on the dock launching our phones into a thirty-mile-long lake." He absorbs them like a horrified therapist.

"So what do you think?" I ask. "Am I gonna be thrown in jail for the rest of my life?"

"No." Marco doesn't quite smile, but his tone is light enough that I'm vaguely comforted. He pulls his phone out. "You haven't Googled it yet?"

"I've been too afraid," I say. Like a total dumbass. "In case our search histories were pulled or something."

"I don't think you need to worry about that at this point." He taps into his phone for answers. "It looks like you could get off with anything from a few years' probation...up to...twenty-five years in prison."

"So twenty-five years in prison." I will plan only for worst-case scenarios from here on out. "I'll be forty-three when I get out."

"You didn't hurt anybody in your fire, right?"

I nod.

"So it's just property," he says. "That's probably a good thing. I'm sure it will all depend on this Richard guy. And on the judge. It will probably take weeks — or months — before you even know exactly what your sentence is gonna be."

"What happens while I wait?" I ask. Even though I'm afraid I might not want to know. "Do I have to wait in jail?"

"I don't think so," he says. "I didn't have to when I —"

"What?" I almost choke on the water I just attempted to take a sip of. "*You* were arrested? When? For what? How?"

"Your mother never told you?"

"No!"

He hesitates for a moment as if he's considering not telling me.

"I got into a fight," he finally says. "I beat the crap out of your father."

twenty-nine

Marco's revelation basically causes my jaw to unhinge from my skull and shatter all over his shiny hardwood floor.

"I was right around your age," he continues. "My buddy and I jumped him one night as he was leaving a bar. I was still bashing his head into the pavement when the cops showed up. I didn't even notice my friend was long gone by then." He acknowledges my shock with a dark chuckle. "I'm not proud. But you know. Your mom was pregnant and alone. He tried to hurt her...and *you*. I could have killed him. I'll admit it was a little out of character for me."

A little out of character? That's the understatement of the century.

And yet somehow it makes so much sense. Nonna has always talked about Marco as if he was my actual father. Maybe—in a fucked-up kind of cosmic way—he is. Maybe when he beat up the asshole who created and then tried to cancel me, he was sending a message to the universe that I deserved to be protected. Or at least, you know: born. He was taking responsibility for a mess that wasn't even his. All because his love for Mom runs *that* deep.

My heart sinks as I think about how we've been taking advantage of it all week.

"I'm so sorry we dragged you into this," I say. "But can you bring me to Bayonne tonight?"

"You sure?" he asks.

"I have to be." I fold up Mom's note and stick it in my pocket. "Don't I?"

thirty

It's *Blair Witch Project*-y as fuck out here in these high-beam-lit woods. The rocky, narrow path from Marco's driveway to the nearest street stretches on for a thousand miles. The sun was barely setting when we left. Now we're in total darkness.

I'm trying to look up tweets and news on Marco's phone, but this is that part of the woods where there's no actual service. What a cruel joke. I finally have access to a phone, and it can't even connect to the internet.

I look at the time on Marco's dashboard. Just past seven.

"When do you think we'll get to Bayonne?" I ask him.

"Usually takes at least four hours."

"When did Mom leave?"

He keeps his attention forward.

"Honestly?" he says. "If that's where she was going, she'll probably be there soon."

I was worried that would be the case.

"What happens after we get to the police station?" I ask. "Like...do I just go up to the receptionist? *My mom and I are wanted for arson. I believe she may already be here*?" I pause. "What happened when *you* got arrested?"

"It's been eighteen years." He sighs. "But I guess—uh—they take your fingerprints and all that. They'll probably throw you in a holding cell for the night."

My throat twists up like a piece of rotini at his mention of the word *cell*.

"I was in there for like a day before I saw a judge," he continues. "You just keep to yourself. Do what they tell you. It'll be over quick."

It's clear from his ultra-careful speech pattern that he's leaving out certain key details in an effort to keep me from totally unraveling. I can't tell if I'm grateful for this.

"You'll be fine," he adds. "This will barely be a blip on your record."

I wish I could believe him. I wish I were still ten years old. Then I would—no questions asked. But I'm not. So I can't.

"Thanks." I wince as I remember that his Google search earlier already gave me a sentence of twenty-five years. "Fingers crossed."

Marco turns on some music. Bruce Springsteen sings that song about the screen door slamming and Mary's dress waving. How appropriate. I've spent the past eight years covering my ears whenever this song comes on—as it often does—in public spaces throughout New Jersey. It brings up too many memories. Marco used to play it around the house every Saturday morning during chore time. Hearing it now slaps me with an image of Mom sweeping the kitchen while he loaded the dishwasher and I aggressively doused all wood and/or imitation-wood surfaces with Pledge in the living room. It's a far cry from the Playlist, that's for damn sure.

"You used to love this song," Marco says.

"No, I didn't," I lie.

"Yes, you did." He laughs. "Maybe you don't remember. You

used to call it 'Mary's Dress Waves' instead of 'Thunder Road.' You *begged* me to play it every weekend."

I can still smell the chemical lemon scent of the Pledge. As a kid I always thought Mom and I loved those mornings in equal measure. Until the day she started hating them. But maybe it wasn't that simple. Maybe she was just weak and got caught up in a series of mistakes and couldn't find her way out. Maybe we trashed Leo's condo not only because he cheated on her — but because she missed those mornings just as much as I did.

"Whoa!"

My eyes are jolted open by Marco's booming voice as he jerks the truck to the side to avoid a pair of oncoming headlights. We barely evade contact with a tree by the time he's done slamming on the brakes. The song ends right as the dust settles.

"You all right?" he asks.

I nod gravely and turn around to see if the other car stopped.

"Oh, my God." I recognize Nonna's Sicilian flag window decal immediately. "Mom."

Marco and I unbuckle our seat belts and eject ourselves from the truck so fast you'd think it was going up in flames.

"Gia!" Marco shouts as she swings the driver's-side door open. "You okay?"

"Joey, thank God." She runs over and pulls me into a tight hug. The scent of Biolage leave-in conditioner in her hair immediately steadies my heart rate. "I'm so sorry. I was scared you'd be gone when I got back."

"No, I'm sorry." Even though she's squeezing me so tight my organs are about to fold into themselves, I can finally exhale for the first time since this morning. Being without her all day was like holding my breath. "I shouldn't have blamed you for everything. That fight was so stupid."

"I was on the highway and thought, 'Why am I doing it this way? Who the fuck leaves a *note* at a time like this?'" Her voice is on fire, like she needs to get this out before she explodes. "I just kept thinking to myself, 'What if that note was the last thing he ever hears from me? What if I go to the police and they don't believe I did it all myself? What if they go out looking for you, and I'm not even there to protect you because I'm locked up? What if we end up telling them totally different versions of the story? What if you get into even *more* trouble because I did it this way?' I just..." She throws her hands up. "I don't know what either of our next moves should be. But we need to figure them out together."

She takes a step back and looks up at Marco. "And I'm so sorry. I lied to you about why we came here. Joey and I—"

"He told me," Marco interjects. "All of it."

"All of it?"

Her eyes dart between Marco and me. "This whole week was so fucked up," she finally tells him. "I've been horrible to you. Honestly? You were right last night." She chokes on her breath. "All you ever did was try to love me. And I fucked it up."

"I'll go wait in the car," I say before she keeps going.

It feels like they're about to have the type of conversation I should only hear about from her *after* the fact. Not while it's actually happening. Or maybe it's the type of conversation I shouldn't hear about at all.

I slide into Nonna's passenger seat. The ratty cloth interior has that same calming effect as the scent of Mom's leave-in conditioner.

There's no music on in here. Was she seriously driving around in total silence for the past four hours? I catch a glimpse of them through the side-view mirror to my right. It's like they're the lead couple in a play. The taillights of their respective vehicles provide the perfect amount of spotlight on their stage of dirt, rocks, and fallen branches. Mom locks like a tiny little ballerina next to Marco — she barely comes up to the chest pocket on his button-down plaid shirt.

And now they're hugging.

I hope this isn't a good-bye hug, even though I know it is.

We shouldn't *need* Marco to come back with us, but he does seem to know a lot about the criminal justice system. And he's the only one with a phone.

They both start walking toward me. Marco taps my window from outside.

"You're gonna be fine," he says. "You got that?"

"Yeah." It's clear he's not planning on coming, and I don't fight it. Whatever disaster unfolds from here on out is purely Mom's and my problem. Which is probably how it should be. "Thanks for everything."

"Anytime." He gives a dark half-smile. "Well. Not quite under these circumstances — but. Well. You get what I mean. I'll see ya."

He taps the hood of the car and runs back to his truck.

thirty-one

Mom orchestrates the world's messiest K-turn, creating a cloud of dust and gravel. We rattle out on the path toward the main road.

"Here." She tosses me Marco's phone. "He gave me this in case we need it. The passcode is zero-seven-one-one."

My face stretches into a melancholy smile. "Your birthday."

I can tell from her voice that Mom's face is doing the same.

"Where were you guys going, anyway?" she asks.

"Home," I say. "Police station, I guess. We thought you had already turned yourself in."

"I was ready to. I *am* ready to. I think."

She pauses in thought for a moment.

"All day I've been thinking about Monica," she says. "How we've always felt so connected to her, you know? Because we know what it's like to deal with the same bullshit she did. The lies, the shame, the bullying..."

"Right." I nod. "Um. How does this help us with our current predicament?"

"So that's the thing," Mom says. "I asked myself, 'What would Monica do in this situation?'"

"She wouldn't be in this situation in the first place," I say. "Burning down the White House wasn't an option. I assume they have a little more security than a garage door keypad."

"Well, yeah." Mom's voice *eeks* into a soft morbid laugh. "But still. Remember in the documentary when she talked about how those Secret Service bitches bombarded her at the mall? She went to the hotel room with them. She eventually confessed."

"To falling in love with a married man," I clarify. "Other than that, she didn't really do anything wrong."

"But we did," Mom finishes. "We let the bullshit drag us down." Her voice tapers as she stumbles upon a new realization about the woman we've spent our lives worshipping. "Monica didn't let the bullshit drag her down. But we did."

We spend the next few minutes stewing in loaded silence until Mom turns onto the main road from the rocky path. The car finally stops rattling and starts gliding. It feels like an opportunity to redirect.

"What if we just keep driving north?" I ask. "What if we go somewhere no one would ever think to find us? Somewhere far away."

"How long could we make that last, though?" Mom asks. "And where is this magical place? Where are we gonna sleep? *How* are we gonna sleep?"

We stop at a red light and I notice a Stewart's gas station on the corner. We're around actual civilization again. Surreal doesn't even begin to describe it. There's a sign that the highway is only ten miles away.

I swipe into Marco's phone to see if it's regained a signal yet.

burn it all down

Service? Yes.

Power? Not so much.

"Shit," I say. "Marco's phone is dying —"

My voice is cut off by the whirling sound of a siren behind us.

A big white sedan appears in our rearview mirror.

Its roof lights up in a twitchy blaze of red and blue.

thirty-two

"What do I do?" Mom screams over the high-pitched blare. "I can't pull over!"

"You have to." My throat feels like it's full of cement, but I need to squeak these words out. "Like, immediately."

Are we actively involved in a police chase right now? Oh my God. We are actively involved in a police chase right now.

Our futures flash before my eyes.

Handcuffs. Prison jumpsuits. Cardboard food. Lots of...concrete, I guess? Metal bars. We'll be totally separated. She'll be having an *Orange Is the New Black* moment with a zany cast of lesbians and ex-prostitutes. Meanwhile, I'll be living on the set of *Oz*—surrounded by Hulk-esque monsters with chips on their shoulders. Reliving my childhood bullying nightmares in a constant daily loop for the next twenty-five years.

"I literally can't pull over!" Mom points out my window at the very obvious lack of a shoulder on this busy main road. "Do I just stop right here in the middle of the street? Fuck! Joey! I'm so scared. It can't be happening like this. I should have turned myself in when I—"

"Here!" I say as we pass under a bridge. A wide breakdown

lane opens itself up to the right of us. Perfect for getting arrested in. "You can pull over here. If we make them chase us, they'll just punish us that much worse."

Mom puts her hazard lights on and comes to a stop after sliding past the thick white line. The blare of the siren gets louder and louder as the cop gasses it . . .

And speeds right past us.

His car vanishes into the black hole of the road ahead.

thirty-three

"You think he ran our plates?" Mom asks.

We're still pulled over with our hazards on. Stalling under a dim streetlight. Catching our breath and counting our blessings. For now.

"I'm sure we'd be in the backseat of that cop car right now if he did," I answer. "He must have been trying to get us out of the way so he could speed off to some other crime scene."

"Jesus." Mom digs her nails into the front of her scalp and blinks really hard. "That was so close."

We remain still in the aftershock for a few more moments.

"But you know?" she continues. "As scary as it was, a small part of me felt…"

"Relieved in a fucked-up kind of way?" I finish for her. "Me, too."

"Something like that."

"We need to turn ourselves in," I say. "The next time a cop chases us, it probably won't be a false alarm."

"You're right." She turns her hazards off and pulls back onto the road. "This was a gift. We can still do it on our terms."

"Maybe they'll go easier on us because we're going voluntarily," I add. "Getting caught in a high-speed car chase would have definitely made things worse."

"Listen to me," Mom says. "I don't care if it was your GPS text that got us caught or whatever." Her voice is a straight line of determination. "When we tell the story, I'm taking full responsibility. Okay? You were there, but I lit the match. We'll tell them you wanted to go straight to the cops, but I talked you out of it."

I consider objecting, since the exact opposite is true. But there's no use. In a few hours we'll be talking to police, and she'll tell the story this way whether I cooperate or not.

"Fine," I say. "But you have to be extremely clear that it was an accident. We only wanted to—"

"*I* only wanted," Mom interjects.

"*You* only wanted to burn some clothes in the tub. You've done it before with no issues, but didn't realize it was a standalone tub without a shower."

"I must have taken a million showers in that bathroom," she laments. "And I didn't put two and two together."

"It was an emotional night." I look down and spot Marco's phone on the floor. I must have dropped it amid all the hoopla. "Want something else for us to freak out about? Marco's phone is almost dead."

Mom sighs. "You've gotta be fuckin' kidding me."

You might think this would cause us to spiral into yet another panic, but we just laugh instead. Our constant misfortune has finally become amusing.

"We have to call Nonna before it dies," I say. "She's probably such a mess."

Mom recites her number from heart as I punch it in. I put the phone on speaker and hold it out in the space between us. Nonna picks up on the first ring.

"It's me," I say.

"And me," Mom adds.

"Cristo Santo!" Nonna sounds like she's actively being electrocuted. "Where are you? You know the police are looking for you? All day I've been worried sick, crying, thinking—"

"I'm sorry," I say. "We couldn't tell you where we were because we didn't want you to get in trouble."

"I knew this would happen," Nonna shrieks. "I knew it. Ever since you called me the other night, I just knew."

"Ma, stop freaking out." Mom sounds more composed than she has in days. "We're going to the police station and we're gonna tell them the truth—it was an accident. *My* accident. Joey didn't do anything."

"Madon'—Gianna Maria—do you have any idea how—"

"Nonna," I interject. "We're fine. We've been at Marco's. He says we'll probably just have to spend the night at the station and we'll be home tomorrow." The phone screen dims slightly. "Listen, Nonna. This phone is dying—"

"Don't go to the police." Her tone shifts from admonishment to desperation. "Come here first and we can figure out what to do. They arrested that *medigan* Richard."

Nonna's bombshell sucks all the air from the car.

"What?" Mom and I wheeze in unison.

My mind goes wild running through possible scenarios that might have led the fire to be pinned on Richard somehow. Maybe we expertly staged it to look like insurance fraud without even realizing it. Maybe he turned himself in because he was guilty of some other crime and didn't want the arson investigation to blow it open. Maybe we've been touched by an angel.

"For the fire?" Mom asks.

"Money laundering." Nonna sounds like she's reading from a piece of paper. "It came out in the investigation, cops say."

There goes my touched-by-an-angel theory. I guess I knew it was far-fetched. Clearly there are others in the world (cancer patients, etc.) far more deserving of divine intervention than a couple of arsonists from New Jersey.

"Oh, my God." Mom hits the steering wheel. "Oh, my God! I knew his businesses were all sketchy."

"You think this will help our case?" I ask.

"I don't know," Mom says. "I hope his ass rots in prison either way."

"Wait," I say. "What if Richard and I end up at the same jail?" I imagine myself having to shower in a big open locker room with a naked, angry Richard scrubbing his balls two drains away from me. The thought gives me a full-body shiver. *"Together?"*

Mom gasps. "Don't put that thought out there—"

"Basta!" Nonna interrupts. I almost forgot she was still on speaker. "Don't go to the police." Her voice is laced with equal parts hope and despair. It's clear she hasn't gotten to the stage of acceptance that Mom and I are at yet. She's probably still somewhere between denial and bargaining. "Come here first. We'll think of something."

"We've already thought of everything," I tell her, recalling the conversation Mom and I just had about Monica. We can't keep running from our mistakes. We need to face them, own them, and move on. "Trust me. We have to just confess—"

"Joey, stop it!" The frustration level in her voice ramps up to a hundred. "Just come—"

The phone goes black and turns off before she can finish her sentence. Everything remains in this state of unfinished quiet until we finally approach the on-ramp to I-37.

"So we're really doing this," Mom whispers. Mostly to herself, I think. "I'm nervous."

"Maybe it won't be so bad," I offer. "Marco said it's like —"

"*Marco* said?"

"Yeah." I sit up. "He told me all about the time he got arrested."

She takes her eyes off the dark stretch of highway for a second to shoot me an apologetic look. We're the only car on the road for miles.

"I know you're not going to believe this," she says. "But I really haven't kept that many secrets from you over the years. Honestly. It's just all this history with Marco. It's...I don't know. I think I wanted to shield you from it?"

"You don't have to explain, Mom. It's cool."

She keeps explaining anyway. "I never wanted you thinking you were the product of some kind of tragic situation — after everything I had been through that year, you know? The parking lot fight was just another disaster to add to the list. But you — you were the opposite of a disaster. You're the best thing that ever happened to me. If I could go back in time to my junior year of high school, I wouldn't change a single thing. All the bullshit — everything." She chokes up. "I'd keep that list of disasters just the way it was. Because it led to a fuckin' miracle."

"Thanks." My mind flashes back to what she said during our fight on the hill earlier. Hurt people hurt people. Maybe it is a cliché. But it's a true one. "I'm sorry I blew up at you earlier. You didn't deserve that."

"I love you." She rubs the back of my neck with her free hand. "We're gonna be fine."

Despite all the reasons not to, I believe her. "I love you, too."

We ride along in silence until we catch up to a car that's going about forty miles per hour — on an empty highway in the middle of the night.

"This bitch," Mom scoffs as she passes it on the right. Her shift in tone makes me laugh through the tears I didn't realize I'd been crying. "Get the fuck out of the left lane!"

thirty-four

So it's not like I was expecting this to be an Instagrammable situation or anything, but still. I look like shit in my mug shot. My eyes are dead, my hair is shorter than it's ever been and yet still somehow looks greasier than a fried eggplant cutlet. I haven't shaved in days. What seemed like organized stubble a couple nights ago now looks like the unkempt beard of an unhinged criminal. And let's not even talk about this atrocious lighting. Honestly — where's the Valencia filter when you need it?

Mom and I were booked separately, so I never got to see her picture. But I'm sure it came out a million times better than mine. Her hair is as sleek as it's ever been, and she cleansed her face with a Neutrogena makeup-removing wipe and did a quick touchup in the car mirror before we came in. (I'm not kidding.)

"I just thought of something," Mom says. "We never got to make a phone call. Isn't that a thing? You get to make a phone call?"

We're alone, locked in a fluorescently lit white room waiting for a detective from the Essex County Prosecutor's Office to get here. We were so out of sorts when we got to Jersey that we forgot our crime was committed in Short Hills — which is in a totally different county than the Bayonne Police Department building we've been confessing in for the past half hour or so.

"Oh, yeah! We should use it to call Nonna. You know she's not sleeping tonight. I feel so bad. I hope she doesn't have to see our mug shots. Those would destroy her."

Mom flips her hair. "I looked kinda cute in mine, actually."

"Of course you did."

We both laugh.

I know, right? Laughing at a time like this. But I have to say. Aside from the unflattering photography, so far the experience hasn't been nearly as traumatic as I expected.

All week we've been so petrified of... sitting around in a sterile office that hasn't had a design facelift since probably 1993? While a pair of doofy overworked cops make phone calls and fill out paperwork? I thought getting arrested would be at least twenty percent more hardcore. I mean, there was a picture of us on the *news*. You'd think we'd be handcuffed or tasered or yelled at or something. But no. Instead it's like we're registering a new car at the DMV. At midnight.

I guess it helps that Mom went to high school with both of the officers. They seemed sad to watch her get in trouble.

The door swings open and one of them — Officer Nelson — walks in with his hand on his duty belt. He's a stocky black dude with a bald head.

Mom and I stop laughing immediately. We are still being booked for arson, after all. And we have no idea what he's about to tell us.

"Good news and bad news," he says. "Which do you want first?"

"Bad," we reply in unison.

"You can't go home. We have to keep you in custody until your arraignment."

"Which is when?" Mom asks.

"That's the good news. The prosecutor is in a rush to sort this out. They think they can fit you in sometime tomorrow morning. We can hold you here until then. Got a couple open holding cells in the basement."

"A couple?" she asks. "You're splitting us up?"

"They're singles," he explains.

"It's fine," I tell her. "We're just gonna sleep."

Mom looks at me and then up at Nelson. "What's gonna happen at the arraignment?"

"Up to the judge," he says. "You might get to go home."

I spoke too soon. His word choice is worse than getting tasered.

"Might?" I ask. "When do people *not* get to go home?"

"If you can't post bail—"

"Bail?" Mom repeats in terror.

Marco didn't say anything about bail! But we should have known. We're over here worried about the one phone call when literally every cinematic depiction of getting arrested always talks about "getting out on bail." Duh. It always comes down to money.

"Yeah, bail." Nelson straightens his posture. "But since there were warrants out for both of you, and you did disappear all week, they might say you're a flight risk and—"

He cuts himself off in that way people do when they realize they're in the middle of a sentence that could destroy you. It's clear he was gonna say they might not let us go at all—bail or no bail.

"And what?" Mom asks.

He doesn't say anything.

"Flight risk?" I ask. "But we just turned ourselves in. That has to mean something."

"It probably does." Nelson tugs on his belt uncomfortably. "Listen, I'm not a lawyer. I really have no idea what they're gonna say tomorrow. If you do have to post bail, I'm sure you'll find a good bondsman. This is Jersey, after all."

"Can we make a call?" Mom pleads. "My mother is probably worried sick about us. I just want her to know we're here."

"We gotta get you in your cells," he says. "But give me her number. I'll let her know."

I consider trying to fight this, but decide it's better this way. Nonna will be kept in the loop without Mom and me having to hear the pain, anger, and disappointment in her voice again. We all win. (Well, I mean. Technically *nobody* is a winner in a scenario like this. But at least it's one less thing to worry about.)

Officer Nelson leads Mom and me back out into the main office where Officer Stamato — a fellow lanky Italian — meets up with us. They exchange glances and seem to nonverbally confirm that their next steps are to guide us to the cells.

The four of us walk down some concrete stairs into a hallway full of motivational posters. There's TEAMWORK, COURAGE, PROFESSIONALISM — but one poster in particular grabs my attention: ATTITUDES ARE CONTAGIOUS. MAKE YOURS WORTH CATCHING. How appropriate. The whole reason we're here is because I forced Mom to catch my attitude that night. Sure, she was reeling from the Richard news. But I know it was my heartbreak that started it the night before. I was patient zero.

The next poster says: ACCOUNTABILITY: THE CONSEQUENCES OF AVOIDANCE CANNOT BE DODGED. Are these bitches trolling us?

We finally reach a fork in the hall. Nelson and Mom go to the left while Stamato and I take a right. Eventually I'm led into a tiny windowless room with nothing more than a twin-size cot built into the white concrete wall. Instead of sheets and blankets there's just a tattered old sleeping bag on top. Overall it looks more like a janitor closet than a jail cell. There are no steel bars; just a big metal sliding door that looks like it weighs three tons.

"Love what you've done with the space." My attempt at a joke lands awkwardly. "Cozy."

Stamato doesn't laugh.

"This is as good as it gets, bud." He reaches for the big iron door handle. "You should see what it's like in actual jail."

I wonder if he's an Asshole in real life. He has one of those deep man-voices that suggests he might be.

"What happens if I have to pee?" I ask.

"Do you have to pee?"

"No. But I might—"

"You can hold it 'til the morning."

He slides the door shut and locks me in for the night before I can start telling him about how I learned from watching *Seinfeld* reruns with Nonna that holding pee in for too long can lead to bladder problems, including involuntary urination. Does this bitch want me to involuntarily urinate? I guess I could always just pee in the corner. What are they gonna do? Arrest me (again)?

I kick my shoes off and stuff myself into the sleeping bag like a piece of manicotti. Have you ever slept on an actual sidewalk? I imagine this is exactly what that would feel like. And don't even get me started on the "pillow." I've seen fluffier piles of rocks.

So I guess that's one jail stereotype that's true. It's not comfortable!

I close my eyes and focus on my heartbeat. I honestly can't remember the last time it wasn't going a zillion beats a minute. I've gotten so used to it by now that "racing" has become my new "resting."

I try to visualize a successful outcome tomorrow. Good

weather. Friendly judge. Speedy hearing. Maybe even some kind of pardon or something. We've already confessed to the cops here, but we made it extremely clear that the fire was not at all intentional. It was just an accident that got out of hand. We didn't break and enter—Mom had the code to Richard's garage because he gave it to her. This was all just an accident and a misunderstanding. Richard's the one who belongs in jail. Not us.

Oh, wait. I forgot I don't do this anymore. I'm a reality person.

But I can be at least somewhat optimistic. Twenty-five years in prison would just be silly.

My mind wanders back to that ACCOUNTABILITY poster. *The consequences of avoidance cannot be dodged.* What a rude-ass quote to have on display at a police station—in the hallway between the office and the cells, no less! Anyone who will ever see that poster has clearly already learned this lesson for themselves. The hard way.

I roll the word "accountability" around in my head for a moment. That's what this has been about all along, hasn't it? We were trying to hold Luke and Richard accountable for what they did to us. If you cheat and lie, there should be consequences.

I still believe that. I really do.

But also? It wasn't worth it. The high of revenge barely lasted a second past the time it took to twist the knife, drag the key, swing the bat. After that, it was all reckoning with the damage—a whole new set of consequences that pinged from Luke back to me. If anything, I gave him a reason to feel less bad about cheating on me. He could tell himself I deserved it.

A better way to retaliate would have been to just block his ass entirely—stop feeding his ego by demanding his approval. Focus on my own healing and allow the real consequences to be enforced by an impartial third party. Like, I don't know, God or karma or some shit.

I roll over to lay on my side, but doing so on this surface makes me feel bones in my hip that I didn't even know existed. I place the back of my head on the pillow and try once more.

Eyelids closed. Deep breaths.

Aaaand now I'm thinking about Will. His voice, his hands, his eyes. I wonder if he's been trying to text me. Or if he's even been thinking of me.

I guess it doesn't matter either way. Even if I could talk to him right now and try to fix things between us...then what? Tomorrow he'll be back in Manhattan living his perfect rich life. Even if Mom and I get sent home in the morning, there's no way he'd want to have anything to do with me. I'd be a hideous reminder of the wagon-trainwreck waiting for him back at his dad's lake house.

But maybe I can find someone else like him after the dust settles from this nightmare. No more Assholes. Only Nice Guys from now on. If nothing else, Will at least helped me understand that *nice* doesn't necessarily mean *boring*. It just means — you know — *not fucking evil.*

You know what? I need to stop thinking about guys!

What I need to do is figure out a way to fall asleep on this unnatural slab of concrete. No matter what happens in my brain from now until the morning, absolutely nothing will change. I'm locked in this closet for at least the next six hours. Six? Maybe seven. What time do they wake you up in jail? Oh, my God. It doesn't matter. Overthinking won't get me anywhere. My brain can't help me. I need to turn it off.

I close my eyes harder and focus on breathing — long inhales, longer exhales. Eventually my heart rate slows down to something that almost seems manageable.

I'm tired.

I can do this.

I'm basically asleep.

And then the words *bail* and *flight risk* barrel into my mind like a stampede of elephants.

thirty-five

A thick wave of fluorescent light pours into my cell all at once.

"Joseph Rossi," a booming voice says as my brain comes into focus. I must have passed out from mental exhaustion at some point during the last few hours. But now I'm awake and there's a new cop standing in the doorway. "Get up."

I rub my eyes until they hurt and peel myself off the cot. You know what would be amazing right now? A giant mug of espresso roast coffee.

"You've got visitors."

Visitors, he said. Plural. Nonna is obviously one of them— I'm surprised they were able to keep her at bay until morning, to be honest—but who else? Maybe Marco? It's gotta be Marco. He must have woken up at the crack of dawn to drive down and come help us get through this whole hearing process.

The cop escorts me through the Motivational Poster Hall of Shame, through the office, and back to that empty white room Mom and I waited in yesterday. It's like he's opening the door in slow motion, I'm so eager to see who's on the other side. But it's empty.

"They'll be right in." He slaps my shoulder blade. "Just take a seat."

The room is just as sterile as it was last night—but now there's a weight in the air that wasn't here before. Maybe it's the light of day. It's making all of this feel so much realer than it did last night after our emotional-roller-coaster ride home from the lake.

The door swings open.

It's Mom. New Cop escorts her to the seat next to me and leaves the room. We look at each other with *don't-fucking-cry-right-now-we've-both-already-cried-too-much* faces.

"You get any sleep?" she asks.

I shrug and shake my head in response.

"Same," she says. "This doesn't feel real, huh?"

"Nope. Were we crazy for coming here?"

Mom shakes her head back, trying her best to look sure. "We had no other choice."

The door swings open again. This time New Cop is trailed by Nonna—she's wearing a jean jacket and carrying a garment bag—and some John Krasinski–looking dude in a suit. Nonna whooshes in like a hurricane, slams the bag on the table, and wraps me in a big hug for about two seconds. Then she steps back, looks at me, and smacks me upside my head. Fair!

"Nice haircut," she says—but it sounds more like a death threat than a compliment.

I open my mouth cautiously. "Thanks…"

"You trying to drive me *pazzo* hanging up on me yesterday?" she screams. "I was trying to tell you that I have a lawyer for you." She hits the suited guy's arm and, like, presents him to us. "Teresa's nephew Michael."

He nods and starts to open his mouth, but then Mom jumps in.

"Are you trying to drive *me* pazzo, Ma?" she asks. "You know we can't afford a lawyer."

"*Madonna mi,*" Nonna moans. "Your picture's been all over the news! You think you can get out of this without a lawyer?"

"But—"

"But nothing," Nonna interjects. "Michael offered his services as a favor. If Joey didn't hang up on me last night—"

"The phone died," I correct her.

She ignores my correction and side-eyes me. "If Joey didn't hang up on me last night, I could have told you to wait. Instead, the two of you come over here on your own, talking to the cops all night without a lawyer present like a couple of *stunads*." She shoots Mom an iron stare. "And you! *Gianna Maria.* How could you do this to me? To your son? What were you thinking? Your father must be rolling over in his grave."

"Good!" Mom barks back. "Fuck him. And his grave."

Nonna puts a hand over her chest as if Mom just stuck a knife in it.

Mom crumples onto a chair and buries her face in her hands. I always knew she held some kind of grudge against Nonno, but damn. That was *way harsh, Tai.* I can tell by the way she's huffing right now that she regrets it already.

"Listen." Michael—our lawyer?—clears his throat. "You can't afford to be fighting with each other right now. I'm gonna do everything I can to help you, but you all need to be on the same team." He loosens his tie and narrows his eyebrows. "We don't have much time."

"Why are you here?" Mom asks. I'm kind of wondering the same thing, but also I'm not about to question our sudden twist of good fortune. "What kind of lawyer just works for free?"

"Gianna," Nonna warns. "Stop lookin' a gift horse in the mouth. *Statazit* and let him talk."

"My firm encourages us to take on a certain amount of pro bono work each year," Michael explains. "And I really do believe I can help minimize your sentences."

He takes a seat across from me at the table and shuffles some papers out of a manila folder. "I talked to the Essex County prosecutor," he continues. "She seems hyperfocused on the unrelated case against your, uh — Richard Massey — which is likely to go to trial in the future. So I think she'll be willing to work out a plea bargain on this one and move on. And I'm sure *his* legal team is more concerned with keeping him out of jail than putting you two in it."

"Is it too late to frame him for insurance fraud?" I joke. Although how amazing would it be if Michael's answer was just, like, *Nope! Framing him for insurance fraud is totally feasible and a great idea.*

"Funny." Michael's face muscles barely move.

I decide to ask the question that is (or at least should be) at the forefront of all of our minds: "So what *is* our sentence going to be? Are we gonna have to go to prison?"

"I'm hopeful it won't come to that." He says it so matter-of-factly that I'm weirdly comforted. He's clearly not just bullshitting to make me feel better. "But you shouldn't worry about the sentencing at this point. The goal today is to get you home until your next court date. Which means you need to come off as apologetic and likable to the judge."

"I brought you clean clothes." Nonna gestures to the garment bag on the table.

"So we get changed and act sorry, and that's it?" Mom asks. A little too hopeful for our own good. "He'll let us go?"

"Given the severity of the charges…" Michael looks down at a piece of paper. "Well. Let's start with the pluses. Neither of you has a record. You have your jobs in Bayonne. Joseph has school. You both have" — he gestures at Nonna — "family in the community."

Hearing an actual lawyer rattle off reasons why we should be allowed to go home feels like putting cool aloe on a blistering sunburn.

"But," Michael continues. Goddamnit. "There are minuses. You've been charged with felony arson and criminal property damage. You disappeared for three days." He clicks his pen. "That isn't a crime in itself, but judges typically don't take well to fl —"

"Flight risks," I somberly finish for him.

The relief is gone just as fast as it came. Back to being burned.

"But we came back!" Mom says. "We turned ourselves in. We told the truth. That has to help our case."

"I'm afraid it doesn't work like that," he says. "If I were here last night, I would have strongly advised you against talking so much — or at all. Now your confessions can be used as evidence against you."

"Fuck me!" Mom shrieks. "I can't do anything right."

Nonna's just sitting on the other side of the table with her arms crossed, biting her tongue so hard it's probably bleeding.

"Listen," Michael continues. "We can argue that you were both under emotional duress and didn't understand the extent of what you were confessing to. You can still plead not guilty today." He pauses. "In fact, you *must* plead not guilty today."

"Joey?" Nonna asks, probably because I'm currently staring at the floor. My sneakers are covered in caked-on dirt from walking up and down that muddy hill yesterday. Hopefully she has some shoes in that bag. "Did you hear that?"

"Yeah. Not guilty." I shift my weight in my chair. "Even though we *are* guil—"

"Please don't say that to the judge," Michael interrupts. "Or anyone at all."

"Right. Got it." I look over at Mom and remember how we slept in separate cells last night. "They're not gonna separate us again, are they?" I ask.

"Since you were charged together, you'll face the judge together as codefendants. And as long as the judge lets you go home today, you shouldn't have to worry about separation." Michael shuts his folder. "But you should be prepared for some fairly restrictive conditions of release. You won't be allowed to leave the state before your next court date, which could be any-where from several days to several months."

"That's fine," Nonna says. "He's going to college in-state."

I can tell she's saying it more for my instruction than his benefit.

"In light of your financial hardships," he continues, "I'm going to ask the judge to let you go home based solely on your promise to appear in court. But given the severity of this crime, you'll probably be required to post b—"

"Bail," I lifelessly finish once again.

"Yes." His eyes dart around the room. "If that happens, you may be able to get a bond, but you'd be responsible for paying ten percent."

"We can't afford *any* percent," Mom says. "Fuck! Fuck—"

"*Basta!*" Nonna says. "Let Michael talk, will you?"

"I'll do my best to ensure bail is as low as possible," he says. "But I would be remiss not to advise you to prepare in the event that it's on the higher side. Is there anyone in your lives who might be able to help?"

"No," Mom says through quivering lips. "We have nothing and no one."

"I have some retirement money," Nonna says. "How much would ten percent be?"

Michael takes a breath. "It could be anywhere from a thousand—"

"Ma!" Mom interjects. "I don't care how much it is. You're not doing that."

If I could bring myself to speak right now, I would tell Mom that now is really not the time to get on a whole *we-don't-need-any-handouts* high horse. But luckily Nonna is prepared to make the argument for me.

"You think I'm going to let my daughter and grandson rot in jail?" She throws her hands up. "I don't have a choice, Gia! *Christ*. You took my choice away when you set that house on fire! You weren't thinking about my life savings then. Were you?"

"There's no need to get hysterical," Michael says calmly. I wish his composure were contagious. "Like I said, I'm going to do my best. Hopefully the question of bail will be a nonissue."

"Right." Mom's voice trembles while I nod along in pure terror. "Hopefully."

thirty-six

If the outside of it is any indication, the Essex County Courthouse is going to be a hell of a lot less like the DMV than the police station was. It looks all grand and fancy and shit.

I trudge up the stone steps slowly — escorted by Mom, Michael, and yet another new cop. Nonna drove separately. (She was very excited to get her car back, you know.)

I marvel at the large lion statue outside the entrance. Who knew places like this existed in Newark? It's like this entire scene was plucked right out of a primetime legal drama.

My sense of awe vanishes, though, the moment we approach the metal detector inside and I remember that we're here because we've been charged with a crime. Nerves wriggle through my veins like tadpoles. What if this is my last time walking into a building as a free man? What if they refuse to let us out on bail? What if I set this metal detector off with a gun I didn't realize was in my shoe? Wait. Do people even keep guns in their shoes? I swear I've seen characters in movies pull guns out of their shoes before, but now that I really think about it, that seems logistically impossible.

The tadpoles multiply and spread through my entire body by the time we enter the actual courtroom.

Scratch what I said out there about *grand*. This place looks like a ramshackle old classroom with rows of wooden benches instead of desks. And criminals and lawyers instead of students and teachers. There are two giant flags—America and New Jersey—on either side of the big judge desk (stage?) in the front, but everything else just looks cheap, dated, and plain.

"Holy shit." Mom squeezes my hand in a direction toward the front. "Look."

It's Richard, wearing a dark-gray suit and a soulless facial expression. Even after looking our way and clearly seeing Mom and me walk in, he's dead in the eyes.

She turns to Michael and whispers. "You didn't tell me he was going to be here for this."

"You're being charged with property damage," Michael replies. "He is the owner of said property. I thought his presence was implied."

Mom rolls her eyes.

"He looks like shit," I whisper. It's the truth. Richard clearly hasn't been getting much sleep. Good! He doesn't deserve sleep. "Where's his wife?"

Mom tugs at her pencil skirt. "If she hasn't left his ass because of all this, then she's even stupider than I am."

"Oh, my God, look." I now draw her attention to a few seats over from Richard. It's the late-night runner who's basically turned herself into the media spokesperson for this entire case. *Joggy McBitch.* She's traded in the purple Reebok hoodie for a taupe blazer, solidifying her status as a total Hillary. She might as well have popcorn in her hand, the way she's clearly here to watch her favorite personal drama unfold like our lives are nothing more than bingeable reality TV to her. "The jogger."

"This bitch," Mom quietly mutters.

We slide into a bench and wait for our case to be called.

What if the judge is a total asshole? What if we don't get to go home after this? What if Marco's experience was only so easy because all *he* did was bash my father's head in? What if turning ourselves in was yet another delusional decision? What if coming back to New Jersey was a huge mistake?

I think about that last one for a second. Maybe it wouldn't have been *that* impossible to start over with new lives. Given how little fanfare there was when we showed up last night, I almost feel like the cops were never even planning to look very far for us anyway.

This feeling—that we *chose* to be here to beg a judge not to ruin our lives over one mistake—is suddenly the only thing I can think about. I consider poking Michael to ask if warrants ever just "expire" when they can't find the suspects, but the room has become totally silent over the past few seconds.

An officer gets up in the front and tells us to "please rise" for the entrance of "Honorable Judge Turner."

Oh! The judge is a woman.

She kind of looks like Beyoncé!

Mom and I exchange quick looks, like, *this is good*. Maybe she'll understand where we're coming from. Maybe she has a lying ex of her own. A knockoff Jay-Z. She'll set us free in the name of *Lemonade*. Blessed Bey.

Our case is the first one called.

"Gianna Maria Rossi and Joseph Anthony Rossi," Judge Turner says from atop her highly intimidating perch. "Are these your true names?"

"Yes," Mom answers.

Judge Turner looks at me. I can't breathe. Michael pats my shoulder, which helps me get just enough air to answer this admittedly very simple question.

"Yes."

"Thank you." She looks down and begins reciting some legal mumbo jumbo. "This complaint alleges that in the early morning hours of April 19th, you initiated a fire on the second level of a residential property located at 33 Marble Lane in Short Hills, New Jersey, in violation of penal code 2C:17-1, resulting in a charge of felony arson in the third degree. It is further alleged that the property, owned by Richard Massey, has suffered significant damage, resulting in a charge of..." She keeps rambling on like this for another few robotic sentences until finally peeling her eyes off the paper and focusing them on Mom and me like laser-beams. "Ms. Rossi. Mr. Rossi. Do you understand the charges as I've recited them to you?"

We both respond with *yes*, even though everything inside of me wishes I could have said no. The way she rattled off the charges — so cold, so matter-of-fact — made it sound like she was taking Richard's side by default. I guess penal codes don't offer much room for the complexity of the truth. (Also, I'm sorry, but why the fuck is it called a "penal" code anyway? That word sounds penis-adjacent, and frankly it's distracting. Especially in a courtroom setting.)

"And have you discussed these charges with your lawyer?" Judge Turner continues.

"Yes," we answer again.

"And do you wish to enter into a plea at this time?"

"Yes."

"Ms. Rossi?"

"Not guilty," Mom answers.

"Mr. Rossi?"

I start to speak, but then I tense up. Suddenly my throat is drier than a slice of stale focaccia. It's almost like I'm afraid the judge is gonna call bullshit on me. *Not guilty? Bitch, I heard all about your confession last night! Now get the fuck out of my courtroom with your lying ass and go rot in a jail cell. To the left, to the left.*

Michael nudges me.

"Not guilty," I choke.

Judge Turner shuffles some more papers as the court-record-taking-guy in the corner types away on a laptop.

Finally she says, "Does the defense have any remarks before bail is set?"

My body twists and pangs with the impulse to scream at the top of my lungs about how setting any kind of bail at all would be akin to a life sentence of its own.

"Your Honor," Michael begins. "As I'm sure you have noticed, this is not a black-and-white case. My clients — neither of whom have any criminal record to speak of — were suffering from severe emotional distress during the event in question."

He sounds super lawyer-y and professional. And surprisingly passionate about defending us. He must have been saving all his energy for the courtroom.

"This fire was an accident in every sense of the word. Their intention was to burn a few garments in the bathtub and put it out quickly — an act of admittedly petty revenge, but one they felt driven to as the result of a personal situation between my client Ms. Rossi and the owner of the property, Mr. Massey, who had been deceiving Ms. Rossi with regard to his marital status for a period of two years."

He pauses to take a breath. A sense of relief washes over me. I still feel like Mom and I are walking on a tightrope from jail to freedom — but this impassioned soliloquy is making it feel just a little less thin. Like we might actually be able to make it to the other side.

"I understand that no degree of interpersonal conflict can excuse an act of arson—or any crime—but I tell you this to explain that my clients are not a danger to society," he continues. "They were caught up in an emotional moment that quickly escalated far beyond anything they had intended. They turned themselves into custody and have been cooperative throughout this process. In light of these factors, I implore you to consider releasing them from custody based on their own recognizance."

Judge Turner doesn't give us so much as a nod, a smile, a look. She just turns her attention to the prosecutor across from us.

"Does the prosecution have anything to add?" she asks.

"Yes, your honor." Her hair is in a messy bun and she looks like she might yawn at any moment. This fills me with hope. Maybe she's exhausted and overworked and won't even bother trying to do her job of prosecuting us. "We are aligned with the defense's proposed conditions of release and are willing to negotiate a plea bargain in the coming days."

"That's all?" Judge Turner says.

"Yes."

The tightrope seems even thicker now. Just a few more steps!

I start thinking about what I'm going to do when we get home—starting with a long shower, some sfogliatelle, and a nap. And then maybe a bottle or three of Luna di Luna.

Just as I'm envisioning Mom's and my freedom celebration on the couch, I notice Richard squirm in his seat from the corner of my eye. My relief is his frustration. He probably wanted the prosecutor to eviscerate us.

"I can appreciate the complicated nature of this situation," Judge Turner says. "But the codefendants' own recorded confession indicates that they made the conscious choice to light a match and throw it in a bathtub. As a result of that choice, a fire was started. As a result of that fire, a house—a very expensive house in a very expensive location—was destroyed." She pauses before turning to address Mom and me directly. "And rather than report the fire to authorities, you made another choice: to leave the state. It was a small miracle that, thanks to a neighbor who keeps a very unusual jogging schedule, this fire was reported at all."

Please stop. Please stop. Please stop.

But she keeps going.

"Other homes could have been damaged. People could have been hurt." She straightens her posture and flips a piece of paper over. She's clearly made her decision. "And the Court just cannot ignore that."

Mom and I interlock our fingers and squeeze each other's hands so tight our palms might form a fire of their own.

"Bail is set at one hundred thousand dollars per codefendant," Judge Turner coolly proclaims.

Nonna gasps.

Richard scoffs.

Joggy McBitch sighs.

Michael shakes his head.

Mom and I collapse into each other.

Turner slams her gavel against her desk—which might as well be our faces, hearts, throats—and calls for the next case.

thirty-seven

"Twenty thousand dollars," Mom whimpers. "It might as well be twenty million."

We're back at the police station, sitting in a tiny basement holding cell while Nonna and Michael try to sort everything out with a bondsman. If they can't come up with ten percent of the bail money, Mom and I are going to jail—*actual* jail—for the foreseeable future.

"What about Nonna's savings?" I ask. Mom is laying against my shoulder while I sit upright in the corner of the cot and play with her hair in an attempt at therapy. It's in decent shape for having been completely neglected over the past twenty-four hours. No split ends at all. Maybe just a little oily. I wrap a curl around my index finger and let it go. "She didn't say how much she has?"

"You *know* she lives from paycheck to pension check," Mom says. "I just hope she has half of it. Then we could at least get *you* home today."

"But that would mean —"

"I'll survive."

But I won't, I think to myself.

I wish I could scream right now. Right in that fucking Judge Turner's face. With her stupid-ass gavel and "the Court just cannot ignore that" speech.

What hurts the most is that I *knew* this would happen. Ever since the possibility of bail was first mentioned last night, I had a feeling that — actually? — it was even before that. I knew from the very beginning that this would all eventually just come down to money. Isn't that how it always works? And isn't that why we ran away in the first place? Because we were broke. And broke people *always* get fucked. It's just how the world works.

It's not that I don't feel bad about what we did. But how does forcing us to come up with money make anything right? As if there's a price tag on morality. I'm not going to do *this* fucked-up thing because then I'd have to pay *this* many dollars. Shouldn't we just *not* do fucked-up things out of the goodness of our hearts?

"That's bullshit," I say. "You shouldn't have to sit in jail just for a stupid mistake."

"Honestly? I think I should."

"Stop—"

"Everything the judge said was right." Mom peers at the ceiling. "It could have been worse. People could have died. *We* could have died, Joey. And for what? Because Richard lied to me about divorcing his wife?" She scoffs. "I'm not the only bitch in the world who's ever had her heart broken."

"We overreacted," I admit. "But obviously we've learned our lesson. Don't you think jail would be a bit much?"

"Burning a house down — even if it was an accident — should come with serious consequences," she continues. "Think about it. What if Marco did that to *me* after I—" She cuts herself off. "You know what I'm trying to say."

I do. And it's not that I disagree — clearly we need to figure out how to process our emotions in a healthier manner. But I also think it's possible for us to get there without having to serve hard time.

"But I will say it's fucked up she set the same bail for both of us," Mom continues. "You're just a baby."

"I'm not a —"

"You're *my* baby." She sits up. "Do you wanna know what I was thinking about when she was giving her speech up there? With that little hammer in her hand?"

"It's called a gavel."

"Whatever," Mom says. "I was thinking about how this bitch is — I don't know — maybe forty? And she's a *judge*. She's not that much older than me! But she did something with her life. And she didn't do it by burning shit down." She sighs. "It's like I was saying last night in the car. We can't let the bullshit bring us down anymore. You're still so young — you could be a judge if you want to."

"Are you high?" I ask. "In what universe have I ever expressed an interest in . . . judging?"

Mom laughs through a sniffle. "You know what I mean."

"And it's not like you've done *nothing* with your life," I offer. "Fire or no fire — you're still the best mom in the world. I consider myself so lucky to have you. Seriously. Can you imagine if I had a mom like Judge Turner? I'd be so boring. Forget about my comedy career. My jokes would be even worse than they already are."

"Shut up." She hits my knee. "You're funny."

"And your work is just as important as hers!" I continue. "Your customers all worship you. You make them beautiful. And you give them free therapy."

"Aw, Joey." Her lips crease into a small smile. "You're such a sweetheart."

An echo of heavy footsteps reverberates from outside.

"Do you hear that?" I ask.

Mom peels herself off the bench and stands up next to me. Officer Nelson slides the door open a moment later.

"Congratulations," he says. "You can go home."

"My mother came up with *twenty thousand dollars*?" Mom asks.

Don't question it, I nonverbally tell her with my elbow. *Just get up and run.*

"I don't think she put it up," Nelson says. "She seemed surprised."

Mom looks at me with what I imagine is the same *holy shit* face I'm giving her right now.

"Then who was it?" she asks.

"Dunno." He shrugs. "I'm just following orders."

It must have been Marco. I knew all along that he'd be coming back here to help us get out of this — it just took a little longer than expected. Traffic on I-87, probably.

As Nelson leads us toward the stairs, my lungs expand. I can breathe — like really breathe — for the first time in days. It's like we've been on a crashing plane all week that somehow just pulled off a miracle emergency landing. Soon we'll be home. We won't have to worry about getting arrested. We've already been arrested.

"You think it was Marco?" Mom asks as we march up the stairs toward freedom.

"Had to be."

We get to the front of the office and see Nonna sitting alone on a wooden bench, clutching her pocketbook and car keys. For someone whose daughter and grandson just dodged a jail-shaped bullet, she doesn't look nearly as relieved as she should.

"Here they are," Nelson says with a silly smile. "Thelma and Louise are free to go."

I give Nonna a giant hug. She reluctantly pats my back.

"So where is he?" Mom asks.

"Michael?" Nonna says. "He's still meeting with the prosecutor about the plea deal. He's trying for community service and probation and some kind of conflict resolution therapy program. He said there could also be fines, restitution payments" — she cuts herself off in exasperation. What a buzzkill. Can't we just enjoy this moment without worrying about what our sentence will be? We were just bailed out of jail! As my favorite Oprah GIF would say: *Let's celebrate that.* "He thinks he can keep prison off the table. You two have horseshoes up your ass, I swear to God."

"I wasn't asking about Michael," Mom says. "Where's Marco?"

"Marco?" Nonna asks. "Why would he be here?"

"He didn't pay the bail bondsman?" I ask. "Then who did?"

"That woman." Nonna flicks her wrist. "She's in the bathroom."

"Who?" Mom asks.

"You know," Nonna says. "Lisa. The woman who—"

"*Hiiii,*" a distantly familiar voice says from behind us.

Mom and I turn around.

Shut the fuck up! It's Joggy McBitch.

thirty-eight

"I'm Lisa." She holds her hand out while Mom and I just stare at each other, then at her, then back at each other, then back at her. She puts her hand back at her side. "You must think I'm so crazy, right? I know. I just *had* to do this."

"I . . ." Mom stammers. "What the f . . . I mean. Why?"

"The money is nothing." Lisa's voice actually makes this statement believable — it drips of wealth. You know those voices? The ones that were just made to say words like *terrace, Jeffrey*, and *sauté*. "I felt for you two in that courtroom."

Nonna's bullshit detector goes off in the form of a suspicious squint in Lisa's direction.

"But why?" Mom repeats.

"Yeah," Nonna echoes. "Why?"

"I have an idea!" I say. "How about we stop second-guessing the motives of the woman who just saved our asses from jail and say *thank you* instead?"

Lisa chuckles at this.

"I'm sorry," says Mom. "It's just —"

"I was seeing him too." Lisa tilts her head in pity. "Richard."

Mom and I exchange stunned looks, the subtext of which are

obviously *holy-shit-the-double-D-bra*. We swing our gazes directly to Lisa's breasts.

Oh my God! They're huge—basically daring the top button of her blazer to pop off. How did I never notice them before? (Oh, wait—duh.)

So Lisa is not *just* Joggy McBitch. She's also Big Tits McGhee. *Joggy is Big Tits! Big Tits is Joggy!*

Mom gasps as she apparently comes to this revelation at the same time as me. "I have so many questions for you."

Nonna straightens her posture. "We can't let you—"

"Too late," Lisa says. "I already wrote the check. I just ask for one favor in return."

"Literally anything," I reply immediately.

She grins. "You must let me take you out to lunch."

Lisa may be the first rich person in the history of the world I don't hate at least a little bit. I mean, how could I feel anything but unconditional love for her? After what she's done for us. We were so wrong about her. She's not just another Hillary. She's not just Joggy McBitch. And/or Big Tits McGhee. She's our savior. I kinda feel bad for hating her and giving her such a horrible nickname all this time. But I guess that's the danger in thinking you know everything about a person just based on where they live and what they look like. You could end up being entirely wrong.

I can tell by the way Mom is letting herself smile as we walk across the street to the mall right now that she's been having similar thoughts. Lisa has officially transitioned from *this* bitch to *that* bitch. Honestly? For twenty thousand dollars? She's *the* bitch.

The four of us get seated in a cozy booth by the window. Lisa orders a round of drinks. The waiter cards me like an asshole, so I make a mental note to steal a sip from Mom's sangria the next time she's not looking.

"So you and Richard," Mom says. "How? I thought all his time in New Jersey was spent with me."

"I'm sure it was." Lisa takes a swig from her wineglass—a very unsurprising Chardonnay (basically rich-white-lady juice). "I settled for scraps from him—a night here, a morning there. I was still going through my divorce when it started. He told me he was dealing with the same thing—splitting up with his wife. It was something we bonded over. I thought for sure we'd be together once..."

"He fed me that same bullshit," Mom offers.

"When I saw the *For Sale* sign go up on his house on Monday, I was flabbergasted." Lisa wipes a stray tear from her foundation-heavy cheek. I'm guessing she uses either Lancôme or Estée Lauder. Maybe Clinique. Definitely *not* drugstore. "He broke up with me later that day, and I swear to God, if you didn't burn that godforsaken house down, I might have."

You'd think someone like Lisa would know better than to get involved with a guy like Richard. She already lives in Short Hills! She's pretty, she's blond. She's got that natural rich-person confidence. She's Hillary to a tee.

Then again. I guess the thing Mom and I tend to forget about Hillary is that she was a victim of Bill's bullshit, too. Even if she would never actually call herself one. He cheated on her. Maybe she was just as heartbroken as Monica. Maybe she just never allowed herself to feel it. Or maybe she did feel it, but figured out a way to heal in private. Without all the hysterics and arson and whatnot.

"I found out the same exact way," Mom says. "And he broke up with me that day. He had the nerve to tell me I was 'too high maintenance' for a side bitch."

"That makes one of us," Lisa scoffs. "He probably loved how *low* maintenance I was. I made it so easy for him."

281

"He's a real prick," Mom says.

"A scumbag," I chime in.

"A rotten rat bastard," Nonna adds.

Look at Nonna! Engaging in man-bashing with us. I'm so proud.

"I trust too easily." Lisa shakes her head. "My ex-husband cheated on me throughout our entire marriage—and I made it easy for him, too. Always had my own life, career, friends. He probably thought I deserved it for not revolving my entire world around him."

"Even when you do revolve your world around them, they still do that shit," Mom says. "You're damned if you do and damned if you don't."

"The humiliation is the worst," I add, thinking back to how bad I felt about myself after I found out Luke was cheating on me. How I ate three plates of Nonna's linguine while worrying about what people would think once I scrubbed him from my Instagram grid. "It's like the whole world gets to see how bad you are at being loved."

"Well here's what my therapist tells me," Lisa says. "It's not that we're bad at being loved. It's that we're drawn to people who are bad at loving. And we have the power to break that pattern."

Nonna hits my arm and then Mom's. "Are you two listening?"

Lisa half-smiles. "Hopefully it's an easier lesson for you to learn than it has been for me."

Honestly? I feel like it might be. Because for some reason, this advice lands with me in a way that no other relationship wisdom ever quite has. There's nothing wrong with Mom or me. And maybe we've known this—deep down—all along. Maybe that's the real reason we've always been so prone to rage in the face of our breakups. Because guys like Richard, Luke, Leo, and whatever-the-fuck-Lisa's-ex-husband's-name is—they make us forget it. They try to make us feel smaller than we are. And we *let* them. And then we regret it after they cheat and we realize we've been shrinking ourselves for nothing the entire time.

"Can I tell you something?" Lisa lowers her voice to a low hum. "I recognized your car that night. I'd seen it in his driveway before on countless other jogs. Deep down, I always knew it belonged to a woman. Which is probably why I never questioned him on it."

She leans forward and touches Mom's hand. "I could see it in your eyes. Both of you. When I ran past you at the stoplight. And then again this morning in the courtroom. There was so much pain. I saw myself in your faces." Her tone deepens into a new level of sincerity. "That's why I pretended not to know the make or model when the investigators asked me about your car. I knew I *had* to report the fire—but I didn't want to be the reason you got caught. You have no idea how horrible I felt after they found you anyway and issued the warrants for your arrest. I'm just glad I was given the opportunity to help somehow."

The waiter brings over a fresh round of drinks. I lean forward and sneak a sip from the long black straw sticking out of Mom's refill.

"There was something so cathartic about seeing that house burn down," Lisa adds. "When I look back on it in my mind, knowing the context now...it kind of makes me smile." She chuckles to herself. "Is that bad?"

"Yes." Nonna sips her espresso and side-eyes Lisa. "It is."

"You've never gotten revenge, have you?" Mom asks Lisa.

"Only in the form of a divorce settlement." Lisa gives a sadistic little laugh. "But it felt empty." She pauses. "There were no *flames.*"

The way she says this makes it so painfully clear. Revenge is best

283

when it's just a concept—something you fantasize about but never actually see through. Kind of like how Mom and I have always loved all those angry breakup songs. It's not because we needed to *actually* get revenge. It's because Carrie and Beyoncé and Rihanna allowed us to experience it vicariously through them—from a safe, comfortable distance. Without the guilt and prospect of jail time.

"You wouldn't have done what we did, though?" Mom asks Lisa. "Would you?"

She seems a little taken aback by the question. "I mean, I wish—"

"But you never actually *would*. Right?"

"I suppose that's true." Lisa places her glass down. "I couldn't bring myself to do something that extreme."

"See?" Mom pokes my arm. "We need to be more like Lisa."

Yes, I reply via knowing head nod. *I just came to this revelation on my own two minutes ago.*

"Well, anyway." Lisa wipes a strand of blond hair from her face and purses her lips in sympathy. "You're both so young. I'm sure you'll find good men in no time."

I wince as I wonder what Marco and Will are doing right now up in Bumblefuck.

Mom reciprocates with a sad smile. "Thanks."

"Let's make a toast!" Lisa exclaims. "To Joey and Gia." She smiles. "For *burning it all down*."

Nonna shakes her head. "You are *not* toasting to that."

Mom, Lisa, and I burst into laughter.

"We weren't going to!" Mom places her non-sangria hand on Lisa's shoulder. "To you. How can we ever thank you for what you did today?"

Lisa dismisses this notion with a fling of her hand. "You wanna thank someone? Thank my ex-husband." She flashes a devilish grin. "I paid for it with his money."

thirty-nine

"You two have put me through hell this week," Nonna moans from the driver's seat of her car. I knew she was being too quiet at that lunch. "God only knows what would be happening right now if you didn't—"

"I'm sorry," Mom cuts her off from the passenger seat. "You have no idea how sorry I am. I messed up big-time. Huge." She pauses in thought for a moment. "And I didn't mean to say what I said about Dad before. That wasn't right. I'm sorry about that, too."

Nonna catches, holds, and releases her breath.

"Your father wasn't a bad man," she finally tells Mom. "I know you always thought he was some kind of monster just because he was...direct. But he loved you. He just didn't know how to raise a girl."

"Direct?" Mom asks. "The man was a fucking dictator—"

"Gianna."

"I'm sorry," Mom repeats. Her new slogan. "I just thought you should have at least stood up for yourself more. That's all. But what do I know?"

"Nothing," Nonna says. Her expression in the rearview mirror has a wistful quality to it. I think she might actually agree with Mom a little bit. She's just too proud to admit it. "You know nothing."

Their mini-spat lingers in the air for a few minutes before Nonna sages it clean with the radio. Dean Martin's smooth voice calms us all down. I gaze out at the side of the highway. It looks different today. The blur of trees and smokestacks out the window captures my attention for a moment. There's a sense of tranquility to the motion.

I look down at my refurbished replacement phone as the number of unread texts balloons into the double digits. It was activated at the Sprint store five minutes ago and has only just now finished loading.

Most of these are from Luke and Will. It's like I've been at the center of a melodramatic love triangle this whole time and had no idea. Luke's texts come in three distinct varieties, apparently depending on the time and/or his mood over the past few days.

The first one is concerned:

LUKE: I just wanna know you're ok
LUKE: this is scaring me
LUKE: Did you turn off your number or something?

The second one is incensed:

LUKE: I can't help you if you keep IGNORING me
LUKE: WHAT THE HELL?
LUKE: YOU AND YOUR MOM ARE BOTH FUCKING
PSYCHO

The third one is sorry:

LUKE: I fucked up
LUKE: you don't have to forgive me
LUKE: but I really am sorry

Seeing all of these come in at once makes him seem...honestly? *Crazy.*

The irony is so delicious it makes the cheesecake I ate earlier seem like cardboard. He's so desperate for the last word. For my attention. I spent ten months making him the center of it — and now that I've withheld it for five days, he's completely lost his mind. Who knew *I* had so much power this whole time? I decide to throw him one final bone in the name of closure.

ME: sorry about your car
ME: bye luke

Will's texts are of an entirely different breed:

WILL: I feel bad about how we ended things
WILL: Can we talk?
WILL: Coming back to NY tomorrow
WILL: would love to start over with you in "real life" lol
WILL: Laugh Loft in the West Village on Saturday???
WILL: Ok I'll stop harassing you now

I get butterflies at the thought of seeing him again. Memories from the lake gently crash into me like waves. I consider texting him back with a long-winded apology and an enthusiastic yes to the comedy club invitation, but then I remember we can't leave the state of New Jersey. Fuck. How do I even begin to explain that to him?

Before I can think of any ideas, Nonna turns the radio back down like she has an announcement to make.

"I threw a chicken at him once." She takes her eyes off the road for just a second to look at Mom. Probably checking her face for signs of life. "Your father."

"You did what?" Mom asks.

I echo her reaction from my post in the backseat.

"I think you were at cheerleading camp," Nonna says. "Or maybe sleeping over with that blond girl in Montclair."

"Brittany," Mom says. "Okay..."

"You know how your father loved my chicken cacciatore?" Nonna says. "I made it for him at least once a week. But there was this one day! I was just *tired*. So I figured, 'What the hell? It's only the two of us.' I ordered a small pie from Da Vinci's. I wasn't even hungry myself." She clenches her teeth. "Well. He gets home from work and the first thing out of his mouth is, 'Where's my chicken?' I told him, 'We're havin' pizza instead.' *Madon'*—you'd think I had just kicked him in the *coglioni*."

Her delivery of that last line makes me laugh.

"So he starts hollering at me," Nonna continues. "How dare I don't make him a homemade meal like his mother always used to do, right? So he goes in the fridge and pulls out the chicken I bought that week. He slams it on the counter and unwraps it. A whole chicken."

She stops herself for a moment, like maybe she doesn't want to keep going.

But she does. "Normally I would have just made it to shut him up. But I don't know what got into me. I turned around and screamed right back at him. I said, 'You want your chicken? Here it is!' And I picked it up—this *raw* chicken. And I threw it as hard as I could." She laughs to herself. "Right at his face."

Mom whips her head around and shoots me a look of disbelief.

And then we both crack up like a pair of hyenas.

"You threw a raw chicken at his *face*?" I ask. "Was he okay?"

"Poor bastard got salmonella poisoning." She does the sign of the cross with her non-wheel hand, I assume to apologize to Jesus for calling her dead husband a bastard. "Otherwise he was fine."

"I can't breathe." I keep seeing this mental image of Nonna—even-keeled, level-headed Nonna!—winding up her arm like a softball pitcher and hurling a whole-ass chicken at Nonno's face. Or maybe it was more of a two-handed granny throw? I suppose she *is* a grandmother. "I'm gonna need more details on the mechanics of the throw."

"It wasn't a big chicken," Nonna says. As if that should tell me everything I need to know. "Probably a two-pounder."

"You are a crazy bitch!" Mom is still laughing and wheezing. "And you've been over here scolding us all day for what *we* did."

"I threw a chicken!" Nonna protests. "I didn't burn down a house." She straightens her posture and raises her chin in pride. "There's a difference."

"Touché, Ma." Mom's wheeze slopes down into a sigh. "Tou-fuckin'-ché."

forty

I could jump out of the car and kiss the sidewalk right now, I'm so relieved to be back on our crummy old block. Who would have ever thought, right?

"Look!" Mom says.

"What?" Nonna and I ask in startled unison.

"I think that's Marco's truck."

She's right. It's weird seeing it here on our street rather than in its natural habitat (a stretch of gravel in the woods), but it's definitely Marco's truck. Nestled up next to the curb outside our driveway.

"He's giving you another chance," Nonna says. "Don't screw it up."

"I already did," Mom says. "It's complicated."

"What, complicated?" Nonna asks. "He took you in this week, didn't he? And now he drives all the way down here. He was probably going to post the bail for you."

"Maybe this week made him realize he wants to get back together," I add. "Him coming here is a grand romantic gesture!"

"Everyone calm down." Mom flips open the visor from the ceiling in front of her and checks her face in the mirror. "I look like shit, first of all. And second of all, Marco lives all the way up there in Bumblefuck." She's trying to sound tough and jaded with her delivery, but there's a hint of excitement in her voice that totally gives her away. She's glad he came. "He's probably just here to get his phone back."

Marco jumps out when he sees us pulling up. He's wearing that same L.L.Bean rugby shirt he wore when we showed up to his place on Tuesday. Five eternities ago, it feels like.

"There you are!" Marco yells at us as we step out of Nonna's car. "I looked everywhere for you. The police station. The court-house. What — h — how'd you make bail?"

"You wouldn't believe it if they told you," Nonna says.

He turns to Mom. "I'm so sorry, Gia."

"For what?" Mom says. "You have nothing to apologize for."

"I shouldn't have let you two leave alone last night. I think I was just in shock." He tugs at the collar of his shirt. "This whole week gave me whiplash."

"I'm the one who should be sorry," Mom says. "We shouldn't have dragged you into our mess."

"Be that as it may..." He flashes a sweet smile. "I'm very glad you did."

"Yeah?"

"I missed you," he says.

My heart swells for both of them. But also I feel like a creepy lurker standing out here with Nonna while they're clearly on the brink of jumping into a cinematic embrace.

"I feel like you guys are about to have a moment," I say. "Nonna and I are gonna go upstairs."

"Will came by looking for you," Marco says. "I felt bad for the poor kid. He seemed torn up. I gave him the CliffsNotes version of your predicament." He shrugs. "Hope that's all right."

Ah. So that explains why he stopped texting. He was probably too freaked out to continue once he realized I wasn't just *any* hot mess — I was a hot mess with a criminal record.

"What did he say?" I ask.

"He asked me a bunch of questions about you," Marco says. "I told him you were a good kid and this wasn't normal behavior." He looks back and forth at Mom and me. "As far as I know."

"Thanks."

"You got it." Marco scrunches his face. "Seems like he really likes you."

"Still?"

"Yeah. Still."

"Another boy?" Nonna whispers as we walk away. *"Ay yi yi."*

"He's different!" I tell her. "It's a long story."

We're greeted into the apartment by the empty wine bottles from Monday, still lined up by the sink. Next to them is the unfinished pot of coffee Mom brewed the morning after. It's astounding to think that while Mom and I were going through everything we just went through, these wine bottles and this coffeepot were just sitting here on the counter. Unmoved. Unchanged.

"I'm worried about you." Nonna plops down onto a kitchen chair. "You gonna be okay after all this?"

"I think so." I really do. "I don't know what's next...."

"College is next," she says.

"Well it might be hard to go to college if I'm picking up trash on the side of the highway in an orange jumpsuit —"

"Don't be a *chooch*. Even if you have to take time off for the sentence, you can't use that as an excuse to never get an education."

"I know." I sit down in a chair right next to her and think about my options. Maybe I can major in something comedy-adjacent.

Use it for material. Or maybe my suspicion has been right all along and college isn't for me. I need more time to think about it. But Nonna's been through enough this week. The least I can do is keep her dream alive another day. "Maybe I'll go to Rutgers after all. Or find another school. I'll figure it out."

"Good." She squeezes my shoulder and smiles. "You know you're *oobatz*. Just like your mother."

"You don't really think we're crazy," I say. "You love us."

"You're right. I don't. And I do." She gets up and leans over me, placing her hands around my face like I'm a toddler. *"Bello di nonna."*

"Nonna —"

"Listen to me," she interjects before I can fully express my faux-discomfort at her doting. "You need rest. Go lay down. I'll stop by tomorrow morning with some pastries."

Oh, my God. I didn't even think about what everyone at Mozzicato's must have been thinking when they saw me on the news.

"Have you been there at all this week?" I ask. "Do they know?"

"Oh, yeah. They asked about you." Nonna's halfway to the door. "I told them to mind their own damn business."

After the door clicks shut, I head into my room and try to become one with my bed. But the second I close my eyes, I think about Will. How he took it upon himself to look for me at Marco's. I pull out my phone and read his texts again. I know it's silly. The odds of anything serious happening between us in the long term couldn't be slimmer. But also. Maybe the long term doesn't matter. Maybe we can just see each other one more time and take it from there.

I decide to call him.

He picks up on the first ring.

"Is now a bad time?" I ask. "Now's probably a bad —"

"Now is perfect." Hearing his laugh in my ear makes me wish

I could see it with my eyes — the way his cheeks dimple and his eyes light up. "I just got home, actually."

"Oh. Good."

"You're not calling me from jail, are you?" he asks. "Sorry, that was in poor taste. I'm relieved you called. It means you're okay. Right?"

"As okay as possible."

"Right." He pauses. "I should confess that I Googled you after Marco told me what was going on." Another pause. "And holy shit, dude. Should I be worried?"

My throat tightens. On the one hand, it's a relief to know everything is out in the open and we can potentially start over from a place of transparency. On the other hand, the guy I like just admitted to scrolling through online news coverage of my arrest warrant. That's not a good look!

"I promise this was not a typical week for me," I tell him. "And to be fair — it was *my mom's* ex's house that we burned down." I pause. "*My* ex . . . we just trashed his car."

"Lucky me — I prefer Uber." He smirks through the phone. "Manhattan parking and all."

I blush. "You must think I'm psychotic."

"That's what's so interesting!" he says. "I've been replaying all the time we spent together this week in my head. I didn't get a psycho vibe from you at *all*. I mean, sure — a little messy. But not entirely unhinged." He chuckles. "But maybe I misjudged. Perhaps I can reevaluate tomorrow night. You know, during your NYC debut at the Laugh Loft."

My entire body melts into a cheesy smile.

And then I remember.

"Shit. So. My mom and I are legally forbidden from leaving the state of New Jersey right now."

"Oh."

"Yeah…"

The line goes silent for a few unbearable seconds as I question my decision to make this phone call in the first place. He's probably actively realizing that he's on the phone with a felon. He had fun joking about it in the abstract, but now he's grasping the fact that it's real. He's probably formulating his excuse for why we need to never speak to each other again.

Is he typing? I hear typing.

Oh, God.

He's writing out his rejection of me long-form so he has something to recite from. Why did I do this to myself?

"So…" he finally says.

"It's fine," I say. "You don't need to —"

"I found a club in downtown Jersey City with open mic at eight. You in?"

forty-one

The line between pain and comedy is so thin, it might as well not even exist. That's what I've learned from all this. Comedy isn't a way to *avoid* pain — it's a way to acknowledge it. My jokes don't need to be perfect. They just need to be honest.

At least this is what I'm telling myself as I sit here in the Comedy Cavern — these bitches love their alliteration! — reviewing all the new material I feverishly punched into my Notes app last night.

I put my name on the sign-up list, but I'm still considering the option of playing dumb when they call it. Letting the moment pass. It's gonna be a game-time decision for sure, but I'm hopeful I'll make the right one. I'm sure I'll gather more confidence once Will gets here. That way I'll have three people at this table to count on for guaranteed courtesy laughs.

Where is he? I scan the club — the red curtain-enclosed mini stage, the uneven rows of tables and chairs, the dimly lit bar — but come up empty.

"You seem nervous," Marco says from across the table. "Remember, you have time on your side. Five minutes will go by like nothing. Even if you bomb —"

"Why are you putting that in his head?" Mom interjects. "He's not gonna bomb!" She turns to me. "You're not gonna bomb."

"I'm not nervous!" I assure them. As my thigh vibrates up and down like a horny rabbit en route to orgasm. "I don't know where Will is. He texted an hour ago that he was on his way."

I pull my phone from my pocket to try him again, but I feel a strong hand grip my shoulder from behind. I turn around and instantly melt like an M&M. He's even cuter than I remember — messy hair, crooked yet perfect smile, genuine brown eyes. Instead of his lake uniform of Nantucket Red shorts, he's in dark jeans and a plain white T-shirt (but like a really nice one). He says hi to Mom and Marco and sits down in the empty chair next to me.

"Sorry I'm late," he says. "Traffic in the Holland Tunnel was unbelievable. And I didn't get cell service down there! They didn't start yet, right? When are you up?"

"I think I'm gonna be one of the first," I say. "There were only two people on the list when I signed up. I still might not do it. I barely have any of my new jokes memorized."

"You have to!" He puts his arm around me and I casually just marry him in my head, no big deal. "You're going to be hilarious." He gives a playful smirk. "You better be — I crossed the Hudson River for this."

"Uh-oh," I deadpan. "Now the pressure's on."

The lights dim a little further and the host of the night jumps up onto the spotlit stage to introduce the first comedian.

"Joey Rossi," she proclaims. Of course.

I look across the table at Mom. Her big hoop earrings peek out and glisten from under her hair. Her glossed lips flash me a loving beam of encouragement. Her MAC-lined eyes brim with confidence in my ability to kill it up on that stage — mixed with just enough nervousness to indicate she'll be destroyed if I don't.

You know what? I am so grateful for this woman. Regardless of what the men in our lives do to us—good or bad—there will never be a love as unconditional as the one we have for each other. I make a mental note to remember this in the event that this whole Will thing ends up blowing up in my face and/or the event that she can't make it work with Marco this time around. It really doesn't matter. We'll have each other no matter what.

Oh, my God. What the fuck am I doing? Now is so not the time to be sentimental—it's the time to literally be a joke machine.

"Joey?" Mom says. "You change your mind?"

Marco and Will just kinda look around like they're minding their own business. It's clear everyone at this table would be supportive if I chickened out right now.

"Joey...Rossi?" the emcee says again. "Bayonne?"

But I'm not chickening out. I'm ready for this.

I sprout up and step onto the slightly raised "stage" area.

Whoa. Okay. This spotlight is gonna take a second to get used to. I squint my eyes until a vision of Will in the audience comes into focus. Now *his* leg is vibrating up and down like a horny rabbit en route to orgasm. Fuck. I'm just standing here and not saying anything. I scan the room. Everyone kinda has that same *oh-shit-is-he-gonna-self-destruct?* look on their face.

"So, first of all," I start. "I know what you're thinking... 'That's the guy who's been all over the local news this week! Isn't he wanted for felony arson?'"

This only gets a few (audibly uncomfortable) chuckles from my table. Maybe the story of the fire wasn't quite as viral as I imagined it was. Shit. This is off to an excruciating start.

"Hold on," I say—into the actual microphone. And then I step down to our table and steal a giant gulp from Mom's wineglass. Hopefully there aren't any undercover cops here! I could have just gotten this place busted for serving a minor. But nobody seems to give a fuck. And I need this liquid courage more than they need their liquor license. "So. Anybody here ever been arrested?"

The wine does wonders. It's not nearly enough to give me a buzz, but there's something about the familiar taste. It relaxes my nerves just enough to let words flow out of my mouth.

I step back onto the stage and allow the spotlight to blind me this time. My mind is a blur. I latch on to the first joke I can think of and just keep talking. My material from last night comes back to me in spurts—not even close to exactly how I wrote it in my phone—but I can remember the basic setups and punchlines. It's almost like I'm on autopilot. I hear myself launch into a bit about how the lighting in my mug shot booth was basically a hate crime. "I should have arrested *them* for that shit."

This actually gets a few laughs. From strangers! I can't even explain the high it gives me. I imagine it's crack-esque. All these years I've been so afraid to get up and tell jokes, I could have been experiencing *this*. More laughs trickle in. Mom howls from our table.

The next joke doesn't land quite as well. It's almost a total pin-drop moment (save for the trio of polite giggles from my table). I try to shake it off as quickly as possible. I do *not* say any corny nonsense like, "Tough crowd." That would just be pathetic. Better to keep it moving. So I switch gears to a bit about the founding fathers. Will came all the way here from the city, so the least I could do is make some historical references for him.

This bit gets a good response, so I stay on the topic. "This country would have been so much better if it were founded by women and gay men instead. You know? Like, founding *mothers* and founding...*guncles*." *Beat.* "Then our exes would be the ones with the mug shots." *Beat.* "And my Mom and I would be over here with Presidential Medals of fucking Honor."

I think I still have a good minute left in my time slot, but that last line seemed to be the perfect finale. I squint past the light at our table and see that Mom is laughing so hard she's in tears. It feels good to know that after a week of crying for all the wrong reasons, she's finally crying for the right ones.

I hand the mic back to the host as the audience applauds me. That's right. There's applause! Nary a *boo* to be heard. I did it! I performed and didn't bomb. Already I can tell you it was the most exhilarating experience of my entire life. Way better than destroying Luke's car or burning Richard's clothes. Instead, I *created* something.

"You were a little rough on Benjamin Franklin," Will cracks as I return to the table. "But you killed it."

"Clearly my killer sense of humor has rubbed off on you," Marco goofily adds and then taps my arm. "You were great up there."

Mom's being suspiciously quiet.

"What did you think?" I ask. "I saw you laughing at the Instagram joke."

"I've always known that once you got the courage to perform, you'd be great." She wipes her smudge-y eyes. "But this blew away my expectations. Oh, my God—Joey. I couldn't breathe, I was laughing so hard."

"Shut up!" I say.

"I'm serious, Joey." She leans back and looks me up and down with love and admiration. "You are *that* bitch."

"No." I smile and throw it all right back at her. "You are."

acknowledgments

I'm gonna try to be brief, but my road to publication was a zillion miles long and I have lots of people to thank! So here we go.

First and foremost, to my amazing literary agent, Elizabeth Bennett. The only reason I've stayed sane throughout the highs and lows of my publishing journey is because of your thoughtful guidance and unwavering belief in my work. I knew when writing this book that it would be an unconventional sell (and a far cry from the rest of your list!)—but you faced the challenge head-on and found it the most perfect home. I can't thank you enough for everything.

When people talk about the importance of finding an editor who "gets" your book, they're so right. And no one gets *Burn It All Down* more than my incredible editor, T.S. Ferguson. Thank you for being such a relentless advocate for this book that you basically moved mountains (no big deal) to acquire it. And thank you for working your editorial magic to help whip it into the shape it's in today! Joey and Gia have grown so much because of your pitch-perfect insights and suggestions.

Speaking of the mountains that were moved to make this book happen! So many heartfelt thanks to Jenny Bak for championing this book through a twisty acquisitions journey, and to the legendary James Patterson for (1) being James Patterson, and (2) getting behind this book in such a big way. I'm still pinching myself!

Thank you to my wonderful film agent, Dana Spector, for your belief in this story and its potential to transcend mediums. And to the rest of the teams at Transatlantic Literary Agency and CAA—I'm so lucky to have such amazing representation all around.

Special shout-outs to Scott Bryan Wilson for the impeccable copyedits (particularly with regards to legal- and wagon-related matters!) and Linda Arends for getting this manuscript past the finish line.

Huge thanks to the world-class publishing teams at Little, Brown and JIMMY Patterson Books, including: Denise Roy, Laura Schreiber, Caitlyn Averett, Erinn McGrath, Josh Johns, Daniel Denning, Charlotte LaMontagne, Flo Yue, Jordan Mondell, Liam Donnelly, Tracy Shaw, Blue Guess, Alexis Lassiter, Shawn Foster, Danielle Cantarella, Ned Rust, Jannelle DeLuise, and everyone else whose behind-the-scenes efforts have gone into the making of this book. It takes a village, and I'm grateful to have the best village in the world!

Huge thanks to my fellow authors (and inspirations!) Hannah Orenstein and Steven Rowley for being so incredibly generous with your support of this book.

To Steven Salvatore: OMG, can you believe this is happening right now? I *can't even know what to say* about how life-changing your friendship and critique partnership has been for me through the years. Our publishing journeys have been so eerily synced—from the blog days to the query trenches to submission hell and beyond—that I have no choice but to believe we were brought together by God (a.k.a. Mariah Carey). I honestly don't know where I'd be without our therapeutic (oftentimes unhinged)

acknowledgments

Gchat sessions. Gandhi! All my books would suck if it weren't for your spot-on editorial feedback. Thank you so much for everything. We did it!

To Julia Foster: Remember when we became each other's first-ever CPs after a short series of blog comments and emails, and then just *assumed* that our first books would go on to be these huge successes, and then slowly had our dreams shattered over the course of hundreds and hundreds of rejections, and then almost gave up about a zillion times each? I'm so glad neither of us ever did. Thank you so much for your always-exactly-what-I-need-to-hear critiques, and for being such an incredible friend and shoulder throughout all the ebbs and flows of this insane journey. We are overdue for another cheesecake date!

To the beta readers and friends who have graciously read my work in its various stages of incoherence and profanity over the years: Fran Ferrara (BFF and first-ever reader!), Dinah Alobeid (eagle-eyed proofreading queen!), Melissa Somosky (character development goddess!), Monsé Barrera (#BikiniCat4Lyfe!), and Katie DiDomizio (love you, cous!!!).

To all the educators who encouraged me to pursue writing back in the day—especially Kristen Hedlund-Esemplare at Western Connecticut State University (who said, "You can and should!" when I told her I dreamed of writing a book one day), and Lynn Talmont at Cromwell Middle School (who sent me to a gifted writer's workshop at UConn in sixth grade, where I distinctly remember using the word "fuck" in a short story for the first time, because I figured what the hell, I was basically a college student for the day).

To all the readers, writers, editors, and others who've played a part in my writing journey—from the blogosphere to Twitter to *Mic* to the world of fiction and beyond. There are too many to list here (I feel like I've been rambling and I need to wrap this up?!), but I'm so grateful to each and every one of you for the support and inspiration.

Special shout-out to the staff at Brewshot Café at Liberty Harbor in Jersey City, who kept me caffeinated for hours on end as I drafted and edited this manuscript.

I'm so lucky to have the most amazing group of family and friends who have kept me going throughout the past decade I've spent pursuing this dream. I wish I could shout out all of you individually, but again: I'm a rambling bitch. So I'll just say that you all know who you are, and I couldn't have done this without you.

To Tony and Cheryl DiDomizio for all the inspiration, laughs, cheerleading, and support (and also Netflix) over the years. And to Wesley (a.k.a. Sir Wesley) and Violette, simply for being the cutest, most perfect godchildren in all the land.

To Dad, for always having such a great sense of humor and passing it along to me. To Laurie, for making the best chicken parm in the tri-state area. And to both of you—I could have never written a book (or done literally anything in life) without your endless supply of love and support over the years. Thank you so much for everything. Next round of keno is on me!

To Mom, for all the obvious reasons. This book isn't *really* about us—but it also wouldn't exist if it weren't for the many adventures we've had together (particularly that one time in 1999 when we shaving-creamed the Cambridge Drive house in a fit of post-divorce rage). Without your unconditional love and guidance, I never would have survived the endless string of Luke-esque assholes I dated circa 2006 through 2013, and I certainly wouldn't have been able to write this (or any other) book. Thank you for being my lifetime best friend and partner in (non-literal!)

crime. This book is dedicated to you, because who else would I dedicate it to?

Finally, to my love—a.k.a. my baben—Graig Williams. There's no one I'd rather meander through this journey of life with. Your love and support over the past six-plus years has kept me going when I wanted to give up, sane when I wanted to fly off the handle, and strong when I wanted to be weak. (Basically the lyrics to "Because You Loved Me" by Celine Dion are how I feel about you.) It still amazes me that you had a front-row seat at watching me fail repeatedly—like, over and over and over and over and over again—for so many years…and yet you never once questioned my ability to succeed. Your belief in me is a gift I'll never take for granted.

about the author

Nicolas DiDomizio holds a bachelor's degree from Western Connecticut State University and a master's degree from NYU. Prior to his career in fiction, he wrote for the internet for several years while also working in corporate roles at Condé Nast, MTV, and more. He lives in upstate New York with his partner Graig and their adorably grumpy bulldog, Tank. *Burn It All Down* is his debut novel.

Follow him on Twitter at @ctnicolas and Instagram at @nicdidomiziobooks.